Judging Meghan

Trudy Adams

Onwards and Upwards Publishers

3 Radfords Turf, Cranbrook, Exeter,
EX5 7DX, United Kingdom.
www.onwardsandupwards.org

This first edition published in the United Kingdom by Onwards and Upwards Publishers (2018).

ISBN: 978-1-78815-688-2
Typeface: Sabon LT
Graphic design: LM Graphic Design

Printed in the United Kingdom.

To Kylie Kelly

For being the first to listen
to and encourage my
stories,

And for that which I thank
God for, always –

The blessing of your
friendship.

1

IT WAS NICK WHO SUGGESTED WE TAKE LUNCH down by the river early one day in September. We'd just come back from church, having spent most of the time after the service talking about Phar Lap's latest win, and I for one had envisaged spending my afternoon curled up in front of the fire, enjoying the faint smell of eucalyptus and reading a good hard-back romance I had borrowed from Helen. But before any of us answered, Nick ran off with a wild grin, found Blacky, our white pony, and hitched him up to the cart. 'Come on,' he called when we didn't move. 'What are you waiting for? It's such a beautiful day!'

Thomas looked up at the blue expanse of sky and bright spring sunshine, and then we glanced at each other and suddenly broke free of our stupor. I ran to find some blankets. Thomas hurried to tell Mum and Dad. Helen took Amy's hand in hers and they went inside to collect what food they could, running through the chickens on the way.

I returned first, and Nick helped me up to sit by him at the front. 'Come on, Meg,' he said, with gentle big-brother ease, putting the blankets in the back. 'Need a good-looking girl in the front to complete the ensemble.'

'Why don't we invite Brigitte along then?' I asked, referring to the copper-headed beauty who had made Nick fall all over himself that morning. He blushed at my comment but didn't answer.

Amy came running out with her arms full of cakes and biscuits and all good things. 'Amy!' I cried. 'Did Mum say we could have all those?'

She looked up at me with soft caramel eyes and a squinted smile. 'She didn't say we *couldn't* have them,' she said matter-of-factly, putting the food carefully on top of the blankets.

Thomas came around from the back of the house, red-faced from running. 'Mum and Dad have gone for a walk up to Craig's Hill,' he said. 'I only just caught them. They said we must be back before dark.' He helped Amy get in the back and then hopped up himself. 'Let's go, Nick!'

'We're still waiting for Helen!'

Helen, at eighteen, never rushed. She seemed to glide through life like an elegant swan rather than stumble through it like the rest of us. She was tall and thin and delicately built, with dark brown curls that fell gently to her shoulders. We hardly looked liked sisters, with her more like the country princess and me fair-haired and getting as plump as the sheep we raised. Or 'cuddly', as Amy liked to say.

Helen came out of the house with a neatly packed picnic basket and something to drink. She lifted her skirt slightly as she walked across the driveway to us and asked Thomas to put the basket into the cart. Then, in a way only Helen could, she gracefully lifted herself up into the back and was about to find a comfortable spot to sit, but Nick, always one to torment, flicked the whip on Blacky's back and sent him forward, causing poor Helen to fall and land with her elbow in one of Amy's tarts.

'Nicholas Manley!' she scolded, though it was only out of a sense of duty. Helen hardly knew how to be angry at all. Even before Nick replied she was laughing at herself. 'At least it's lemon meringue and not custard!'

We turned down the dirt track towards the river. The pastures where Dad kept his sheep were in front of us, broken by the brown river which was edged with tall green brushy trees. Beyond that was our small town, Harrington, but only the church, with its tall steeple, really stood out at that distance. Behind us, to the left, was our stone home, just big enough for the seven of us and as cosy as a cottage. The chimney smoked a bit – Dad always lit a fire before he and Mum took their routine walk after church every Sunday, so it would be nice and warm by the time they got back for lunch.

Amy and Thomas started singing *Road to Gundagai* in the back and it wasn't long before we were all belting it out in between giggles and laughter. We passed some of our sheep who paused, mid-bite to look at us. 'Just you concentrate on getting nice and fat for us!' Nick called to them. 'Look at their fleeces,' he said to me. 'Prime stuff, that.'

I nodded vaguely and started singing *Waltzing Matilda* with a voice I hadn't inherited from my musical father.

We arrived at our spot by the river under a plump willow tree and started unpacking the food. I spread out the blankets, Thomas tethered Blacky and Amy began throwing rocks into the river, falling forward at one stage and nearly getting soaked. 'Amy, be careful,' Helen said half-heartedly and only because she knew Mum would make her take responsibility for any of her sisters' misbehaviour. 'Come and eat with us.'

We settled down on the blankets and Nick poured us some tea. Once we all had a cup, he raised his and said, 'To Amy, who turned thirteen yesterday and is now officially a rambunctious teenager like the rest of us.'

Amy's lips, like a red rosebud, opened slightly and she laughed. 'But you're not a teenager any more,' she reminded him. 'You're all grown up!'

Nick did not look so sure about this. 'Only on Mondays to Fridays, when I help Dad on the property. Other than that, I'll be young forever!'

'I could still race you to the top of the tree,' Helen told him with an un-ladylike grin.

'Never!' But even as he spoke, they were both on their feet and racing up the willow.

Thomas was watching them with a smile.

'What were Mum and Dad doing for lunch?' I asked him. He shrugged his shoulders and scrunched up his face as if he'd just been eating something disgusting. 'What is it?'

Tom was fifteen, just a year younger than me but smarter than any of us. He was forever pushing his dark shaggy hair off his forehead, but he refused to have it cut. He was thickset for his age and the best cricket player in the district, even better than Nick, although Nick said it was because he was too busy to practise.

'I was just thinking of Mum and Dad holding hands as they went off on their walk,' he said. 'I can't imagine liking anyone that much.'

'That's because you're still a kid.'

'I am not!' He threw an almond at me, but I didn't retaliate.

'One day you will understand,' I said, as if I had all of the world's mysteries figured out.

I looked up at Nick and Helen, who were at the top of the willow tree now. Nick, with his tanned, outdoorsy look and biceps that gripped the tree's branches like an ape, was shaking Helen's branch as vigorously as he could while she ignored him, her skirt tucked up beneath her and her long white legs hanging down like a melting ice-cream.

Thomas made a small fire, even though it was such a fine day we weren't in need of one. Amy 'helped' by collecting twigs. 'Just like a girl,' Tom muttered. 'Why don't you find something decent like a log?'

'You've got to have something to start it with!'

Nick, who was hanging upside down now, told them they needed both, but didn't volunteer to help. I left them to it and walked up the river a bit, until I came to a nice clear pool that always formed next to the river whenever it rained a bit more than usual. I knelt beside it and watched small insects buzz over the surface. I studied my own reflection – a sixteen-year-old girl who was the middle child of a loving family, but who was not sure of her own strengths or whether she really had anything to offer the world. I mean, it was Nick who was most needed on the farm and Helen who helped Mum with everything else while keeping the local boys on their toes. Thomas looked after the horses and helped Nick, and Amy was still at school. I had finished with school but I was too plain for the boys, not strong enough for farm labour and not good enough with my hands for domestic chores. I collected the eggs in the morning and the rest of the day was filled with odd jobs. I know my family loved me. I loved them too but part of me worried that they would suddenly realise they had no real use for me. I put a dried piece of bark on the pool and watched it quickly sink, taking an ant with it.

'Meg?' Helen called, coming up behind me.

'Did Nick shake you out?'

'No, he'll be the one with bruises tomorrow.' We both laughed and walked farther along the river together.

'What do you think of Brigitte?' I was keen to hear Helen's opinion of the girl who had rendered Nick speechless. Nick and Brigitte had been friends all through school, but she had been in the city for a year and returned a woman, with a touch of class I wasn't sure I liked.

'I think it is quite possible she may become family.'

'Does Nick really like her that much?'

'I think so.'

I pursed my lips with disgust. Not because I resented Brigitte in any real way but because I hated the thought of losing Nick. 'Perhaps she'll go back where she came from.'

'Meghan, that's not fair. Harrington is her home too. And what would we do if Nick followed her back to the city?'

'She's from a rich family, I suppose...' I said vaguely.

Helen sighed, and put a hand on my shoulder. 'Come on, let's go back to the others.'

After we had run ourselves ragged up and down the river and eaten all of our supplies, Nick drove us home. Helen was the only one who sang now, and it was the old hymn, *It is Well.* She sang softly with Amy curled up under her arm and Thomas gazing out over the distance like a contented man considering his lot.

When we pulled up outside of the house, the first thing we noticed was a motor vehicle parked in front, which meant that either Brigitte's family or the bank manager, Mr Willis, had come to visit. No one else could afford a car in our town.

Nick hoped it was Brigitte, but it was Mr Willis who came out of the house. He was a short man with a grey felt hat and a small black moustache. His daughter, Victoria, was like one of those burrs that gets stuck in sheep's wool, the kind you spend hours trying to get out, and even when you do, you end up with cuts on your hands. She wasn't with him now, thank goodness, but she was a stuck-up, snobby know-it-all whom I detested.

Mum and Dad followed Mr Willis out with their arms around each other. They smiled at him, but we could tell it was forced. 'You remember our children, Mr Willis?' Dad asked. 'This is Nicholas, Helen, Meghan, Thomas and Amy.'

'Why does he never start with me?' Amy whispered crossly to me.

'Yes, I remember.' He gave us a curt nod and got into his car.

We walked over to Mum and Dad on the verandah and watched him go. 'Come inside, all of you,' Mum said, her eyes watching Mr Willis' car drive away, as if to make sure he didn't turn back. 'It's still getting chilly at night.' She put an arm around my shoulders and we walked in together.

2

MY FAVOURITE TIME OF DAY IS DUSK, WHEN everything in the world settles and calms. The sun, often so bright and overbearing, begins to sink, but it leaves behind a last breath of heat that hangs in the air just long enough for all the wrens, rosellas and magpies to find a comfortable spot for the night. Kookaburras laugh one last time while insects, made golden by the last rays of sunshine, float about in the heavy air. Sometimes a gentle, warm breeze tricks the gum trees into shuffling one more time, and every now and then it also produces a wonderful waft of sweet wattle mixed with the smell of sheep. Soon even that subsides, and there is stillness.

I watched this stillness descend over our land, and then followed the others into the lounge room. We sat by the fire later that evening, me finally reading Helen's book and finding it as good as it promised, Helen stroking Angel, our new grey kitten, and Amy and Nick playing a board game on the blue rug in front of the fire. Dad was reading the kind of newspaper that was so big that when he held it up, he disappeared behind it. Mum was darning a pair of Thomas' pants and mumbling something about boys and their fathers.

I adored both my parents but I was especially proud of Mum. She had such a gentle nature, which she had passed on to Helen along with her warm looks. She also had a surprising strength. I often found myself wishing I could be more like her. Out of the two, I looked more like Dad, but Dad was handsome and he had a great talent and love for music, neither of which I had inherited. He was tall and built strongly – a man in his prime, or so I'd heard people say – and he didn't have a grey hair, even at forty-two. What was most important to us was that he could work from dawn to dusk and still have energy to spend time with us. He often told us how proud he was of us all, and he always listened to us with great interest, but it was no secret that Mum held his heart and always had.

Though only a bit shorter, Mum was much more delicately built than him and she had dark brown, wavy hair that she mostly wore up or at least tied back. She had long, slender fingers that were good at healing injuries, wiping away tears and silencing conflict. She was quieter than Dad, but she knew what she thought and who she was and wasn't easily moved. When we had a problem we needed advice for, we went to Dad. When we had a problem we needed sympathy for, we went to Mum.

Thomas was practising the piano. It wasn't really a passion of his but he was pretty good at it simply because he was just so clever at everything. He began to play a waltz he'd never played before, so there were a few slips and upside-down chords. Dad put down his paper and smiled at Mum. She didn't return his gaze but she smiled slyly. 'The Harrington Ball,' Dad said with great feeling.

'*The Blue Danube*,' Mum added with a nod, looking up. She brushed back a strand of dark hair from her forehead and seemed to be remembering something.

'The first time we ever danced.'

We all stopped what we were doing and looked at them, knowing there was a story coming, one that we had heard, but one we would never tire of hearing.

'Well, what happened?' Amy asked for us.

Mum put down her sewing and looked at Dad, encouraging him to tell the story. He grinned and settled back into his chair. My father was a great storyteller, and we all enjoyed hearing him, even Mum.

'Your mother was courting Frederick Hanson, a townie.' Dad rolled his eyes as if the very idea was preposterous. 'A boy who wouldn't know the difference between a sheep and a cow!'

Mum clicked her tongue. 'He was a fine young gentleman – credit me with some taste!' We laughed at her mock indignation.

'And what's he doing now?' Dad asked, as if he didn't know.

'He owns a department store. Richest man in the city or something.'

'*Pfft!* A real man works with his hands – remember that, Nick.'

'*Nathaniel!* A real man simply cares for his family. Nick, Tom, you will be respected as men no matter what you choose to do as an occupation.'

'Unless you open a department store in Harrington,' Dad added under his breath.

'Nathaniel!' she chided, and Dad laughed with satisfaction.

'Can we get back to the story, please?' Amy asked impatiently.

'Yes, sorry, Amy.' Dad winked at her. 'So, I arrived at this ball without a girl by my side and feeling particularly aware of it, watching the prettiest girl getting twirled around by some bloke who...'

'Nathaniel...'

'My mates all knew how crazy I was about her, but I wasn't brave enough to actually do something about it.'

'You must have been,' I said. 'Otherwise we wouldn't be sitting here now.'

'Well, Meg, things changed when Fred stood on your mother's toe. He helped her take a seat and then the swine left her there – went and took another girl onto the floor, obviously on a mission to bruise as many toes as possible. He didn't come back for her at all.'

'Yes, I was a little put out that he just left me sitting there, as if he'd gone off me and orchestrated it so he wouldn't have to dance with me.'

Dad reached over and took her hand in his. 'No man in his right mind could do that.' He kissed her hand and held onto it as he continued, and Mum now had the young glow I'm sure she must have had that night. 'So, I went straight over to her – I don't know what gave me the courage!'

'He forgot my name,' Mum said. 'Just came over and stood in front of me like a gaping cod fish.' We laughed at the thought.

'All I could think of was what an idiot I'd feel like if she said no. But I finally spat out my question, and to my amazement she said yes. It was the most beautiful moment in my life.'

'He finally remembered my name. "Miss Wright... Evelyn, would you do me the honour of giving me this dance?"' Mum re-enacted. 'I'll never forget how pleased you looked with yourself when I agreed.'

'They played *The Blue Danube,* a grand, magical dance that allowed me to get closer to your mother than I'd ever been. She was wearing a beautiful burgundy gown and had her hair flowing down.' Dad used his hands to bring his memory to life.

'He swept me off my feet, almost literally. I had never enjoyed dancing as much as I did at that moment. I forgot all about my sore toe.'

'So, I thought I'd ask her for the next one, and the next one... And then I casually guided her steps outside for some fresh air...'

'But I don't think our children need to know all the details,' Mum said quickly with a slight blush as she returned to her darning. There was a series of groans, but Mum can be unmovable when she wants to be, especially when she's embarrassed.

'Why did you love her?' Helen asked Dad.

Dad gazed at his daughter wistfully. 'I'd been watching her from a distance for a while. She was – is – beautiful, but she was also elegant and clear-minded. She attended church every Sunday and had no doubts about who she was or what she believed in. And she was obviously intelligent. I've seen many men brush off an intelligent woman in favour of dominating a girl with a head full of air, but I hope, Nicholas and Thomas, that you both see the value of having a woman with a good mind by your side. And Helen, Meghan and Amy, I hope you find men who will also value you for this. As a farmer, I needed a wife that wouldn't faint at the sight of a dead animal, who would help me run the business side of things, and who would also bring our children up in the ways of the Lord. I wasn't afraid to have a woman point out my faults, as your mother frequently does...'

'Out of love, of course,' Mum said.

'But that's all part of being partners in life. Asking your mother to dance that night was the smartest thing I ever did.' Dad pushed his glasses up the bridge of his nose and went back to reading his paper as if he had just solved the answer to life and was content to move on.

I know that when their marriage was published in the local paper, he was quoted as saying that marrying Mum was 'the Wright and Manley thing to do'. He still used that phrase to remind us of what we stood for as a family, to always act with integrity and do what is right, and to ensure we each became the best man or woman possible. They guided each other and together they guided us.

Later that night as I was getting ready for bed, I glimpsed them dancing slowly in the lounge room, Mum with her head resting against his chest; his arm about her waist.

———————————

Two days later, while Helen and Mum were cooking dinner, I found Dad and Thomas drinking tea on the verandah. I sat with them and poured myself a cup while Dad opened a long envelope with his ivory letter-opener. He pulled out an official-looking piece of paper and smoothed the creases. As soon as he started reading it, Dad began to frown.

'Evelyn?' he called. I knew something was wrong because of the way he enunciated each syllable. 'Evelyn? I have a letter from Mr Willis.' He went back inside and into the kitchen. Thomas and I followed, and everyone stopped what they were doing. Mum wiped her hands on her pink apron and eyed him carefully. 'Evelyn, I need to talk to you.'

She followed him into the study and they closed the heavy wooden door behind them. After a minute, the rest of us pressed ourselves up against the wall next to the door but it didn't help much – we only heard something about 'deficit', 'lay-off', 'one month', and then we thought we'd risked getting caught enough so we went back to fixing dinner. Helen started clearing the bench and I set the table while Thomas went to look for Nick and Amy. After all, we were sure Mum and Dad would tell us in their own time.

They eventually came out, but we had almost all finished eating dinner before Dad finally spoke. 'We've decided to lay off two men. Well, we have to.'

Mum reached across the table to take his hand in hers. We all knew how much of a responsibility he took on himself for the men he employed. But since the crash in America in '29, almost two years earlier, we innocent farmers across the world were starting to feel the pressure. The farm had started running at a loss – wool was selling for less than half of what it used to. Even though we used to own the place, Dad had to take out a small loan to survive, which meant that every month became a struggle to meet the repayments. Mum had started washing and ironing for the workers for an extra shilling or two and that seemed to grate on Dad more than anything. He had never wanted to see his wife be a servant.

'If we don't catch up on last month's repayment as well as this one's within a month, they will foreclose on us,' he continued. 'Recall the loan.'

'Can they do that?' Nick asked indignantly.

'Mr Willis can.'

Nick's face darkened. 'He's always had it in for you since you got the highest price at that auction for the best ram. I remember his spiteful comment about you being on the front of *The Valley Herald*.'

'Yes, but also his cousin, Frederick Hanson, told him we were crooks after your mother married me instead of him. Any time we needed financial help… well, it was like getting blood out of a stone. But still, we've done alright.'

'Until now,' Helen whispered.

'What do you think will happen? Will you be able to make the repayment in time?' I asked.

'I don't know, Meg. I just don't know. We'll do our best. We will have to sell some of the sheep, of course, maybe call in a few favours. But I don't know.'

'Will I have to leave school?' Amy asked hopefully.

'Not unless it's absolutely necessary,' Mum told her. 'Now, just remember the most important thing is that we are still together. I've heard horrible stories of families being pushed to travel for work and losing touch with each other. That is not going to happen to us.' She took her plate over to the kitchen bench and busied herself with the dishes before any of us had even finished. I knew she was worried, and that worried me more than anything.

Later that night I returned to the verandah at the back and sank down in the hammock we had tied up there. Swinging myself gently backward and forward, I wondered what it would be like to lose our property. It was everything to me. It was my home. It was who I was. It was my parents' hard work, our hard work. It was our living, our reason for existing, our key to belonging in Harrington. No, not just belonging – mixing with the farming gentry, like Brigitte's family. Who would we be without our land? The thought was incomprehensible to me, so I brushed it off and told myself it could never happen anyway. Over the last few years or so, we'd had a few men drop by, desperate for work, and Dad usually helped them out until they moved on to the next town unless he saw them as a threat to his women. There was no way that Dad would suddenly become one of those men, desperate to just get a quid or two.

Amy wandered out eating some fudge that she assured me Mum had given her. 'You can have some,' she offered, but as it was already mostly smudged over her hand and face, I decided against it. 'Megsy, why do you never worry about anything?'

19

'What?'

'You always seem like nothing ever affects you. Even when Barney died, you didn't even cry!' Barney was our beloved pony, the one we had before Blacky.

'Oh, Amy, I hated it when Barney died.'

'But we would never have known.'

'Do you need to know things like that?'

'Well, just to make sure you're still normal and all.' She licked her hands and smiled at me as if to see what I would say to that.

I glared at her a little and then did the only thing I could – I tickled her until she regretted having ever come out.

My best friend ever since I could remember was Julianne Young. We went through school together until we were fourteen, at which point we both had to leave to get jobs. I, of course, worked on the farm and she found employment at the post office.

I went into town the next day to see her for lunch, walking all the way in and enjoying the September sun. Thomas came with me, since he had to go to the produce store for Dad.

Julianne lived on the farm next to ours and closer to town, and much of my childhood consisted of me running up the lane to see her, or her coming over to see me. She was always bright and cheerful, and she often got me into trouble with some of the schemes she came up with, like secretly taking one of the new lambs as a pet, dressing it up like a doll, and feeding it Mum's freshly baked blackberry pie. Dad found us with berry spread all over our hands and faces and in the wool of the lamb. Then there was the time we imagined Dad's new horse to be an untamed brumby, so we climbed onto its back and pretended we were horse whisperers. Everything would have been fine, had the horse not broken into a run and had Julianne not fallen off and broken her wrist. It took a long time for our parents to forgive us that one.

We were partners in crime, self-made sisters. I had been there for her when the first boy she liked told her she was stupid, and she had been there for me when a school teacher, Mr Timms, told me that as a girl, the only way I could earn my keep was to bear children but that no one would ever marry me.

I didn't like Mr Timms much.

Seeing Julianne whenever I could was always the highlight of my day. I loved her as much as I loved my family and I was the closest thing she had to a real sister. So, when we greeted each other in the post office with a warm embrace, most people would've thought we hadn't seen each other for a month.

'Come on, Meg,' she said, linking her arm through mine. 'Let's eat outside.'

We sat on a verandah chair that linked the post office with the rest of the shops. I must have given the impression that I was in a bad mood because Julianne chewed her sandwich thoughtfully and watched me. 'One of your cats didn't die, did they?'

I shook my head and she didn't say anything else. She'd known me long enough and well enough to realise she couldn't force me to talk. She ran her hand through her thick, shoulder-length auburn hair. Julianne's fringe, which fell like a red curtain over her white forehead, was tousled by the wind. Her blue eyes, highlighted by her blue skirt and jacket, shamed the sky. In fact, I was always a bit envious of her pretty looks. Just sitting next to her made me deeply aware of the extra pounds I was carrying around my middle. I didn't think of myself as ugly, but neither did

I ever consider that anyone might think of me as beautiful. I certainly didn't. Rather, the word that came to mind was ordinary. My hair was an ordinary dark blonde colour that didn't make a statement like Julianne's did.

Actually, nothing about me made a statement or said to the world, 'Here is a girl worth noticing.' I was of an ordinary height, and didn't appear to be growing any taller. I had sloping shoulders, freckles that came out whenever I was in the sun for too long, and deep set, light brown eyes. The only thing I liked was my complexion – a sort of tanned, healthy outdoors look. I was pretty fit, but with arms that were perhaps a little too muscular, or 'not entirely feminine', as Julianne would say. I just couldn't lose that baby fat around my stomach. Julianne was always fiddling with her hair and her clothes, forever thinking that people were watching her. I was a bit like that too, but for the opposite reason – I was trying to work out if people saw me at all.

'Julianne! Meghan!' a voice called. It was William, and Jeremy was with him. They had been two years ahead of us in school, and as it was a small town, we saw them often, at least from a distance. I also knew why they had come over to us – William had always had his eye on Julianne. He invited her over for dinner that night, and I watched as his face lit up when she said yes.

Jeremy met my eyes for a moment. His were a deep brown, like Thomas'. He gave me a weak smile and held my gaze for a moment longer. There was something about the way he looked at me from under his eyebrows that made me self-conscious.

'Did you hear that, Jeremy? Julianne will be coming over tonight!' Will smiled and stood a little taller while Julianne just grinned at him. They were both tall boys, and still growing. William was a thin blond and a little bit cocky, but Jeremy was broader, sturdier, although a little clumsy whenever he was nervous. He had been orphaned young, and somehow that gave him a depth others lacked.

'Good,' Jeremy said. Will and Julianne chatted for a moment more while Jeremy and I sat there trying to avoid further eye contact with each other. I was glad when the boys finally moved on.

'Oh, Meghan! Can you believe it?'

'Of course I can. You're the prettiest girl in town!'

'Oh, Meg, you can be so frustrating. You are pretty too! You just hide it, that's all. I mean, you didn't even try to talk to Jeremy!' Julianne was always emphatic in the way she spoke, as if everything she said was of the utmost importance. She frowned at me now. 'So, what do you think of William? Do you think he's good for me?'

I hated those sorts of questions. What would I know? 'I don't know him well enough to say, Jules. But you're my best friend and I'm happy for you if things work out with him.'

She didn't look happy though. 'If you are my best friend, why don't you tell me what's bothering you?'

'Because you wouldn't be able to do anything about it.'

'That doesn't matter. Being a friend means just being there for each other when it matters, not having all the answers. Now, what's on your mind?'

So I told her about the farm, Mr Willis and the letter, my heart sinking as I spoke.

Julianne leaned into me out of sympathy and sighed. 'I'm sorry, Meghan, that this is happening to your family. I know how much it means to you all. I've never seen so many people desperate for work. They say there are thousands of people out on the track now, all just trying to earn a crust to get them by, living hand to mouth until the next dole ration comes in. I hope that doesn't happen to us.'

'Friends no matter what?' I asked as she hugged me.

'Friends no matter what,' she echoed.

'Anyway, if things get bad, you'll just have to marry Will as soon as possible! His dad owns the general store, so they will always have money!'

'Meghan! Sometimes I wonder about you! I hope you fall in love with someone who's dirt poor just so you understand that love conquers all.'

'You've been reading too many magazines about film stars.'

'You can't talk! You've been reading that book of Helen's. You told me! Where are you up to in it now?'

I laughed and we talked about it until she had to get back to work.

———————

I found Thomas and we collected Amy once school had finished for the day. The three of us walked home. The road was dusty but it had green grass tufts growing high in the middle, which Amy insisted on walking through. Before long the paddocks beside the road were ours and we could see smoke coming from the house over the hill. Thomas wanted to call on a friend on the next property, so he ran off down Paterson's Road, leaving Amy and me to take the things home for Dad.

We were not far off and there was no reason for anything to go wrong, only something caught my attention – the bleat of a distressed sheep, a sound I was trained to hear. I glanced across the green paddocks, scanning them once, twice, looking for something out of the ordinary. Just as I was about to forget it and keep walking, I saw a man right across the other side of the pasture, standing amidst our sheep and trying to catch one.

Without even thinking about it, I jumped our fence, ripped my dress, gouged my hand and leg on the barbed wire, and fled across the paddock whilst yelling at Amy to fetch help. I nearly reached the man without him noticing me. By then, he had a sheep between his legs and was about to slit its throat. I was so angry that he would even consider stealing something my family had worked hard for, and more than that, he was doing it in broad daylight as if he wasn't even ashamed of his actions. It wasn't until I screamed at him to let it go before I set the dogs on him (who were with Dad, who wasn't even in sight), that he became aware of me racing towards him. The man flinched and looked behind him, as if considering an escape route, but then he realised I was just a girl, so he took on a more casual air. I remember feeling a bit insulted by that.

'Put down that sheep, you mongrel!' I yelled, forgetting all about my churchly upbringing in the heat of the moment. 'Get off our land before we hand you over to the police!'

'You talk pretty tough for a sheila,' he laughed. 'Why don't you go back up to the house and play with your dolls?'

'Don't insult me you good-for-...'

I was in such a passion I didn't see him reach for me, but he grabbed my wrist and gripped it tightly, bringing my speech to a sudden stop. I don't know how he managed it – he was so quick and it took me completely by surprise. I gasped at the shock but didn't dare show any fear. When I tried to resist him, he tightened his grip. *You're so stupid!* I thought to myself, staring at his scraggy grey beard, his yellow, crooked teeth and his little eyes that made my skin crawl.

'Look, girly, do you know what it's like to eat nothin' but rabbit for weeks on end, being homeless and as hungry as I am?' He spat as he spoke.

I glared at him, trying not to let on that he was really hurting my wrist. 'Well, thieving from good people is not the answer!'

'Good people!' he scoffed. 'You'd be the daughter then?'

'What's it to you?'

'Nah, can't be you – they tell me she's a beauty. They didn't tell me nothin' about a lunatic.'

'Better a lunatic than a thieving tramp,' I said, now more angry and offended than scared.

'Tramp? I'm nothing but a victim of society! And you talk about your family as if they're good! Just this morning the man here told me to push off, even knowin' 'ow desperate I was for a couple o' bob! Said he didn't need none of my help!' He twisted my wrist and I felt the blood drop from my face. 'Well, now's my chance to show him!'

3

I TRIPPED OVER A TUSSOCK OF GRASS WHEN HE pulled me closer, and fell to my knees. Totally desperate, I pushed at his legs with all my strength. To my surprise and relief, I shook him enough for him to let me go. I struggled to my feet, tasting dirt and grass in my mouth, and felt my wrist throbbing. He got to his feet as well and I was trying to make a rapid decision whether to make a run for it or stand and fight. Even though I was petrified, I still couldn't bring myself to let him get away with stealing. Then, because I didn't decide what to do quickly enough, he turned with his knife and slit the throat of the sheep anyway. Its dying bleat of distress filled my ears.

'*No!*' I yelled, and I was about to rush towards him again, but someone grabbed my arm from behind. I turned, about to shove whoever it was away, but then I realised it was Nick. He let go of me and flipped the rifle he carried over his shoulder into his hands.

'Get off our land.' Nick aimed the gun at the tramp. The man stood staring at him to see if he meant it. Blood was dripping off his knife and onto the grass. 'You've committed a criminal offense and you'll pay for it.' I rubbed my wrist and got out of the way, feeling both angry and nervous as I watched Nick. 'This is the second time you've been told to push off, and there won't be a third.' He released the safety catch on his rifle.

The man's gaze turned back to me and he spat on the ground. 'Won't always have your big brother to keep an eye out for you.' He stared at me as if he wanted to remember my face. Then, with one last dirty look at Nick, he let out a humph and walked off. Nick made sure he was off our property completely before returning to me. He slung the rifle over his shoulder.

'Meg, I'm not sure if you're foolhardy or brave, but I'm pretty sure I know which one Mum and Dad will think you are.'

'Meghan Manley!' Mum cried as soon as she saw me. She was cross but I knew it wasn't too bad because she hugged me straight away, and it was only then that I realised just how scared I had been.

'Did he hurt you?' she asked, looking me over and seeing the cut on my leg. 'Come inside – we'll clean that up.' Mum sat me down on the couch and clicked her tongue over the state of my skirt as she bandaged me up, mumbling something about this being a bad time for me to need a new one. She decided that Helen would have to lend me one, then cupped my face with her hand. 'I'm proud of your courage, Meghan. I want you to know that, although sometimes you worry me more than all the others put together. Now, if your father gets angry with you when he gets home, it's only because he loves you.'

'I'm sorry if I worry you,' I said a little sullenly. She only smiled and kissed the top of my head.

Amy, Nick and Helen came in and sat around me after Mum left. 'I ran as fast as I could!' Amy said keenly.

'And I came as fast as I could,' Nick said.

'I was fine, really,' I said, and immediately wished I hadn't spoken. After Helen and Nick finished explaining all the terrible things that could have happened to me, I said with irritation, 'Well, next time I see someone stealing our sheep, I'll tell him, "Don't stop at one!"'

Helen, who didn't like conflict, suddenly faded away from the room. Amy realised Tom was home and that she had a moral duty to fill him in on what was going on as soon as possible, and Nick drew a breath to say something depressingly sensible but Dad hurried into the room and filled it with such a determined presence that even he slinked away. I refused to meet Dad's eyes, even when he sat beside me. 'They tell me that you demanded that thief to get off our land,' he stated.

'Yes.' I looked up and realised he was trying to hide a grin.

'They also tell me you were lucky that Nick was able to come and scare him off.' Dad stroked his moustache.

'It wasn't luck, Dad. I knew he'd be coming – I'd sent Amy for help.'

He sat there and gazed at me. 'Well, I'm proud that my daughter cares as much about our land as I do, and I find it interesting that you, at sixteen, have more guts and conviction than grown men like Mr Willis.'

I smiled then. 'Thanks, Dad.'

He squeezed my hand. 'Of course, I'd be no kind of father if I didn't say at least once that you should be more careful, especially when it comes to men like that.'

'I know, Dad.'

'Show me your wrist.'

I held out my left arm for him to have a look at.

'Bruises showing already. Well, he's been reported, so hopefully he'll get what's coming to him.' Dad shook his head. 'That man was lucky it was Nick and not me who went after him. I think I would have succumbed to temptation and left him with a few bruises myself.'

———————————

All too soon, things smoothed over again and the whole event was almost forgotten. Mum and Dad spent most evenings surrounded by paperwork, trying to figure out a more sustainable way to run the farm, or just a way to get us out of trouble. Dad also had many meetings with Mr Willis, in an attempt to find a way to extend the time and to pay him back, to satisfy both parties, but it just didn't work. Mr Willis was heartless. Dad would come home angry and annoyed after seeing him. His sense of defeat hurt us all and for the first time, I started to feel uncomfortable at home.

Julianne had dinner with William's family, and after telling me all about it, I realised she already liked him a lot more than I had appreciated.

'Is your wrist all better?' she asked me two weeks after the event as we walked through town. She looked at it with concern.

'Yes, it's fine. Just a bit tender, but fine.'

'Weren't you scared?'

'Yeah, I was a bit.'

'A *bit!*' Julianne rolled her eyes at me as we passed a group of young boys.

'Hey, Meghan,' one of the younger ones called. 'Scared off any tramps lately?'

'Meghan scares off all boys without even trying!' another taunted.

'Shut up!' Julianne said fiercely in my defence.

'What?' the same boy whined. 'It's true, isn't it?'

'Meghan, the mad mistress!'

'Harry, get out of here!' an angry voice yelled from behind me.

I turned, expecting to see one of my parents' friends, but it was Jeremy. 'Just ignore them, Meghan,' he said. 'They're all bags of wind.' Without another word he disappeared into the bakery, tripping slightly up the step on his way in.

Julianne gave me a cheeky grin. 'I think he likes you!'

I ignored her as we walked into the general store.

'What can I do for ya, young Meg?' William's dad, Mr Cale, leaned over the counter with a warm smile.

'Mum's given me a list. Here it is.' I took the creased piece of paper from my jacket pocket.

He took it in a meaty hand and unravelled it carefully. 'Ah, I'm ever so grateful that there's one woman in Harrington who can still write clearly! Let me get these things for your mother – won't be a moment. Oh, and how are you, Julianne? You must come over for dinner again!'

Julianne chatted with him for a moment while I stepped outside for no particular reason, but perhaps because I wanted to see if Jeremy was still around and if he had William with him. But I found neither of them and regretted having come out at all when Mr Willis appeared beside me. Victoria was with him. She looked at me like she'd been sucking lemons. Her blonde hair fell stiffly around her shoulders as if she'd stolen it from a scarecrow. All bones and elbows, she had a mouth so full of teeth that people called her a shark behind her back, which I personally thought was very appropriate. Victoria had nothing going for her – she was neither pretty nor intelligent, nor friendly – and yet she thought she was the most eligible girl in town, and worst of all, she bragged about it. She was intense, overwhelming and bossy, and she'd put people down, and I would have preferred to chat to a murderer than bump into her as I had done now.

Taking off his hat, Mr Willis greeted me like I was an old friend. 'Miss Meghan, what a pleasure to see you!' His sickening tone made me even more uneasy than the tramp had.

'Have you put on more weight?' Victoria whispered to me while a passing friend distracted her father. 'Or is it just those hideous clothes?'

I gritted my teeth and could not answer.

'How's your father?' Mr Willis asked, returning his focus to me again. 'Do you think he will be able to make his payment in the next two weeks?'

I stared at him but said nothing, knowing that he was baiting me.

'Hmm, well I suppose he wouldn't talk about that with his daughters.' My stare gradually became a glare. 'Oh, have you met my cousin?' he asked suddenly, gesturing to someone behind me. I turned to see a tall man with thinning hair. 'This is Frederick Hanson.'

Frederick was dressed in a suit that loudly announced his affluence to the world. I could tell, by the way he held his head and narrowed his eyes at me, that he was used to looking down at people. He touched his ear uncertainly as he studied me for a moment, then extended a fine hand that was made for a pen and not shears. 'Lovely to meet you, Meghan. I see you've inherited your mother's eyes.'

Under other circumstances I would have been complimented. Mum had beautiful, honey-coloured eyes. But at that moment, all I wanted was to go home.

'Thank you. And how is Mrs Hanson?' I asked with a slightly arched eyebrow.

His face darkened. 'There is no Mrs Hanson, Meghan, which I think you know.'

'Mr Hanson is already organising what will happen to your farm, once your family is forced to leave,' Victoria said, and I felt my eyes widen with shock, not only because of what she said, but because she smirked at her father and Frederick and the three of them seemed to be enjoying my discomfort.

'Which won't be far away, if I can help it,' Frederick muttered.

'Thank goodness Mum chose Dad,' I said under my breath, but I think Frederick still heard me. The smile suddenly left his face anyway.

I was glad when Mr Cale and Julianne came out looking for me. 'Here you are, Meg.' Mr Cale handed me a box of flour and sugar and things. 'Shall I just put it on the tab?'

Victoria's snide, muffled laugh reached my ears, as if she thought we would never be able to afford it. It was all I could do to not scowl at her. I fished around in my pocket. 'Here you go,' I said, putting the amount Mum had given me into Mr Cale's hand. 'Right down to the last pence.'

'I'm sure it is, Miss Meg, knowing your mother! Best wishes to the family!' He patted my shoulder and returned to his shop.

'If you can afford these extravagances, you can afford to pay off the house,' Frederick said.

'We have to eat! Anyway, I thought finances were a matter between a client and his bank manager,' I said tightly. 'How is it that you know so much about my parents' affairs despite rules of confidentiality?' Mr Willis tugged at his collar self-consciously. 'It has nothing to do with me and it certainly has nothing to do with you, Frederick Hanson. Now, good day to you!' I walked back onto the road with Julianne just behind me, feeling a deep anger beginning to flicker somewhere inside me and not knowing quite what to do with it.

4

LATE ONE THURSDAY IN OCTOBER, THE DAY OUR month had passed, I came back into the house after tending to the chooks to find Nick and Helen sitting silently in the lounge room. Helen was trying to read something, but really she was just staring off into the distance, and Nick was concentrating hard on polishing his shoes.

I heard voices behind the closed study door.

'It's Mr Willis,' Nick said without looking up. 'Mum and Dad are both in there with him.'

I sat next to Helen, and she suddenly hugged me. 'What do you think, Meghan? Will we be alright?'

'How can we not be, if we're together?'

Amy had gone to find Angel the kitten and Thomas was raiding the kitchen for something to eat, but I decided to stay with Helen – she looked like she needed company.

When it grew dark outside and they still hadn't come out, I asked Helen to help me with dinner. I knew that it was better than sitting around dwelling on our fears, and Helen especially needed something to occupy her mind. Amy had returned with Angel and was getting some food for her.

'Nick, Thomas, can you set the table please?' I asked.

But the study door opened suddenly and Mr Willis was in the doorway. He stared at us all, one by one, with a smug look on his face. He held my gaze with a smirk. Then, without a word, he let himself out. The study door closed again and that made me nervous. Mum and Dad weren't even prepared to face us. Helen stifled a sob and returned to her cooking. Amy was very quiet, and Nick and Tom were broody.

'Nick, could you say grace for us, please?' I said when dinner was ready, as it seemed I was the only one still functioning. He did so, but before we began to eat, the door opened and Mum and Dad came out.

I could tell Mum had been crying, but she tried not to show it. Dad looked sick.

'Well, it's done,' Dad said, getting straight to the point. 'We have lost the farm.'

Those five words hung in the air like the smell of a wet sheep in a small room. He hung his head and I tried to work out what it was I could see in him. It was something I'd never seen before. It wasn't anger, guilt, fear or bitterness; all the things I was feeling at that moment. No, it was shame. Mr Willis had beaten him.

We have lost the farm. It echoed around and around in my head. I tried to catch the words to find out what they really meant. To lose the farm was one thing. To lose pride and respect, that was another. To lose touch with Julianne, to lose our home, our town, these were the things that mattered to me. I knew we wouldn't lose each other, but could we still love each other when we had lost our right to self-respect? A gloomy sense of regret descended upon me. Had we really appreciated anything before this?

The tears Helen had been holding back now flowed and she went to her room, with Mum just behind her. Nick stalked outside and made short work of the wood-chopping that had to be done anyway. Amy held Angel close and took her to watch Nick, while Thomas cursed out loud and said he was going for a walk. Dad went after him.

I sat at the table, now by myself, and poked at my dinner. I could hear Mum trying to comfort Helen in her room without much success. Outside Nick was snapping at

Amy and telling her Angel was a stupid cat. Amy burst into tears – a real dramatic wail that she had perfected years ago. I couldn't hear Dad and Tom. The dreadful impact of what Dad had said weighed my heart down, but there was no one to share it with. I looked at the other plates of food, now going cold, and let out a long, frail sigh. I was as scared as anyone else. I didn't know what was going to happen. I pushed my dinner away, looked around at the empty room and table, and suddenly felt very alone.

'I thought I'd see you today,' Julianne told me the next afternoon, coming up our driveway where I was taking Blacky back to his stall. She was carrying her small bag and her red hair seemed even brighter against the grey sky. I indicated for her to follow me to the stables. I made Blacky comfortable, spreading out some new hay, giving him his feed and a special treat from me. I could feel Julianne watching me. 'You have to go, don't you?' she whispered.

I was still facing Blacky, but I nodded.

'Oh, Meg.' She reached out and put a hand on my shoulder.

To have someone finally express sorrow on my behalf was enough for tears to spring to my eyes. But I could not fall apart now. I blinked them away and turned to her, surprised to see that Julianne had tears of her own. 'We're going too,' she said.

'What?' I thought she was joking.

'My parents have had to give up our house to the bank too. We're going to travel to find work for Dad.'

'All of you? I mean, Peter too?' I asked, referring to her older brother.

'All of us.'

'What about William?'

A tear rolled down her rosy cheek. 'Well, if it's meant to be, it will happen anyway, somehow. But to be honest, that's not what really worries me.'

'What does worry you?'

'Losing you,' she whispered. 'Friends no matter what, we said. And now we will probably be forced to go in different directions.'

'Oh, Jules,' I said affectionately, embracing her.

'You're like a sister to me, Meg,' she choked.

I held her closer.

'We're heading towards Coolibah,' I said. 'Which way is your family heading?'

She hesitated for a moment. 'We're going to Coolibah too!'

'Well, there you go; that's not so bad.'

She smiled and wiped away a tear or two. 'Maybe our dads will both find work there and we'll see each other just as much!'

'We can only hope.' I took a deep breath. 'I'll really miss Harrington, but remember how much we thought we'd miss school?'

'Oh, yes! But just think, now there's no more Mr Timms trying to tell us that education is wasted on girls; no more Mrs Phipps telling us we can't cook properly and that therefore we are failures as women.'

'No more Mrs Taylor speaking to us in a language we could never understand.'

'French, which you could speak better than any of us!'

'Au contraire!' I said, and we both laughed. 'Will you miss William?'

Julianne forced a smile. 'I was only just starting to really get to know him. But, I did hope that... Yes, I will miss him, Meghan. Jeremy's already in Coolibah. Did you know?'

'Really?' I said flatly, failing to hide my disinterest.

'Uh-huh. Left here to go and work on a property there.'

'Well, that's good for you.'

'How so?'

'Because William will want to visit him sometime, and then you'll be able to see him!'

Her face brightened up at the thought, and we talked about the possibilities until it was time for her to go home.

'What are you doing here?' I asked with a ferocity that Frederick Hanson seemed to coax from me. I was on my way back to the house later that day when I saw him riding up the driveway. Rusty, our cattle dog, started growling at him.

'Evicting your family,' he replied calmly.

I dropped the bag of food I was carrying. 'What? Already?' I asked in shock. 'We were only told about it yesterday! We need time!'

'Emotion doesn't get far with me, Miss Meghan.' He dismounted his horse and towered over me. 'I take it you inherit this impertinence from your father. Your mother was never so forceful in the way she spoke.'

I swallowed the curses I wanted to spit at him. 'They say you loved her but now you're prepared to turn her onto the streets. Do you think that will make her regret choosing my father over you?'

His eyes settled on me with a disturbing coolness.

'Meghan?' I heard Mum call, and then I heard her light steps behind me. She faltered when she saw whom I was talking to and put a protective hand on my shoulder.

Frederick's eyes moved to Mum's. They did not greet each other – I think Mum was shocked to see him and he was remembering. 'Seven days,' he told me suddenly, and then he remounted his horse and left.

———————————

At first I worried that both Mum and Dad were sinking into a depression – it was such a blow for them. Dad had left his parents' farm to build this one with Mum when they married. But then, somehow, they both started talking positively again.

'You know, Meg,' Mum said one time while I was helping her decide which clothes to take, 'I think God has given me the strength to do this. Perhaps we need the change. Perhaps it will bring us closer together.'

'God?' I scoffed. Having always been to church, I had never really questioned that God existed, but last Sunday I actually paid attention to what we were singing – hymns about him being a friend, a mighty fortress, helping us in times of need. For the first time, I felt bitter when I thought of him, because friends, like Julianne had said, were there for each other when it mattered most. Losing our farm, having to go on the road, seeing my dad look ashamed – that all mattered a lot to me and my family. So where was he now?

Mum squeezed my shoulder. 'He is the only one that never changes, the only one we can hang onto through all of this. Don't deny yourself that, Meg.'

'I think you should take this skirt,' I said to her, pointing at a grey woollen one and deliberately changing the subject. 'It'd be nice and warm.'

'Yes, but we're heading into summer now.' Still, she folded it up and put it in her suitcase.

'What do you think Dad will work as?'

'Oh, no doubt he'll work on the farms with Nick and Tom. I'll look for work too, though God knows, it's ever so much harder for women.'

'Helen and I will help. I'm sure Amy will too.'

'Yes, I know you will. I am blessed with good children.' She winked at me and tried to close her suitcase. 'But you'll soon realise that not all men are like your father. Many are respectful, but many others are like that tramp you scared off. Or like Mr Willis, or Fred.'

'Yes, but what will happen, Mum? I mean, we all start earning money, but then what? Buy another house? Come back here? Just keep drifting until this financial whatchamacallit is over?'

'Meghan, I don't even know what we'll be doing tomorrow let alone when your father and I get jobs, or even *if* we will get jobs. More and more men are travelling the roads every day, looking for work.'

'And I thought you knew everything,' I said with a grin that she returned. 'Did you hear about those unemployed men in Perth? Demanding to see the premier?'

'Yes. I'm afraid the situation is getting a little desperate.'

'And it's finally hit us.'

Mum's suitcase slipped off the bed and burst open again. 'I think I might have to sacrifice some more things,' she said with a laugh.

'You can put some in my case – I don't think I'll use it all.'

'Meghan, I must say, you are taking this better than anyone.'

'What has to be done has to be done. I just want to get on with it.'

40

She eyed me carefully and with suspicion, as if she thought I was being a little too clinical about it, but she decided not to say anything.

I ran outside when I heard Nick and Dad coming home. They had gone into Harrington to sell and buy some things for the family. The first thing I saw was that the old cart was gone and had been replaced with a rather large rig or van and a new Clydesdale horse.

'We've got two tents as well!' Nick sounded almost as if he had been enjoying himself. 'Enough room for us all. Mum and Dad will sleep in the van, of course, and we'll travel in it as needed.'

I nodded my approval and patted the horse. 'What have you called it?' I asked Nick, as Dad went to fetch Mum.

'I was thinking either Clyde or Dale. What do you think?'

'Not very original. And pretty odd for a mare, isn't it?'

'Oh!' He reddened and double-checked the horse.

I laughed. 'Just kidding, Nick. It's a he, as you knew very well.'

'Meghan! For a second there, I thought I'd failed as a farmer's son!' He shoved my shoulder and I think he would have chased me right up to the letterbox, like he did once when I cracked raw eggs in his boots, but Dad returned with Mum.

'What do you think, Evelyn?'

She looked in the back of the van. 'Well, I've always wanted to be a gypsy!' At first I thought she was being sarcastic, but then they both laughed. 'Tomorrow then?'

'Tomorrow.' They kissed, and seeing them, Nick and I quickly went inside.

———————————

That night, just after we had finished dinner, we heard a car pull up. 'If that's Mr Willis, just you let me speak to him,' Dad said firmly to no one in particular. I shuddered to think I might have to see Victoria again. We heard the rattly motor switch off and the sound of young people. A faint look of hope passed over Nick's face as he went to the door.

'Mr Robinson!' he exclaimed, greeting Brigitte's dad. 'Come in, please.' Mr Robinson's wife came in next with a shy smile, followed by their three children. Emily was their youngest, at only eleven. As she was seven years behind her brother, James, there were some rumours suggesting that she may have been a surprise. Brigitte, the eldest, came in last, wearing a deep purple coat. She smiled warmly at us all and I was suddenly aware of just how pretty she had become.

My parents invited them all to take a seat and join them for a cup of tea. Soon the room was full of chatter. Amy immediately adopted Emily and went to show her Angel and Clyde, while James and Thomas began talking about whether or not Donald Bradman would help us win some match. Not feeling particularly social, I busied myself with making the teas. I was surprised when Brigitte came to assist me. 'How are you, Meghan?' she asked softly, and I had a feeling she really wanted to know.

'Fine, and yourself?'

'Good, thank you, though very sorry that Harrington will be losing such a fine family tomorrow. I shall miss having you all around.'

'Any of us in particular?' It was a leading question, and not one I had the right to ask. Nevertheless, Brigitte was honest.

'You know I like your brother. Men like him don't come along every day.'

It was funny to hear Nick be called a 'man' – it all sounded a little too grown-up for the big brother who had been hanging upside down out of trees so recently.

'But we're nobodies now,' I said. 'We'll be living in tents tomorrow night.'

'Do you think that bothers me? Or my family?' She brushed back her beautiful copper hair, her hazel-green eyes trying to work out what I really thought of her. 'We are not all like Mr Willis.'

'I hardly know you, Brigitte.'

'I know, but I want to get to know you – and Helen and your parents and the others.'

'And how do you intend to do that? We'll be on the road tomorrow while you get to sit in your comfy chair by the fire, eating lamb roast or something equally hearty. We'll be brushing the charcoal off our damper and soon you won't even know where we are.'

'Nick is going to write to me, Meghan.'

I stopped pouring the tea and started setting them all onto a tray.

'And you cannot blame me for what is happening,' Brigitte added quietly.

I realised I had been unnecessarily harsh. 'I… I don't. I just… I'm not ready for all these changes. And I don't understand why you're telling me these things. I'm just Nick's little…'

'Like I said, I want to get to know you a bit.'

I picked up the tray, glad when Helen came in to find out what was keeping me, because Brigitte began to talk to her, allowing me to escape.

When I walked back into the lounge room, Mrs Robinson was giving Mum some homemade hand towels to take with her, while Dad and Mr Robinson discussed the future. 'I only wish I could offer you work myself,' Mr

Robinson said. He was a level-headed lawyer who employed a farm foreman to run his property while he indulged in other business, both in Harrington and in the city. 'Seems such a shame to have a man of your knowledge and calibre leave the district to find employment. It's not fair.'

I approached and handed them their cups of tea.

'Yes,' Dad said, 'but as my Meghan here says, what must be done must be done.'

Mr Robinson took a sip of his tea and looked at me. 'Sounds a bit... callous.'

I bit my lip. I was already feeling out of sorts after my talk with Brigitte and I didn't need her father judging me. What did he know of what I felt? Did he think I was looking forward to the next day? Dad noticed my silence and covered it with a laugh. 'No, just practical,' he said warmly, which helped a bit.

But then I saw Nick going out onto the verandah with Brigitte. I realised that, since Helen had joined the mothers, I was on my own again. I don't know what happened next, only that my hand shook a little and when I went to hand Thomas and James their cups, I tripped on the mat. Although I did not fall, all of the teas did. Some of Mum's best china smashed on the ground with a shattering sound that stopped everybody's conversations like a brick wall stops a paper plane.

I watched the black tea swirl around and sink into the mat like a big bruise. I was still clutching the tray, now much more tightly than necessary. I looked up slowly and saw everyone staring at me, including Nick and Brigitte, who had come back in at the sound of the crash.

I forced myself to walk away from them into the kitchen, where I put down the tray. I could hear either Mum or Helen coming after me, but I slipped out the back door and ran down into the nearest paddock. I was scared of what I had done, of why it had happened, and afraid that the emotions I now felt would somehow be the end of who I thought I was.

———————

Nobody found me hiding amongst the long grass like a rabbit. I heard them calling me, but I couldn't face the Robinsons. I waited until they left and then until the last light in the house was switched off before I made my way back. Creeping in through the door they'd left open for me, I went to my room, trying not to make the wooden floor squeak. I closed the door and turned on the light. When I turned around, I saw Mum sitting on my bed and I jumped with fright.

'I'm sorry about your china,' I blurted straight away. 'It was an accident.'

'I know it was, so why did you run off?'

'Because I... I was scared.'

'That's not like you.'

I didn't know what to say to that, so I said nothing. I just wanted to go to bed, to spend one last night in my room. Mum watched me for a moment and then walked over to hug me. Dad came into the room and hugged us both. Then he put an arm around Mum's waist, so I knew that what he was about to say came from both of them.

'We know this is not easy, Meghan, but we will be doing it together. It'll be just like camping, only all the time. We'll get used to it, and it could end up being a bit of fun.'

'Yes, I know,' I said, hoping they would just leave me alone. I don't know why I wanted them to go – I didn't understand anything I had been feeling for the last seven days.

'We love you, Meghan.' Mum looked as if she was really worried. 'A lot.'

I weakened a bit then. 'And I you.'

The next morning, just as we took the last of what we could out of our house, Frederick Hanson, Mr Willis and two other men arrived. Without a word to Dad they went into the house, started carrying out furniture and dumping it on the driveway. 'What are you doing?' Dad asked Mr Willis, grabbing him by the shoulder.

'You won't be in need of these anymore,' Mr Willis said. 'We'll auction them off.'

'Can't you at least wait until we're gone?'

It was one of the most demoralising things I had ever seen. There was a cry from Mum inside the house, and Dad shoved Mr Willis out of the way and went in for her.

I heard another pair of footsteps coming up behind me. I turned, and my heart sank when I saw it was Victoria. I took a step towards Nick, instinctively seeking him for protection, but Victoria reached me first.

'Well, Meghan,' she crowed softly, 'it's funny to think that when we went to school together I thought you may have been better off than me. And now look at us!' Another man dropped my bed onto the driveway. 'I bet this is one of the worst days of your life.' Her tongue touched her top lip as she waited for my response.

'Victoria, what are you doing here?' Nicholas asked, coming over. 'I don't see why they needed to bring you. I think you should leave.'

I was gripping my hand into a tight fist, trying not to show her how much she had upset me. How dare she mock us when we couldn't be brought any lower anyway? 'This property belongs to my father now,' she said, her eyes still fixed on me. 'I have a right to be here. It's your family that has to go.'

She swept past and paused by my side to intimidate me. 'I hate you,' I whispered.

'God bless you, Meghan.' Victoria's throat made a guttural sound that I think was supposed to be an attempt to stop herself laughing out loud. She deliberately bumped my shoulder as she walked into the house. Nobody else noticed. I watched her go, no longer thinking of her as a shark, but as a vulture, scavenging and picking away at the remains of what was once my life.

Amy was hiding her face in Helen's waist while the boys looked like they wanted to kill someone. I could hear Dad shouting now, and Frederick Hanson shouting back. We all knew that Dad only ever really yelled at someone when they had upset Mum. The other two men came out and dumped Mum's dressing table out on the driveway, a present from her father upon her engagement.

'I'm sure Miss Victoria would like to have that,' one of them remarked. Next came the beautiful piano. Then Dad's desk.

'All our things,' Amy whispered. 'Why are they doing this to all our things?'

Before any of us could respond, Dad, angrier than a lion whose pride has been threatened, stormed back out of the house leading Mum by the hand. She was white and trembling, and Dad indicated for us all to get into the van. We scrambled in, but I glanced back. Dad held Mum closely and then they both turned and took one last look back at the house as the pile of furniture at the front grew.

'First they took our house,' Mum said to Dad. 'Now they have taken our home.'

5

SITTING IN THE BACK OF THE VAN, I WATCHED the last view of our home disappear behind the hills. I felt a deep, strange fondness for it; more so than I ever had when it was still 'ours'. As we drove our way to town, Rusty lying with his head in my lap, I kept thinking things like: *That's the tree where Amy broke her arm when she was seven, and Nick carried her all the way home. This is the paddock where Julianne's parents' cart broke and we had to come and help them fix it. Here's the stretch of road where we found our dog Lazy dead, and Dad just said, 'Oh well, saves me shooting him myself.'* That had made Helen cry. *There's the lane where we found Thomas after he walked eight miles without us knowing when he was only six.* We'd spent ten hours looking for him and when we found him he looked at us in surprise and asked, quite innocently, 'What?' It was the only time I could remember Mum losing her temper.

'That's the spot where I got my first and only kiss,' Helen said, pointing to a patch of grass by a small creek.

'What?' I asked with surprise – as far as I knew, Helen had never been interested in a bloke. 'Who was it?'

'Tommy Maxwell – we were five.'

I rolled my eyes. 'That doesn't count.'

'That's where you were born, Meghan,' Dad said, joining in our reminiscing. He pointed to a small cottage not far off the road. Mum and Dad had been on their way to a charity-do in town when Mum suddenly went into labour. I came so fast they didn't have time to get her to hospital, so Megan Bell, Jeremy's mum, who was also pregnant at the time, brought me into the world in that little cottage where she and her family were living. Mum first told me the story when we visited her grave in the town cemetery. She had died in childbirth, which was, as Mum put it, 'one of the more poignant injustices of life'. Jeremy was only two when she was lost along with his baby sister. His father looked after him, but he died himself when Jeremy was nine. Mum never forgot how Mrs Bell had helped her though. She put flowers on her grave at the anniversary of her death every year and she'd also named me after her. Except she added the 'h' – 'for hope,' she said.

'That's where your father proposed to me,' Mum said as we came into the outskirts of town, indicating the park on the river.

'What did you say?' Nick asked Dad.

'"Come on, ya old sheila, you'll do for me."'

We laughed, and I heard Mum hit him. 'He did not. Otherwise I certainly would not have said yes!'

'True,' Dad said. 'I dunno, Nick, just told her she was beautiful and that I wanted to spend the rest of my life with her. The usual spiel. Turned on the charm – got what I wanted.'

Although I couldn't see Mum's face, I knew she'd be glaring at him, but I also knew that Dad was just doing it to help her forget what had just happened back at the house. She cleared her throat and recapped the proposal in a classy voice: '"Evelyn, you know I've loved you from the moment I met you. You are beautiful and warm, clever and interesting. I cannot imagine life without you, so I hope you will consider being my wife. As your husband, I will love and protect you, provide for you and always be there for you. Will you marry me?"'

'I said all that?' Dad feigned surprise.

'*Yes!*' Mum emphasised the word as if he should remember, which I suspect he did.

'Well, don't go telling too many people. I've got my reputation to keep up!'

We turned into the main street of Harrington, which we had to travel through to get to Coolibah. There were a few people walking up the road, but it seemed strangely quiet. Then, an amazing thing happened. At the last bend, where the last shops of Harrington were, there was a small crowd standing outside the bank. When they heard Clyde clopping along, pulling the van behind him, they took off their hats and waved at us. Some shouted well wishes while others cheered.

'Mr Willis is no friend of ours!'

'You'll be missed around these parts, Nathaniel!'

'The next town will be lucky to have ya!'

'Good luck, Evelyn!'

We waved back and called our final goodbyes. I saw Julianne standing amongst them with William behind her. Since Mum and Dad were distracted with their friends, I jumped off the back of the van and ran to her for one last hug.

'I'll see you soon, Meg,' she promised.

I squeezed her hand and ran back to the van. I didn't realise that Nick had also jumped off and made a beeline for someone else. He was hugging Brigitte, and when he stood back and tenderly brushed back a stray hair, I realised that he was beyond the point of help. He loved her, and she him. I would now have to learn how to love her too. He squeezed her upper arm and hurried back as I had, but then a wild grin passed over his face and he suddenly raced back to her, cupped her face with both hands and kissed her right there in front of everyone.

The people whistled and barracked as Nick ran back to the van in a daze. Brigitte laughed as she waved to us. I caught her eye and she mouthed, 'Goodbye, Meghan.' I smiled at her, and Brigitte smiling back at me was my last memory of Harrington.

It was around dusk when we pulled into Magpie Reserve at Coolibah. There were a fair few people camping there. They all stopped and stared at us as we drove in, the pots and pans in the van rattling and drawing even more attention. Some of them had crying babies. Some were just men on their own, and they seemed to stick together. Others were young couples without kids, but there were lots of children younger than Amy. They all ran around through each other's camps so it was impossible to see who belonged where. Most of them looked like they needed a good feed and a bath.

Dad picked a flat spot under a huge river red gum and cheerfully went about setting up camp. 'Nick, can you set up the girls' tent first? Meghan will give ya a hand. Tom, I reckon you could make a good fire with some of the bark from this tree. Amy darl', could you fill this bucket with water from the river? Oh, and Helen, what are you like at cooking damper?'

'What do you want me to do?' Mum asked.

Dad put his arms around her. 'Enjoy the fresh air?'

'Nathaniel...'

He kissed her quickly. 'Tend to the horse. I'll set up everything else.'

Once we were settled in, some of the other campers came over to visit us. There was Molly and Dave, who were newly married and who both worked at a local cannery. Molly had just found out she was expecting, so things were about to get a bit tough for them. There was old Mrs Fletcher, whose husband had just died of pneumonia so she was on her way to stay with her daughter's family. Mum straight away gave her a bag of tea out of sympathy. There were brothers, Jack and Larry, and a red-haired girl called Jenny who reminded me a bit of Julianne. She was older though and married to a bloke called Ian. They had a little tacker named Danny. And there was Emma Wales, who was just a bit older than Nick and on her own. She didn't say much and didn't introduce herself, but we heard from others that she had no family and had been fending for herself for some time. Mum made her a pie and Dad began to worry that we'd run out of food and supplies after that first day.

Dad found temporary work pretty much straight away – shearing at a farm with Nick – but it was poor money, only enough to keep us in flour and other basics. Mum spent eight days going to every place within walking distance, with Helen, Amy and me only half a step behind her. The dairy was going to be the last place she tried, partly because she was starting to lose heart, and partly because there was nothing else left anyway. We came to the dairy and told the owner, Mr Johnson, about our situation.

'Sorry, ladies, but I don't need much more help here, at least nothing permanent.'

'We'll take anything,' Helen begged. She had taken the change worst of all and was tired of scraping for work, especially when just weeks before we had been in a position to offer it.

'Sorry, miss. Don't mean no offence, but you hardly look fit for work.'

'Excuse me?' My tone immediately made Mum reach for my hand. 'Look, we all grew up on a farm! We're used to working. We may not be the best at it or look like we

impossible. I thought I'd either be separated from the kids somehow or they'd get sick or we'd end up beggars... I am lucky that they aren't young. Nick is a grown man and Helen almost a woman. They are all capable of good work and this is proof that we can do it. We have to. There isn't a choice.'

'But what changed you?' Molly asked. 'I mean, you don't seem too worried now.'

Mum laughed as if it was absurd. 'Don't I? Well, I still am, but I guess I just know that God would never put us through this alone. It's not all bad. What do you think, Nathaniel?'

He smiled tenderly at her. 'As much as I regret losing the farm and our way of life and our respect, I don't mind this. It's an adventure, if nothing else. Not ideal and not forever, I hope, but I still reckon we're blessed.'

Once the chatter around the fire died down, I went to bed, stepping past Helen and Amy on the way. As I lay down on the thin mattress, I realised that it was soaked through. The rain we had had that afternoon had gotten in and wet everything of mine. I grabbed my pillow and headed back out to sleep next to the fire in the open air. *Blessed,* I thought cynically.

———————

I spent my days at work with Mum and Helen. They both milked cows at the dairy but I spent most of my time cleaning the milk cans and milk shed, wondering if I'd prefer to marry a dairy or sheep farmer. Every day, as we walked back to camp, I'd hope that Julianne would be there, that we would be reunited. I missed her so much. She was the only one I could tell everything to and I longed to share with her things about work, Mr Johnson, about how we were doing okay, how Nick wrote to Brigitte every other day, how Mum ran a bit of a school when we got back from the dairy every day, and how Emma always listened in from a distance. I wanted Julianne to be there when the whole camp gathered and sang around the fire or shared stories about how they lost everything and ended up on the road. But she didn't come.

I wrote her a letter, but I had no way of telling if she'd received it. Although I didn't speak it, I started to worry because this was not like her. She had said she'd meet up with me and I trusted that. Had something happened? Was she in trouble? The thought took up a permanent residence at the back of my mind, but more than that, I was worried because even if she was in trouble, what could I do?

So, although I anticipated her arrival every day, she didn't come, and soon Dad and Nick finished with the shearing and we had to move on.

'She's a pretty girl with red hair. Not red like fire, but red like a sunset. And blue eyes, like a wren. She's as tall as me.' I waved my hand just above my head to emphasise what I meant. Mrs Fletcher listened to me patiently. 'If you see her, just tell her that we've had to move on to Gracechurch.'

'Okay, Megsy dear. Your mother has been so kind to me, I'd do anything to repay the debt. But I won't be here much longer myself. Nearly saved enough to get to my daughter's place in Darralong now.'

'Well, here's a letter for her in case you do see her.' I handed her the rough bit of paper with Miss Julianne Young written on the front, wondering if she would ever be Mrs Julianne Cale. I felt sad at the thought that I may be missing something major in her life but reassured myself that she wouldn't do anything without talking to me about it. We were still best friends, after all.

'Thanks, Mrs Fletcher. I hope you get to your daughter's soon.'

Our camp was already packed up, but I wasn't keen to move and start the hunt for work all over again. Helen appeared shaky and I knew she hated it most of all, or at least it frightened her the most. Only Thomas was faintly interested in the idea. I think he just wanted new things to think about. I settled into the van with my legs hanging out the back and Rusty sleeping beside me. The green grass spotted with gums soon became open paddocks that reminded me of home, but I knew that, like it or not, the road would be my only home for a while yet.

6

'MEGHAN!' HELEN YELLED AT ME. I FLINCHED AT the sound. 'Why is there no wood for a fire yet?'

I opened my mouth in surprise. We'd been at the Jasper Recreation Park just outside of Gracechurch for two days and yes, we'd all become a bit tired of having to live so close to each other. But none of us had bothered yelling.

'I got some just this morning!'

'Well, we've used it all!'

'Well, I didn't know that.' I was annoyed at her tone. Who did she think she was, my mother? 'Since when did it become my job anyway? I thought making fires was Tom's job!' We were standing about twelve yards apart and attracting attention from some bystanders.

'Yes, but he's in town with Nick and Dad, so please just help me out and do something constructive for once.

How dare she? I thought, my anger flickering again. Do something constructive? I'd been working as hard as anyone else! More than her, I knew that for a fact. She was too busy sulking about the injustices of losing the farm and being away from her friends to put her mind to work. And what about me? I missed Julianne like crazy, was seriously worried about her and deeply homesick, but did I complain?

I cursed under my breath and headed for the gum trees on the other side of Jasper Creek. I slipped over in the creek and ended up with mud all up one side as well as a nice graze on my right upper arm. I sat there for a moment until I realised what had happened and the pain in my arm started to sink in. Grimacing, I tried to get up and slipped again. I kept doing so until I ended up crawling to the side and onto the bank, my new shoes filling up with water on the way. *Why does everything have to be so hard?* I finally managed to stand up, pretended that neither my body nor my pride was hurt, and kept going.

I was so annoyed at Helen that I walked and walked. Once or twice I broke into a run but tried to restrain my anger, which meant slowing down. I walked past a cluster of mossy rocks, a tall stringy bark, a wombat hole and a small billabong. When I was far from the camp, I found a single, tall tree fern and sat down under its long fronds. The grey clouds started to spit on the earth and I was grateful for the shelter, even though I was pretty wet from the creek anyway.

Whenever I got angry on the farm, I would go down to the willow on the river and just watch the creek flow, smoothly but certainly. I would clear my head and not think about what had upset me, and soon I would be my usual calm self again. I now watched drops of rain drip from the end of the fern's fronds, and it had the same effect on me. I pulled my grey woollen jacket closer around me, as if that would coax its wet fibres to warm me.

I don't know how long I sat there, but I was considering heading back when I heard footsteps. Whoever it was, they were just behind me. They were walking quite purposefully at first, but then, for whatever reason, they stopped.

My heart quickened. Ever since the incident with the tramp I'd become much more nervous of strangers, and men particularly, especially when I was on my own. I was far into the bush where no one could hear me even if I did yell. I gripped my jacket lapel tightly and didn't move.

I was too late. Apparently, they had already seen me. I heard them approach me carefully, like Dad used to approach a ram that had to be gelded. Wondering if they were as worried about me as I them, I jumped up suddenly and turned to face them, figuring surprise was my best method of attack.

I raised my hand – I'm not really sure why – and then dropped it. It wasn't a man so much as a boy, and one I recognised from somewhere. He recognised me too, so we stood there staring at each other, trying to decide how we knew each other.

'Meghan?' he asked carefully.

'Jeremy?' I scrunched up my face, trying to see if it really was him underneath the tan and behind the weary gaze. 'Jeremy Bell?'

'Yes. Meghan, are you hurt?' He approached me with concern. He slipped on a patch of wet leaves but recovered quickly and stepped closer.

'No, I'm fine.'

'You look terrible.'

'Just fell in the creek.'

He hid a smile. 'Are you lost?'

'No, just hiding. My family is camped somewhere over there.' I pointed to where I meant.

'Really? Could I see them? I guess I'd... I'd feel like I was back at Harrington again.'

'Sure, they'd love to see you too.'

I was a little perplexed at this new Jeremy. The old one hardly put two words together let alone spoke in full sentences to a girl. My parents knew Jeremy better than I did. He'd worked for my father occasionally and Mum always chatted to him in the streets because she knew his mother, but I didn't consider him a friend at all. He used to spend all his time with William.

'William!' I said suddenly. 'Have you seen William or heard from Julianne or anything?'

He shook his head. 'Last I heard, Will was heading north to stay with his cousin for a while. Don't know anything about Julianne. Surely you do, though?'

'No, no, I haven't heard anything.' Tired tears sprang to my eyes as I thought of her, but I blinked them away. *What's happened to her?* I thought for the thousandth time. *What if she's not okay?*

'I'm sorry, Meghan. I'm sure she has a good reason... You two were like sisters.'

'Friends, no matter what,' I mumbled quietly, but then for the first time, I felt a little confused. Julianne was supposed to be my friend, my best friend, a position I didn't offer freely. And yet, not only was she not there when it mattered to me, she hadn't even written to tell me why. It was the not knowing that was killing me. Did she hate me for some reason? Did she not want to see me anymore? Was she ever really my friend at all, then? Or worse, had something terrible happened? In which case I should be there for her and I wasn't, so did that make me a bad friend? I sighed heavily, forgetting all about Jeremy for a minute and wondering why friendships were so complicated sometimes.

'Perhaps we should head back to your family,' he suggested. 'You should dry off, clean up a bit.'

'I was supposed to be getting firewood,' I remembered suddenly.

'Let me help.' He gathered some branches as we walked back towards camp. I stopped at the stringy gum and collected some bark that had fallen around the base.

'There she is!' Amy said when we made it back to the creek. I walked across more carefully this time.

'You didn't have to run off,' Helen said stormily as I dropped the bark and wood around the fire. Jeremy did the same, but one log landed on his foot. He crinkled his nose to try and prove it hadn't hurt. Then he greeted Helen and Amy. Tom, who had been visiting one of the other campers, realised he was with us and ran back to say g'day.

Dad must have heard us talking, as he came out of the van. 'Jeremy Bell!' He immediately went to shake Jeremy's hand. 'Well, Mr Bell, it's good to see you!'

Mum, who was scrubbing our clothes in the wash-basin a few yards away, looked up and brushed her hair back with soapy hands. She seemed weary but smiled when she saw him. 'Jeremy?'

He walked over to her, grinning like a kid in a lolly shop. 'Mrs Manley,' he said.

Mum hugged him tightly. I think Jeremy must have been pretty lonely for the last few months and she somehow knew this, because she held onto him for a moment longer. He relished all of it. I knew that he couldn't even remember his own mother. Moments like this which I often took for granted were probably precious to him.

'Jeremy, come and sit by the fire that Tom's about to make, and tell us what you've…' She saw me and stopped. 'Meghan! What have you been doing?'

I looked at my hands guiltily and realised they were brown with mud. I probably really did look a mess. Mum sighed and went back to the van. She grabbed some soap and a towel as well as other clothes for me to change into. 'Meg, go and clean up and I'll wash your clothes for you. Make sure you clean out that gash.'

I took my time back down at the creek, liking the feeling of the water lapping my legs, although I was only in up to my knees. It made me feel clean and a part of the land. I watched the dirt run off me and back into the river where it belonged. It was swept away in an instant, bending to the will of the current. With a bucket, I washed my hair thoroughly and tried to decide what colour it really was. Mum called it honey and Dad called it mousy. I decided on dark honey and tied it all back with a clasp.

I put on the clean clothes, tied up my shoes and leaned against the river gum that grew steadily by the water. I could hear chatter coming from the campsite and smell the smoke from the campfires. It was a real thick eucalyptus smell, the kind that is familiar and good, rather than the bushfire kind.

I got back in time to hear the end of Jeremy's story, how he'd had a rough time at Coolibah and moved on to Gracechurch fairly quickly. 'And today I was just coming back from work when I found something that I wasn't sure of at first.' He looked at me and his brown eyes sparkled. 'But it was the most welcome sight I ever saw.'

I smiled politely.

'Well, she doesn't look half so scary now.' Mum winked at me.

'Quite the opposite,' Jeremy mumbled.

'What do you intend to do now?' Dad asked him.

'Keep working, I guess, while the going is good. There's an orchard about three miles away. I help pick oranges. There's quite a few of us there.'

'Do you reckon there'd be room for a few more?'

'Well, I don't see why not. You, Nick and Tom, you mean?'

'We're looking for work too,' I said.

Jeremy grimaced. 'Yes, but I'm afraid Mr Rogers, who owns the place, doesn't hire women.'

I rolled my eyes and was about to criticise.

'I don't make the rules, Meghan,' Jeremy added. 'Nor do I always agree with them. But there might be work in the town itself, in Gracechurch.'

63

'We'll be sure to check it out more thoroughly tomorrow,' Mum said, looking at me steadily. 'In the meantime, Jeremy, where have you been sleeping?'

'Oh… here and there.'

'Well, stay with us tonight. You can sleep under the van – it's quite cosy, actually. Or perhaps we could persuade Nick to clean up his half of the tent and you can squeeze in there.'

Nick was about to agree but Jeremy shook his head. 'Under the van sounds great. Much better than on the side of the road, anyway!'

He stood to put his swag there while Mum went to finish the washing.

'You could clean up your stuff anyway,' Tom suggested hopefully to Nick.

Nick just grunted and pretended not to hear him.

———————————

By the end of the next day, everyone had work except for Amy and me. Mum said she'd keep asking for me but in the meantime I was to help Amy with her French. I had no idea how French was going to be of any use to us, but I think Mum wanted to know that her kids were still as educated as any others, and French had a certain class about it. It was also the only thing I was good enough at to pass on to someone else.

Towards the end of the second week at Jasper Reserve, I was running her through a new set of verbs when we heard Dad's voice just after midday. That was real unusual. We were into December now and the days were hot and humid, so much so that even walking became a burden. Yet Rusty was barking loudly and when I saw Dad he seemed to be running awkwardly with someone in his arms. Fear passed through me like quicksilver as I thought it was Mum or Helen, either dangerously ill or hurt. But when he came closer, Amy and I realised that it was Emma, whom we had met at Magpie Reserve.

'What's wrong with her?' I asked as Dad lay her down in the van.

'Not sure. We found her lying on the ground just outside the fence at the orchard. She had an orange in her hand so I think she might have been stealing. I don't know if it was a bad one and she's poisoned by it, or if she was sick with hunger before she even got it. Jeremy's gone to fetch the doctor and your mother.'

'Why Mum?'

'Because Emma will want her more than any of us. Now, Meghan, I have to get back to work or I'll lose my job. Can you stay by her and keep her warm until Mum and the doctor arrive?'

I nodded and hopped up into the van next to Emma. Dad smiled weakly at me and was off. Amy went up to the road to keep watch.

Emma was perspiring. She had blonde hair and very pale skin and she was mumbling in a daze. Not knowing what else to do, I took her hand and got a bit frightened when she gripped it so tightly. If I'd had more faith in God I would have prayed, but I didn't. He never answered my other prayers so why would this one be any different? The only bit of the Bible I even remembered was 'hope deferred maketh the heart sick'. Prayer created hope, so it seemed best to avoid it.

Even so, I was feeling lonely there with Emma. The breeze outside picked up and whistled past the van. Camp seemed unusually quiet. I put my hand over her forehead like Mum always did when any of us were sick, and realising just how hot she was, I fetched a damp cloth and put it over her forehead. She settled for a moment at the touch of it. I lit the kerosene lamp and tucked Mum and Dad's blankets tightly around her. Then I propped Emma's head on a thin pillow, dabbing the cloth on her forehead again. Although her breathing was heavy, she seemed to fall into a light sleep.

It was another fifteen minutes before Amy pulled up the back canvas and told me she'd seen Mum hurrying back on her own.

When she finally made it, Mum was puffing and tired. Still, she got into the van with me and looked at Emma with concern.

'Where's the doctor?' I asked her.

'He wouldn't come. Said he was too busy and that it was probably just the common cold, even if it is summer. He may be right, but I think a lot of it is hunger as well.' She squeezed my shoulder. 'You're a good girl, Meghan. She looks very comfortable. Just keep dabbing her forehead like that and I'll make her some porridge and brew some tea. I think a good meal will help her more than anything.'

'What about your job?' I asked. Mum and Helen worked at the hotel in town.

'Mrs Jenkins gave me an hour off, and only because I was insistent after Jeremy came to tell me what had happened. I'll have to go again soon, Meghan.' She spoke as if she deeply regretted it. Mum wiped some sweat off her own forehead and her face seemed a little grey.

'Why don't I go and finish the day for you? You're tired from running here and you'll know how to look after Emma better than me.'

Mum bit her lip as she considered the idea. I could tell she was about to say no, but I also knew it was tempting to her. She looked a bit haggard, like she was drained by it all: being on the road, struggling for money, looking after us all.

'Come on Mum, you look done in. Take it easy for the afternoon and let me help out. Please.'

She gritted her teeth but quickly said, 'Alright, go, before I change my mind.'

I said goodbye to Amy and headed over to the road.

'Meghan!' Mum called behind me.

I turned and she brought me her thinning sun shawl. She gently wrapped it around me. 'Thank you,' she whispered, resting her hand on my cheek for a moment.

———————

It took two days for Emma to start to improve. We figured it must have been more than hunger because she was so sick, but the doctor, who apparently was not a philanthropist, refused to see her. The nearest hospital was too far away so we never really worked out what it was. Mum nursed her into health and I went to work in Mum's place the following day and the next.

I was glad to give Mum the rest – she was not herself either and I was worried that she was getting sick too. I think Dad was worried as well because after dinner one night, when we had pretty much all the camp gathered around one fire, singing songs and trying to keep high spirits, I saw him draw her away early and settle her into bed. When he returned he tried to sing along with the crowd again, but his heart wasn't in it.

That was the first night that Emma moved more than a few yards though. With a blanket wrapped around her shoulders, she stumbled over to the fire. Nick got her some damper and a cup of tea.

'Thank you,' she said weakly. It was the first time she'd really spoken to any of us.

'Meghan?' Thomas, who was sitting beside me, asked. 'Do you think we'll ever get the farm back?'

I looked at him in surprise. I had dropped the idea soon after we'd left it. 'I don't think so. It's possible, I guess, but I don't think so.'

He turned his gaze back towards the fire. 'So long as it's possible.' I wished I could have been as content with that as he seemed to be. 'I miss school, you know,' he said, 'and the boys, and the sheep, and the river. Remember that last picnic we had there? I'm sorry we never did that more often.'

'Me too,' I said truthfully. We had taken so much for granted.

'But I enjoy this too,' Tom added. 'Every day's different. I mean, I know it's always a worry with the money and all... But, I kinda like the way we live, for now. Don't you, Meg?'

'I think I'd enjoy it more if I knew where Julianne was and if she's okay.' Each day that passed was another day of not knowing if she was alright. We had never been apart without communication for such a long time before and, on top of the worry, I just really missed her.

Jeremy, who'd been talking to Nick, overheard my last comment and sat down on the log on the other side of me. 'Meg, I'm sure you worry too much. Julianne's just fine, I bet she is.'

'Then why doesn't she tell me so? Why wouldn't she contact me if she's okay?' Somehow the thought of such deliberate neglect was worse than the idea of her being in trouble.

He threw a twig into the fire. 'I don't know. But I know how you feel. I haven't heard anything from William either. He was my best mate.'

'Do you think they're together then?'

'I don't know, Meghan, but I'll tell you one thing: I'm not into speculation.'

7

THE THINGS WITH ORANGES IS THAT IT'S TEMP-orary work – there's only so many to pick. So, when the work dried up after a couple more weeks, we moved on. A new town. A new campsite. A new creek. New faces but some familiar ones too. Emma and Jeremy came with us but supported themselves mostly. They seemed to have adopted us as family, and my parents them as children. Emma was better, though Mum still coughed a lot.

We were at a campsite at Kently now, except it wasn't really a campsite; rather, just lots of people who'd pulled up next to a nice river not far off the track. Molly and Dave were there – Molly's pregnancy advancing well – as were Jenny, Ian and their little son, Danny. I kept glancing at Jenny whenever I saw her, since, with her red hair, she reminded me so much of Julianne. The air was heavy with December heat and overall the camp had a lethargic feel about it.

We'd hardly been there five minutes when a bloke called Samuel came over. He tilted his worn brown hat at my father and greeted Mum with a friendly nod and, 'G'day.' He stood with his foot up on a log and seemed a real comfortable sort of person, like he could stay and chat with us for hours. Only young, he had the kind of cheeky grin you had to return, and he'd charmed us all into liking him pretty much two seconds after he arrived.

'So, what'd you used to do?' he asked. 'How many children? Five? But there's seven... Oh, I see, they're mates. Been travelling long? Nice strong horse you got there – how old is he?' His questions all ran together, and Mum and

Dad answered with two words or less since that's all they could fit in.

Then he put his hand in his jacket and produced a small bag of flour. 'House-warming present,' he said, but instead of giving it to Mum, he handed it to Helen. I glanced at Nick with my mouth open slightly. He raised his eyebrows back at me. We both knew that giving flour to the daughter was just a way of saying, 'I like the look of you and I'm a man looking for commitment.'

Helen blushed, and Mum and Dad glanced warily at each other.

I think they wanted Sam to go then but he didn't. He helped us set up camp, chatting the whole time like he'd been expecting us and wanting to catch up. 'I work at the sawmill,' he said, when Dad was actually able to ask him something. 'It's good, steady work. I've been there a few months. Might even be able to afford a room in town soon! The boss is fair, plus he pays a decent wage. He'd be happy to meet you; I know that for a fact.' Funny how boys know that to win a girl's heart they first have to win over the father. But I know that at the mention of 'sawmill', Dad wasn't thinking about Helen any more. I saw the glance he gave Mum and how she seemed to brace herself for something.

Knowing them as well as I did, I could read them like a book. See, Mum's dad, Grandpa Wright, was killed in a machinery accident working at a sawmill. It was just after Mum and Dad were engaged, and Mum, her two brothers and Grandma Wright were devastated. Dad told us that story only once. Mum never spoke about it at all and that's how I knew it must have been bad.

So, it was virtually written in the fine print of Mum and Dad's marriage contract that Dad would never work in a sawmill. His glance at her was a display of guilt because he knew it would be the best job around, would pay the best, and would be the steadiest. But he'd have to go against that unspoken agreement in order to get it. And Mum tensed because she knew he was actually considering it. The whole thing was a taboo subject in our family and as soon as Sam did leave, the rest of us faded away to let Mum and Dad talk about it.

Except they didn't talk about it. They hardly spoke to each other at all for the rest of the day and that placed a huge strain on all of us.

'Do you think Mum will let him ask for a job there?' Helen whispered to me as she made her daily damper.

I was kneeling next to her beside the fire and handed her the salt. 'Depends how desperate they are for money, I guess.'

Amy came and kneeled on the other side of me, not about to be left out of what she thought might be an important discussion. 'Do you think it's possible that what happened to Grandpa could happen to Dad?' she asked.

'Surely, things have improved since then,' Helen said quickly.

'Accidents can still happen though,' I said. 'Even Uncle Leroy detests sawmills – I remember him saying so once.' Uncle Leroy was Mum's younger brother. He lived in the city with his wife, Jane, who was incredibly stingy with her money to the point where, even though they had always been wealthier than us, she had restrained Leroy from helping us at all with money. Not that I think Mum and Dad would have accepted their charity, of course, but I know that Leroy regretted not being able to help, especially when he had only two children. But then, even with money, I had heard they were starting to feel the pressure like everyone else and Mum had said that Jane would only be interested in making sure they didn't lose their townhouse.

'I don't know, Amy,' I went on. I remembered what Jeremy had said to me about Julianne and not speculating. 'But we can't keep trying to guess. Let's just see what happens.'

I left Helen with the damper and went to find Nicholas. He and Thomas were trying their hand at a bit of fishing in the river, even though that part of it was just about fished out with all the people coming by with the same idea. 'Caught anything?' I asked.

Thomas proudly led me to his bucket. 'I caught a trout! We could eat it for dinner. Nick can cook fish pretty well.'

The fish wasn't enormous, but it would be a nice change. 'Good on ya, Tom. What about you, Nick?'

He shook his head. 'Nothing.' He put down the rod he'd borrowed from Sam and gave up. 'Want to come into town with me, Meg? I wanna see if there's a letter for me at the post office.'

'Sure.' I was keen to get away from Mum and Dad for a while.

'Maybe Helen can help me then,' Thomas said.

I laughed. 'Not if it involves anything wet and squishy.'

Tom rolled his eyes. 'She's such a girl! Glad you're not as painful as that, Meg.'

I wasn't sure how to take that, so I said nothing and followed Nick up to the main road where we walked together into Kently.

Kently reminded me a lot of Harrington. At least the main street did, with its small country hospital, all its little shops and cheerful people. Nick and I went into what looked like a brand-new post office. We soon found out the last one had burned down. He was elated to find out that a letter had just arrived for him from Harrington. I knew he'd have to read it before we headed home again. We sat on the step of the post office and he tore open the envelope.

'It's from Brigitte,' he said, as if I hadn't worked that one out already. I watched his face as he read. Nick blushed at first, then smiled and laughed. He looked a bit more serious, then concerned. At last he laughed again.

Must be entertaining, I thought.

Nick drew a deep breath and looked at me. 'Meg, here. I think you ought to read this bit for yourself. Don't read anything else, mind, just this paragraph.' He handed me the paper with the cursive writing and I read what he'd pointed out.

When you last wrote, you asked about Julianne Young on behalf of Meghan. I've made some enquiries for you both. I'm afraid she's gone towards the city and when I asked friends of her parents why they didn't head to Coolibah as planned, they told me there'd never been any intention of that. In fact, her brother and parents have gone to Gale Ridge, which is, of course, nowhere near either Coolibah or the city. I'm almost certain that Julianne went to the city not only with William Cale but also with Victoria Willis, who I fear has been a bad influence on Julianne ever since Meghan left. I'm not sure how Meghan will take this, so look out for her either way.

If it had not been Nick's letter, I would have screwed it up. Gone to the city? With Victoria, whom she knew very well I hated more than anyone? And she never intended to go to Coolibah? How could Julianne talk to me about friendship and the like, tell me we'd see each other soon, then go off with my enemy while letting me believe a lie? I was angry, hurt and disappointed all at once, then embarrassed when it all leaked out through a couple of tears. I brushed them away and tried to laugh it off, but

73

when Nick put an arm around me, I suddenly felt real sorry about it.

'Well, at least I know,' I said.

'I'm sorry, Meg. I know you would have risked your life for her. She's been unfair to you, if nothing else.'

'I would have done anything for her. It's been months! She's left me hanging for months! I was almost convinced that she was near death or something! And all this time I've been worrying about her, she's been off probably having the time of her life, not thinking of me at all. To think that she went to the city with William! She's only sixteen, like me! Nearly seventeen, but still! She knows what Victoria's like! The Julianne I thought I knew would never have done anything like that. She would have been hot on my heels to get to Coolibah.'

'I'm sure there's more to it.'

'Even if there is, that doesn't excuse her.' Something was hurting inside of me and I knew it was resentment already eating away at me.

Nick didn't read the rest of his letter. He just took my hand and walked back to camp with me.

———————————

Mum and Dad were being painfully polite to each other when we got back. It wasn't until the next morning when Dad came out of the van with his work pants and brown boots on that Mum finally spoke up. 'So that's it, then? You're going anyway?'

We kids were all sitting around the fire trying hard to appear busy and uninterested, while also trying hard to hear every word. Mum never got angry, so it always shook us to hear her use that I'm-not-pleased tone.

'Evelyn, you know that if I got a job there, it would be steady work. We wouldn't have to move for a long time.

We might even end up being able to rent a house! This could be our only chance for a better future!'

'I'd rather spend the rest of my life on the track than have my children fatherless!'

'That's not going to happen! Evelyn, that was a long time ago. Things are different now. Sam says there hasn't been a single problem in the history of this sawmill. They know what they're doing and so do I.'

'What's more important to you, Nathaniel? Having a house again or your family? Is this the Wright and Manley thing to do?'

'Evelyn, that's not fair! You know I care for this family more than anything! That's why I'm prepared to take this job to give them and you the best they deserve.'

'Even if it means putting yourself in danger?'

'I'm hardly going to war!'

Samuel walked up as if he had no idea what they'd been talking about, which was probably true. 'Ready to go, Mr Manley?' he asked cheerfully.

Dad stared right at Mum and said, quite firmly, 'Yes.'

I saw Mum's body tense up and knew she wasn't impressed. Still, Dad left with Sam, and Jeremy, which surprised me. I think if Nick had known Jeremy was going, he might have gone too.

Since arriving at the campsite at Kently, Emma had been spending more and more time with Jenny and Ian. She still slept near us but ate with them. I think their son Danny made her smile. Still, that afternoon she came over to see us. She inquired about Dad and Jeremy's absence and then she chatted to us a bit about Kently and the people there. It was the most I'd ever heard her speak.

As she talked, Mum suddenly broke into a fit of coughs. Helen patted her on the back but there didn't seem to be much else she could do. After a few minutes Mum caught her breath again, but it worried all of us. Emma glanced away guiltily, since it seemed she'd passed her sickness on to her carer.

'Are you okay, Mum?' Nick asked.

She smiled at him. 'Yes, just a bit tired is all. I'm going to go for a short walk. Might help clear my head.'

Nick was about to protest, then decided he'd better not. We spent a while talking about how different this coming Christmas would be from last year and what we'd do for presents. Mum only got back just after Dad, Sam and Jeremy returned from work. She seemed to be in a better state and mood. She even smiled at Dad. 'How'd you go?'

'Well, Jeremy and I got a job,' he said. Mum paled. He took her hand in his. 'Loading the wood for travel, that is.'

She faltered for a second and asked, 'You mean, you won't be working with machinery?'

'Not of the sharp kind, no. And Nick, there's a job for you too if you want it. It's not much, but it's better than nothing.'

Mum opened her mouth to say something, but then just hugged him tightly. 'I'm sorry I was...'

'No, I'm sorry Evelyn.' He kissed her, and they went for a walk along the river. I knew they wouldn't be back for a while.

We ate dinner without them. It was then that Helen said Nick had told her about Julianne. 'I'm so sorry, Meg.' She looked at her plate of peas and potatoes sadly.

'Me too,' Jeremy said with feeling. 'I'm pretty disappointed in Will too.'

'What happened?' Amy asked, and we had to fill her and Tom in. She screwed up her face and thought that criticising Julianne would help me to feel better. It didn't, but everyone caring did. They all seemed to know how important it was to me.

'What did the rest of Brigitte's letter say?' I asked Nick, to take the attention off myself. 'Anything exciting?'

His eyes suddenly lit up. 'Yes, actually! She and Emily are coming to Kently!'

We were all excited for him. When we settled down he went on. 'They have a cousin here – which I did know but I'd forgotten – and they've been invited to come and stay! It's holidays at school, which is why Emily can come. Oh, and Brigitte says that Emily's looking forward to seeing you again, Amy.'

Amy glowed with pride. I knew she'd look forward to it too.

'Mr Robinson's going to drive them here, but he can't stay. He'll pick them up again in three weeks. Then they're going to stay in the city for a while and Emily will study there for a bit over the summer. They're not sure when they'll get here but I hope we stay put for a while! Can you imagine? Three whole weeks with Brigitte just up the road!'

I was proud of Nick at that moment, not because of his excitement to see Brigitte but because I realised that he'd sat silently on something that was extremely important to him to make sure that my feeling of hurt would not be over-shadowed. I loved him for it, and I loved Helen, Thomas and Amy too. I'd forgotten that, but sitting around the fire chatting together like we used to back home in Harrington filled me with a renewed sense of it.

When Mum and Dad finally returned with their arms around each other and a refreshed inability to stop smiling, I spent the rest of the night humming to myself. I joined in when they sang *Daisy* and even managed to put aside my grudge against Julianne.

Mum and Dad both kissed my cheek when I went to bed. Dad even made sure that everything was nice and dry for me, even though we hadn't had any rain lately. Mum tucked Amy in, thanked Helen for keeping the home fires going, and then she tucked me in too. It made me feel young again, but I still liked it.

'I'm sorry about Julianne,' she said, brushing the hair off my face. 'But know the fault lies with her, not with you. When someone hurts you, don't punish yourself and hurt yourself as well.' She smiled at me with her caramel eyes, squeezed my hand and went to bed.

'Meghan! Meghan! It's Christmas!' Amy yelled in my ear just after dawn on Friday seven days later. Already the air was heavy with moisture and I knew it would be a terribly hot day. I hardly felt like getting up at all, but Amy tugged at my hand until I did.

Walking outside in a bit of a daze, I realised that everyone else was up already, even Mum and Dad. We wished each other 'Happy Christmas', but my heart wasn't really in it. Last year we'd woken to the smell of a hot breakfast, pine and tinsel. Now all I could smell was horse manure.

Jeremy invited me to sit next to him. The tradition in our family was to spoil one person at a time, and this year they decided to start with Helen. Mum and Dad gave her a beautiful, small wooden box that Dad had made for her with 'Helen' engraved on top. Inside was a scarf Mum had made. I gave her a necklace I'd prepared, Tom had written her a poem, Amy had picked her some lovely flowers and Nick had found a small mirror and framed it with cedar wood, again with Helen's name engraved in it.

After her, it was Nick's turn, then Amy's, Thomas' and mine. I was given a brand-new skirt from Thomas, Mum and Dad combined, since I always wore mine out more quickly than the others. Nick had made me a beautiful wooden hair clasp. I also received flowers from Amy, and the last gift was a small leather book of the Proverbs from Helen.

After Mum and Dad had had their turns, I thought it was all over, but then Mum and Dad pulled out two more presents. One, they handed to Emma. It was a small bracelet, another fine example of Dad's craftsmanship. I was beginning to wonder where my parents had found the time to make all these things without us knowing. The second present they gave to Jeremy, who was particularly touched that he had been thought of. It occurred to me that it was probably the only present he would receive. He was hardly game to open it, but when he did he was even more touched. It was a pocketknife, not new but still pretty good. He pulled out all of its knives, admiring it carefully. When it finally sank in, he shook Dad's hand gratefully and kissed Mum's cheek. 'Thank you so much,' he said. Mum squeezed his hand.

Most of the campers joined in when we sang carols around the fire that night. Even I joined in for my favourite one, *Hark, the Herald Angels Sing,* but I think it was *Silent Night* that brought everyone together. Sam and Helen sat closer than they ever had before, and Mum nestled her head into the hollow of Dad's neck contentedly. It was a fine summer night and the stars shone brightly. A cooler breeze rustled through the gum trees and I heard a friendly mopoke somewhere on the other side of the river, in which the five of us, with Jeremy and Samuel, had spent most of the day swimming and throwing mud at each other.

While everyone was distracted I went up to my tent to get a drink of water. I didn't realise until I turned around that Jeremy had followed me.

'Sorry, Meghan, I don't mean to keep you. I just… I just wanted to give you your present.'

'My present?' I echoed with surprise. Jeremy hadn't given anyone else a present. 'But I don't have one to give you.'

'Your family is the best present I could ever get,' he said shyly. 'You don't know how I thank God for all of you.' He dug in his shirt pocket and pulled out a thin leather necklace with a small metal cross on it. 'I made this for you at the sawmill. I wanted you to have it, sort of like protection.'

I laughed. 'You think I particularly need protection?'

'Perhaps,' he smiled. 'Nah, it's just in case.' He put it over my head and I moved it into place. 'Nick was telling me that you doubt God,' he went on, 'but I made this for you anyway, as a reminder that God loves you no matter what.'

I fiddled with it, avoiding eye contact with him. 'If he loves me so much, why has all of this happened?'

'To help you grow into a better person. Years from now we'll say that it was times like this that made me a man and you a woman.'

'Surely, there are less painful ways,' I muttered.

Jeremy thought about this. 'The metal in that cross was two old nails. I had to heat things up for them to change their shape and shine up. We're not so different.'

I smiled faintly and finally met his eyes. 'Thank you for the present, Jeremy. I shall treasure it, even if I don't always treasure the God it represents.'

He touched my cheek briefly and we both walked back to the others.

8

THE WEEKEND WAS FULL OF FUN IN THE RIVER and games of cricket that Tom kept winning. Each night Mum tucked us in as if we were young children again. She still hadn't shaken her cough and neither did she look particularly well, but she was always in good spirits.

But then, on Sunday night, she started coughing violently, so much so that Dad had to hold her to keep her upright. She went to bed early and didn't get up in the morning. Nick and Jeremy were waiting for Dad to go to work but he took longer than usual getting out of the van, and when he did he was stressed. 'She's not well,' he said to Nick. 'You know your mother. Normally she has to be physically restrained to stop her working.'

'Dad...' Nick began, but he wasn't prepared to argue with him.

Even so, Dad grimaced and reconsidered. 'Helen, Meghan?' he called, and we both looked up. 'I want one of you to be with your mother at all times, okay? If she even hints at worsening, you get Thomas to ride Clyde or something and get me, okay? Don't take any risks.'

We didn't see Emma that day, and in the end, we decided that she must have gone to town. Helen and I did as we were told and stayed by Mum, while Amy played games with the other children.

I couldn't remember Mum being sick before. Helen tried to remind me of one time when she'd had a real bad fever, but it was when Helen was six and me only four, so I'd forgotten it. Dad hadn't been sick much either – he'd always said that it was Mum's good cooking that kept him healthy – but he'd broken his collar bone once coming off a stallion. 'That's not the same thing,' Helen said indignantly. We were sitting either side of Mum and I saw her smile faintly. Her eyes were closed and her breathing shallow, but she was still aware of us. She was half asleep, and very weak and faint, but I decided to keep talking, and after half an hour Helen and I had recapped every sickness our family had ever gone through.

But there's nothing quite like having your own parent sick. I guess growing up you think of them as invincible and all-knowing, and it's a shock to think that maybe they're not. To cheer myself up, I started thinking of how Mum must have been at my age. She was good-looking now, let alone then. I imagined her being a bit like Helen – soft and only strict when it was really, really necessary, and even then it was an effort. Dad was proud of Mum, and so were we. I wondered if her life had turned out the way she'd wanted, and decided I'd ask her when she was better.

It was a pretty boring morning mostly. Helen and I took turns walking up and down the river just to get out and stretch our legs. I got Amy to practise some French and Thomas to read some of his poems to Helen. But I was with Mum when she first woke a bit.

'Meg?' she whispered hoarsely.

'Yes?' I gave her my hand and she took it weakly and groaned.

'Prop me up a bit, will you, to help my breathing. And please, get me some water.'

I did as she asked, and she drank a bit, but most of it just ran down her front.

'I feel so cold, Meg.' She was sweating and shivering at the same time and her grip on my hand suddenly tightened, then slackened altogether. I put another blanket over her and rubbed her hand to keep it warm. Her teeth started chattering and it was then that she slipped into a fever.

I tried to cool her down, but nothing seemed to work. She was trembling enough to scare me. After half an hour passed, when nothing I did seemed to help, I called for Helen. I heard her run to the van.

'Mum's burning up,' I said. 'Dad won't be home for ages. I reckon we should take her into that small hospital in town.'

'Emma was okay without a hospital,' Helen said.

I made myself consider this. Was I overreacting? But Mum's pale, sweaty face concerned me, and I could hear Dad's voice echoing in my head, 'Don't take any risks.'

'Helen, I think she might be worse than Emma. What if she gets pneumonia? Mrs Fletcher's husband died of pneumonia!'

Helen stared at me and then at Mum. She seemed to take forever to say anything, and even then, it was only another question. 'How?'

'We'll take the van. Mum can stay right where she is. You ride with her and Thomas can drive. Amy and I'll find Dad and meet you there.'

She wasn't sure about this. She brushed Mum's hair back from her face and rested her hand on her forehead for a moment. I thought she was hoping I'd just go away, but then she said quietly, 'Okay. I guess even if they don't take her in, they may be able to give her some medicines to help.'

That idea made sense to me. 'With any luck that's all she'll need.'

'I hope we're doing the right thing, Meg.'

'The Wright and Manley thing...' I mumbled distractedly, then said, 'I'd rather try and be embarrassed than do nothing and see her fall beyond help.'

'Yes, you're right of course.'

I think Thomas was actually excited by the idea of being trusted to drive the five miles into town on his own. Amy and I travelled with them for the first two miles, and then we had to take another road to the sawmill. As we walked, Amy gripped my hand tightly, taking one-and-a-half steps to my every one. I was worried we'd get lost and not even find the sawmill, but as it happened, we couldn't miss it. I wasn't sure where to go – it all looked so big and complicated – but Samuel saw us.

'G'day, Meghan, Amy!' he called cheerfully, leaning over the wire fence. Then he frowned when he realised that we weren't quite so cheerful. 'What's wrong?'

I quickly briefed him and asked him to take us to Dad, when his boss came over and interrupted.

'Samuel, who are your young friends?'

'Oh, ah, this is Miss Meghan Manley and her younger sister, Amy. This is Mr Long.'

'Manley?' Mr Long repeated, stroking his jaw in thought. He wasn't a real old man, but he looked too serious for me. 'Oh, you belong to Nathaniel. Well, I'm sorry but I can't let you in here.'

'But our mum's awful sick and we need Dad.'

'Sorry to hear that but a lot of my workers have sick relatives. They still work. I'm afraid I can't bend the rules for your dad. If he left, I would have to…'

'Alright, alright,' I interrupted, perhaps a little rudely, but I was too tired and worried to listen to a long drawn-out speech about why he was allowed to be unfeeling and why we should just shove off. 'Sam, could you please just tell Dad that we've taken Mum into town? Don't make it sound terrible or anything – I don't want him to stress about it all day. Just ask him to come to us as soon as he's able.'

'No worries, Meghan, will do. Hope she gets better real soon.' He looked at me like he felt bad that Mr Long hadn't been more easy-going. I gave him the best smile I could and with Amy's hand still in mine, we began what suddenly felt like an incredibly long walk back to town.

'Why did he have to be so mean?' Amy asked me, and I realised she had tears on her cheeks. 'Doesn't he know she's our mother?' I put an arm around her as we walked, trying not to feel bitter myself.

'Do you want me to tell you a story?' I asked. Amy nodded, so I recapped what I could remember of *Pilgrim's Progress*.

When we made it into Kently, sore and tired, we saw two men lifting Mum out of the van. I let go of Amy and ran to Helen and Thomas. 'What's taken so long?'

'They wouldn't take us seriously,' Helen said, 'but they are now.'

I saw that Thomas was smirking. 'What?' I asked him.

'Helen yelled at them!'

I shared his utter surprise.

'Well,' Helen said hotly, 'I'm sick of people treating us like idiots.'

Amy and I smiled at each other as we tried to imagine what she must have said.

One of the staff, Nurse Doncaster, told us that they would check Mum out and let us know what was happening. We had to wait in the foyer, something else that seemed to make Helen angry. 'We're her children, for goodness' sake,' she muttered under her breath when Nurse Doncaster left and we sat down on hard, wooden seats that were about as friendly as a brown snake. Thomas couldn't get comfortable and decided to pace the foyer instead. Amy snuggled in between me and Helen as we waited.

And waited.

'Excuse me,' Helen called when another nurse walked past. 'Can we see our mother yet?'

'Who?'

'Mrs Evelyn Manley.'

'Oh. One moment and I'll see what's happening.' She hurried off between two white doors that flapped behind her like someone waving away a bad smell.

'I'm hungry,' Thomas said.

'You're always hungry,' I said offhandedly.

'It is getting around to dinner time,' Helen remarked. 'I'm surprised Dad and Nick haven't shown up yet.'

It was another half hour before they did. Dad came into the hospital looking as mad as an ant's nest after it's been poked with a stick. He still had his hat on and his work clothes were covered in sawdust. His face had a faint covering of brown over it, giving him a dirty, haggard look. At first, I was worried that he was angry with me for bringing Mum in, but then he told us how Mr Long had kept Sam away from him so he couldn't pass on my message until after work. Even then, he was deliberately delayed.

'Where is she?' he asked a little curtly. Nick was standing behind him but a bit away, as if to give Dad extra space.

'We don't know,' Helen told him. 'They took her behind those doors and that was the last we saw of her. No one will talk to us.'

Nurse Doncaster came out and seemed surprised to see us still there.

'Where's my wife?' Dad demanded, standing right in front of her so she couldn't walk past him. She looked so small standing next to his tall, brooding figure. Dad seemed even bigger than usual and part of me wondered if it was because all the emotions he was feeling suddenly couldn't fit inside him.

'I assume you're Mr Manley. Either way, there's no need to take that tone with me. Your wife has the beginnings of pneumonia and we'll be keeping her in. She'll receive the best care, I assure you.'

'Well, can I see her?'

'She's sleeping.'

'I just want to see her.'

Nurse Doncaster said nothing for a minute but then nodded. 'Don't wake her, mind.' I got the feeling that she spent most of her time arguing with patients and their relatives to the point where it had made her tough. She was only in her thirties, but I reckon she could've told anyone off easily enough.

Dad followed her through the doors and the five of us were left to ourselves again.

'Well, come on, you lot,' Nick said.

'What?' Thomas asked.

'In the van – let's go back to camp and make ourselves something to eat. No point moping around here. They won't let us kids in any time soon.'

'What about Dad?' I asked.

'They won't let him stay late, and it won't get dark for ages yet anyway. He can walk back when he's ready.'

Nick and Tom drove home while Amy, Helen and I sat in the back of the van with nothing to say. I leaned against the wall, just listening to the rhythmic walk of Clyde and feeling the gentle rocking of the van as it made its way over the countryside. Soon it started raining a bit and then it got heavier and wilder. When we got back to the campsite we saw that it had been windy there for a while – there was leaf litter all over the grass and a few people were propping up their battered tents. One lady was trying to calm a crying baby while her husband and six-year-old tried to get their tent up again so they could get out of the rain.

Nick and Tom pulled up, saw to Clyde, then hopped in the back with us. We sat together in a squished circle chatting about nothing in particular and waited until the storm passed. Rain poured down the canvas on all sides like the sun was crying on us, but then, like most storms, it dried up as quickly as it had started. We pulled back the canvas and got out one by one, looking around at the damage. There wasn't much really – just lots of campfires that had been doused and a few more sorry-looking tents. Tom and Amy got our fire going with difficulty while Helen started unpacking some food. Nick was fixing our tent – the boys' one was fine – and then I saw Sam and Jeremy coming up the road. Sam was grinning as usual and they were both soaked.

'Did you get caught in that?' I asked them.

Sam nodded emphatically. 'Too right.'

'We had a fallen log to hide behind,' Jeremy said with an unsure smile. He looked at me from under his ragged, brown akubra and a small waterfall fell off the front, dripping in front of his face. He adjusted the swag he had over his shoulder with a shrug and his eyes settled on me with a comfortable gaze. His mouth twitched on one side and I found myself smiling at him.

'How's your mum?' Sam asked.

'Yeah, not good. Dad's still with her.'

'Yeah? Geez, that's no good.' He shook his head but was distracted. 'Hey, Nick! Should you be playing with something you don't understand?'

Nick was having trouble with the tent and Samuel went over to him, but Jeremy stopped by me for a second. 'Meghan,' he began, but then he just smiled and walked over to our two tents.

'What?' I whispered after him, not sure if I wanted to ask the question out loud.

The fire was going now, and Samuel was actually trying to dry off by it rather than help Nick, partly because he was wet and cold, and partly because Helen was also standing there. He'd become a bit of a shadow as far as she was concerned. Helen handled it all a little too coolly, but she had told me that she was interested. Well, 'he's not bad' were her exact words, but that meant he had potential.

Nick was cursing the tent. He didn't usually fight with tents – he just wasn't concentrating properly. Jeremy took pity on him and had it up in seconds.

It was a pretty ordinary scene: people walking in and out of each other's tents, helping each other, sharing food and stories. The fires were smoking again in no time and soon there was that evening smell of cooking. The sun was shining through the clouds in one or two rays, and gum trees were rustling in the wind.

Jeremy was asking me for something, but his voice was just a muffle. Something had caught my eye. He was standing with the five of us and we were all near each other, but someone was getting out of our van. I squinted to better see the broken shoes, then the torn skirt, then the stained shirt descending the three stairs. As the shoes landed on the wet green grass, I realised it was Emma. What's more, she was tucking away a few quid into her shirt, a few quid that Mum and Dad had kept aside – their savings. It wasn't much, but we didn't have much to start with. That made it everything.

I felt my face crumple with anger. She must have felt my negative energy swarming towards her because she looked up and met my eyes. Helen was touching my arm, trying to attract my attention to something, but I just stood staring at Emma. Then I burst into a run. A split second later, Emma did the same.

I heard the others calling after me as I chased her onto the road and away from town. She was fast for someone who was supposed to be sickly and hungry, but I knew that a lot of it was sheer desperation. She looked back at me a few times, her eyes alight, but she put her head down and kept going.

Already my lungs were resenting me and my legs starting to burn. But anger is a powerful tool and soon I was gaining on her. I ran up beside her, grabbed her arm and pulled her back. Emma wrenched herself away from me but stumbled and fell to the ground.

'Give it back, you little cheat,' I puffed, trying to find which pocket she'd shoved the money into. Leaning over her was like trying to pin down a fish out of water.

'Meghan, I need it to get home!' she gasped as we struggled.

'Need it? You're stealing money from the very people who offered to look after you! My mum is lying in hospital with the sickness that started when she helped you, and you repay her by stealing from her?' I was yelling now but was surprised to see her look at me in fear. I worried for a moment that I was becoming something horrible. 'You give it back now or I'll report you to the coppers!'

Even at that moment, I knew I was projecting on her the pain I felt from Julianne. After all, they'd both betrayed me in some way.

'Meghan, I'm hungry and I need to get home to the city.'

'That's no excuse to steal from good people!' I shook her by the shoulders, remembering both Julianne and the tramp. 'What is this country coming to? Losing our homes and jobs, that's one thing, but to lose our respect for each other, to stoop to this level to survive – it's... it's primitive! If we can't keep our dignity and integrity through this depression, or whatever name they have for it now, then what's the point? You think things are bad now? Well, how you act now will determine where you'll be when this is all over.' I was quoting Dad then. *Your present determines your future,* he'd always said, particularly when he was planting trees on the property.

Emma was still staring at me strangely and I knew she didn't get me. She had an odd snarl on her face and then, to my complete disbelief, she hit me. I felt the bracelet Mum and Dad had given her graze against my cheek. It took me so much by surprise that I fell away from her and she got up and ran, taking the money and leaving me on the side of the road holding my face.

It was starting to rain again. I sat for a moment in bewilderment, but when I heard Jeremy calling me just up the road, I quickly scrambled up and began walking back.

'What happened?' He handed me a hanky to press on my bleeding lip. When I told him, he instantly turned to rush after Emma, but I stopped him.

'Are you okay?' he asked me. 'Did she take much? You took off like a...'

'I'm fine,' I said. *I'm just becoming an impoverished, crazed legalist.*

We got back to find the others waiting to hear what had happened and why I'd chased Emma.

'Stealing?' Amy breathed with wide eyes, like she'd never heard of the concept before.

Thomas mumbled under his breath and snapped a twig with his boot. Nick was the most disgusted, but I think he was making more out of it because Sam and Jeremy were there. He started talking heroically, saying things like,

'We'll be alright. She'll get what's coming. We can manage.'

Helen was looking at my lip with concern, just like Mum would have. She wet a cloth and insisted on cleaning the lip properly. 'You have courage,' she said, 'I'll give you that.'

'No, I don't. I have anger.'

She crinkled her nose. 'Because of Julianne? Or losing the farm?'

'No.' I stared intensely at a nearby tree while I thought. 'I think I'm more angry at myself, and I don't even know why.'

9

'MEGHAN, I'M PROUD OF YOUR GUMPTION,' MUM said when Thomas, Jeremy and I went to visit her three days later. She'd had a few rough days, which meant we were forever walking between camp and town and trying to keep Dad sane, while stopping Mum worrying about how things were going without her. She'd been pretty out of it, and we'd all been worried, but she was coming through it now.

Jeremy went to put some wildflowers he had picked for her in a vase but accidentally knocked the vase over instead. The sound of the smash on the ground made us all jump.

'Sorry!' Red-faced, he looked apologetically at the others in the ward who were now glaring at him.

'It's okay, Jeremy,' Mum said. 'See if you can find a broom.'

He nodded and left.

Mum touched the bruise on my face with the back of her hand. 'That poor Emma.' She clicked her tongue like she used to when Dad told her how one of the lambs had been rejected by the flock.

'Poor?' I echoed with a frown.

'Yes. I mean, to be so desperate.'

'Mum, she stole from you and Dad!' Sometimes I wondered about Mum.

'I know, Meghan, I know. But I don't hate her for it.'

'But she did the wrong thing! Definitely not a Wright and Manley way to act.'

Mum smiled now. 'You're so much like your father sometimes. Everything's black-and-white to you. Right and wrong. But sometimes life is a little more complicated than that. And we can't hold everyone up to our family's creed.'

'So, she wasn't wrong?' I was getting confused.

'What she did was wrong, yes, but I'm just saying I understand why she did it. And, as they say, to understand is to forgive.'

I was still frowning but said, 'Maybe that's why I'm beginning to really hate Julianne. Because I don't understand why she'd deliberately hurt me like that.'

Jeremy returned and started cleaning up the broken vase with a small broom and dustpan. Shards of glass scraped against the floor.

'Hate is just love distorted by hurt, Meghan. You can focus on the hurt and hate forever if you want to, or, with God's help, you can let it go and learn to love again. I don't hate Emma. Neither should you or anyone else. Isn't that also Wright and Manley?'

A bitter taste developed in my mouth and I think a part of me knew then that I just wasn't that good. I wasn't like Mum and Helen, who'd forget what they were upset about the next day. I took things much more seriously, so much so that it annoyed me because it made everything in life so much more difficult to deal with. But if I gave up my anger, what would I have left?

No, I just didn't have it in me to forgive like that. If I stopped being angry with Julianne, I would be excusing her for what she did. I'd be saying that lying to your best friend and then abandoning them is totally fine.

I'd rather live with bitterness.

Jeremy found another vase to put the flowers into, successfully this time, while Thomas chatted to Mum about how he'd become a member of the Kently library. He was going to pick up either a Charles Dickens novel or some poems by Banjo Paterson.

'It's up to you, Tom,' Mum said. I could see she was getting tired, so I made Tom say goodbye.

'We'll see you next year,' Jeremy joked, since 1932 would begin the next day.

She smiled weakly. 'May it be a better one.'

Being late afternoon, everyone was at their tents when we got back. Sam was playing his harmonica to impress Helen, while Nick started chatting to Jeremy about which wood was best for houses. Amy had the children all involved in some intense game of hide and seek.

Dad was lost without Mum. He didn't chat as much, and he would wander aimlessly around camp. He whittled away at some wood in the evenings or went and talked to the other men in the camp. Then he'd come back because they were talking 'some union nonsense'. When he was really bored, he'd father us like we were five again. 'Amy, have you washed your hair lately? Meghan, don't forget to wash the plates.' As I always did the dishes, the plates weren't something I was likely to forget. 'Thomas, did you check on Clyde today?'

'Yes, Dad,' Tom would drawl, and so it went on until he realised he was becoming unpopular with us, but I knew things were really bad when I caught Dad having a good old conversation with the horse.

When Mum came home the day after New Year's Day, still with a cough but on the mend, Dad finally left us alone. He sat her down, gave her a short log to rest her feet on, wrapped a blanket around her shoulders even though the days were hot and the sun crisp, and handed her a cup of tea. She gripped it with both hands as if she was afraid she'd drop it, but her face got some colour back as she drank.

Helen was brushing Amy's wet hair, but I sat by myself, thinking how nothing had changed much since we'd left the farm. I still felt most useless. Thomas had his writing as well as everything else now, Nick could do anything with his hands, Amy was a natural leader and Helen was a domestic genius. All I had was determination to not stoop to people like the tramp and Emma. Maybe I was like Dad. He was most proud of the fact that we hadn't had to draw on a dole card as yet, even though we'd been on the road for three months. Self-respect – that's what he had, even after losing everything, and that's what I was lacking after losing everything. Self-respect was a valued treasure for men – they fought for it, sometimes literally. But women… men didn't often respect them, so why would they respect themselves?

But not all men were the same. Dad was an exception – he valued Mum more than anything. Nick and Sam were different too, which, I think, is why Brigitte stayed loyal to Nick even after they'd been separated, and why Helen was beginning to come round to Sam's advances. And Jeremy, he was a real exception.

I couldn't make him out. He was two years older than me but sometimes that seemed like a sea between us. Sometimes, with that gaze of his, he seemed about thirty. But then, when he went fishing with Nick or sang around the fire or got a compliment from Mum, he glowed like a child. He came to love our family, and Mum and Dad always encouraged him. When you lose everything that gives you a sense of purpose and identity, you need family, you need friends – you need somewhere to belong to make it through. It's what gave Mum the strength to get better. It's what gave Dad the determination to work hard every day and save money, even after the last of it had been stolen. It's what made Nick think about building his own family, with Brigitte.

So, if nothing else, I respected Jeremy because he understood all this, which is why he was loyal to us. He knew what mateship was all about. I knew that if it came to the crunch he'd be there for us.

At least I thought he would be. After Julianne, I didn't have much faith in my sense of judgment anymore. But I guess deep down I knew. It was in the way he chopped wood and neatly stacked the blocks. It was in the way he eagerly got ready for work in the mornings, then patiently waited for Dad, Nick and Sam. It was in the way he smiled at me, as if he trusted me to understand him more than most. That was a trust I came to value.

'Meg? Are you still in the land of the living?' Helen poked me with a finger.

'Huh?'

'I didn't think so.' She invited me to walk with her down to the river, where we wandered along the bank. 'What do you think of Sam?' she asked quickly, almost as if she didn't really want me to hear her question.

'You know I like him. We all do. He's a real character. Fun but works well too.'

'He's Nick's age, you know.'

'Yeah...?'

'I'm pretty sure Nick will propose to Brigitte soon, when she comes to stay in Kently.'

I tried to think how this related to Sam but failed.

'So you... you like him, then?' Helen probed again.

'Yes. Do you?'

She blushed. 'Well, to be honest, he's not exactly what I was looking for in a man.'

'Let me guess, you were looking for a businessman; someone with a secure job who could provide for you and your ten children, who would always be courteous and follow etiquette without slipping up.'

'You make it sound awful! But yes, I guess you're mostly right. Sam is so… unpredictable and spontaneous.'

'Helen, if anyone needs more spontaneity in their life, it's you.'

'So you think… you think I should encourage him?'

'I can't tell you if you should or not! If you like him, go for it. If not, you'd better at least make that clear.'

'I do like him, you know. I think most of what I'm worried about is that the family won't approve.'

'I just told you we all like him.'

'Yes, as a friend. But as part of the family?'

'Helen, stop getting ahead of yourself. If you like Sam, just go from there.'

She sighed heavily, as if this was something that'd been weighing her down for ages. I could tell she still didn't know what to do because she gave up and changed the subject. 'What about Jeremy?'

'Well, he's already part of the family, really – don't think you'd have any trouble there.'

'I meant you and Jeremy!'

'What?'

'Don't tell me the idea never occurred to you.'

'I'm too young, I think.'

'You're seventeen soon. He's very good-looking, you know.'

'Too good-looking for me,' I muttered. I didn't think Helen heard me, but she suddenly took my hand and led me back to camp. She wouldn't answer my persistent repetition of, 'What are you doing?' It wasn't until we got back to the van and she collected some soap and things in a bucket that I realised what was happening. She took me back to the river amidst my protest and sat me down on an old stump.

'Meghan, whether you believe it or not, you are beautiful.'

'Not like you and Mum.'

She rolled her eyes. 'Meg, I've never met a girl who wasn't pretty. With some of them, their looks hit you in the face, like Brigitte's. Some, you have to search harder to find it, but it's always there. You're like that. You're pretty but just don't present yourself well. Take your hair, for example.' She picked up my ponytail and dropped it again as if it was poisonous. 'Rats' nest,' she pronounced with an uptilted nose. Helen filled the bucket up with water and started washing my hair and trying to comb it out. 'You need to take pride in yourself.'

'Come on, Helen – we're camping, for goodness' sake.'

'That's not the point! You smell like smoke! And if you lose your pride...' She grunted as she tried to pull the comb through a rough patch, and water filled my eyes at the sting. In the end I lost a clump of hair. 'If you lose your pride you don't feel good about yourself and your beauty won't radiate.' Once she'd finished combing all the knots out, Helen braided my hair, leaving a few short strands out. 'To embrace your face,' she said.

She then got me to stand up. 'Your posture is terrible.'

'You know, I don't remember enrolling in finishing school.'

Ignoring me, she pushed my shoulders back. 'Put your chin up. See, huge improvement already.' She rested a hand on my shoulders. 'Meghan, I am glad God gave me you as a sister and I want you to know that.'

'God? How can you speak of him so fondly when he has reduced us to this?'

'This is not his fault, Meghan, and you should not hate him for it.'

'"As flies to wanton boys, are we to the gods."'

100

'You're smarter than that, Meg.'

'Smarter than Shakespeare? I don't think so.'

'Miss Helen,' Samuel said politely when we came back from the river. 'I was wondering if you'd come with me into town to get my rations and see if there are any letters?' He was grinning widely and had his hands on his hips, like he was prepared for whatever she said. He didn't have a hat on, for a change, and his dirty blond hair was sticking out a bit wildly. I wondered if he'd get dragged down to the river soon too.

Helen looked at me and bit her lip. I gave no indication of what I was thinking because I wanted her to make the decision for herself.

'Yes, well, I don't see why not.' She asked Dad for permission and then the two of them left.

When they returned, there was a letter for me from Emma. That surprised me more than anything. I quickly went inside my tent, since Amy and Helen weren't in it, to read it alone.

Meghan,

I have been thinking about your words ever since we parted ways. I'm not going to write a bunch of excuses – this is only to enclose the amount of money that I stole, since I've managed to earn it here in the city. I want you to give it back to your mother.

I know you think I did the wrong thing, but you don't know what it's like to be so empty, so lost and aimless with nothing to live for, except to somehow find food to get by just another day. You are surrounded by people who love you – doing the right thing is easy for you. My dad was killed in the Great War and my mum died when I was two. I said

I wouldn't make excuses and I won't, but it's not easy to feel bad about taking a little from someone who has a lot, just to survive. I'd probably do it again. That's how desperate I was – but I'm sure God will forgive me, even if you won't. I know what I am, and that's not good, but I'll soon rectify that.

Emma.

It was the strangest letter I had ever received. I honestly didn't know what to think of it, only that I was confused that God would forgive someone who did the wrong thing while he'd ignore those who always did their best. Maybe that was Emma's best. I don't know. At least now it seemed she was going to try and be good. I gave the money to Mum, who was as surprised as I was. Then I put the letter inside my pillowcase and left it there until it was forgotten.

'Meghan? You need a hand?' Jeremy asked as I virtually dragged a heavy bucket of water up from the creek.

I shook my head. I'd just been thinking about what Helen had said about me and him. The idea both worried and intrigued me. *Does he even like me? What if he does? What do I do?* I wished for a moment that Helen had left me ignorant.

But then I could see him smiling to himself as he watched me struggle and I decided not to dismiss the idea. 'Am I the only entertainment you have at the moment?' I asked.

'Nope, but you're the most interesting.' He folded his arms and kept watching, as if waiting for me to trip.

'So, you think I can't do this without you?' I stumbled closer to him.

'I reckon you can, actually.'

'Well, feel free to leave me to it.'

He grinned at me. 'What if I don't want to?'

I paused mid-step and pretended to be thinking about something. 'Hmm,' I said, tapping my chin and walking up to him. 'Well, I think you may regret it!'

'Oh, really?' he taunted as I rested the bucket on my hip.

'Uh-huh.'

'And what is it you reckon I'll regret?'

With a heave, I lifted the bucket and threw the water all over him, making him slip over into what was now wet grass. 'Any regrets, Mr Bell?' I was not even embarrassed by the people around the camp laughing with me.

He looked up with a surprised and unsure smile. Jeremy ran his hands through his thick brown and now wet hair. Suddenly he got to his feet, snatched the bucket and raced down to the creek.

'Jeremy, don't you dare!' I called after him, but he didn't stop. I hurried back toward the safety of our camp, looking over my shoulder. He ran up the bank of the creek towards me, water splashing over the sides of the bucket when he stumbled over a fallen branch. He'd almost reached me when Dad stepped out of the van.

'Jeremy, what are you doing?' he asked.

Jeremy stopped mid-stride and stared with an open mouth. I gave him a 'so there!' glance with a grin.

'Oh, I… I, uh… I was just getting you some water, since Meghan said you needed some.' He tried to glare at me but the gleam in his eye gave him away.

'Right.' Dad looked him up and down over the top of his reading glasses and glanced at me with a raised eyebrow. 'Carry on, then.' He went back inside the van.

Jeremy and I laughed.

————————

The next Sunday evening, as we were all eating dinner from the plates in our laps around a small cooking fire, Jack and Larry, the travelling brothers, arrived in Kently and came out to the campsite. After they'd greeted Molly and Dave, Ian and Jenny and a few others they knew, they came over to us. 'Heard you was sick, Evelyn,' Larry said. 'Ya better now?'

'Yes, much better, thank you.' Mum smiled up at them.

'The story was that that Emma had it first – yeah?' Jack asked.

Mum chuckled. 'I don't know who tells these stories, but yes, Emma was sick too.'

'Oh, we heard it from Ma Kearny, who heard it from Harry Lane, who heard it from Sam, didn't we, Jack?'

'Yup. And then it was Harry Lane, who heard from Jane O'Connor who heard from Will Pearce, who told us about what happened, how she won't be getting sick anymore.'

Mum chewed slowly as she tried to work out what he meant. 'What?'

'Gone to earth and all.' Larry looked at us and realised we had no idea what he was talking about. 'You didn't hear? She died not long after she got to the city.'

Mum dropped her fork on the ground and I choked on my bit of bread.

'Died?' Amy repeated, with wide eyes.

'What do you mean, she died?' Dad asked, since none of us could.

'Took her own life. No one knows why.'

'Was it definitely Emma?' Mum asked, reflecting the utter shock we all felt.

Jack nodded and took off his hat. 'Afraid so, Evelyn.'

It seemed too terrible to be true. Mum met my eyes with a fear I hadn't seen before.

'Was there… was there a funeral?' she asked, with her hand on her heart. Dad reached over and took her other hand in his, but it didn't stop the tears forming in her eyes.

'They buried her at the local cemetery. Since she had no family to speak of, and no friends, I'm told it was just the gravedigger and the parson who were there.'

I felt like I was going to be sick. I felt shaky like I had the night before we left the farm. All of us felt real sorry for the loss, of course, but there was something nagging me at the back of my mind, something that was telling me I had caused it, that I had been too hard on Emma, and that now she'd killed herself because I'd made her feel so terrible.

I'll soon rectify that! That's what she had said. Had she really meant she was no good and that she was going to kill herself? How could she give up like that? I didn't want to be hard on her all over again, but it just didn't make sense. I knew straight away that Mum would feel she hadn't done enough for her, hadn't loved her enough, and I wanted to tell her that it was me. I hadn't loved her at all. I wanted to cry but I didn't. I didn't feel I had a right to. Emma's death was upon my head and I'd have to live with that. Tears couldn't help me.

But why did she do it? Why did she and Julianne not want to exist in any world where I was?

Nicholas reached over and squeezed my shoulder, but at that moment I didn't want to be loved. Being lonely forever was my penance. I went to my tent and sat down but Mum came after me. Without a word, she knelt in front of me and hugged me. I let her. I held onto her for a long time because I really didn't want to be alone, not for a moment, because Emma had been alone. She had died alone, and I didn't want that to happen to me.

10

WHEN I GOT OUT OF THE TENT THE NEXT MORN-
ing there was a bit of a commotion going on, but it sounded
like a happy one. My family were surrounding someone,
and I glimpsed copper-coloured hair.

Thomas saw me standing there. 'Meghan! Look, it's
Brigitte and Emily!'

Brigitte, wearing a beautiful blue dress and summery
scarf, smiled at me. She came over and I had to let her hug
me because everyone was watching.

'You look very well,' she said to me, as if this brought
her some relief.

'So do you,' I said politely. 'When did you arrive in
Kently?'

'Only yesterday. Emily and I thought it would be a
lovely day for a walk, so we set out to see you all as soon
as we could, before everyone went to work.' She was
talking to the whole group now. 'I'm glad Nicholas told me
where to look, since I was expecting an official park or
something. But this is much nicer!' She looked so pretty,
she didn't seem to fit around us poor campers, but it didn't
appear to bother her. Emily's hair was styled in beautiful
ringlets that I could see Amy eyeing off with a bit of envy
while Brigitte started talking about Harrington.

'Fred Hanson and John Willis have been causing
people a lot of grief and everyone's glad Victoria's in the
city, though she's developed a terrible name for herself –
claimed to be engaged to someone who we found out didn't
even exist! Mr Hanson was called into the city too, for
"family business", but no one knows what, which is

unusual. I mean, you know what the grapevine's like! But at least everyone's been able to relax some more.

'No one's moved into your farm – seems no one wants to. I mean, they do want to but they won't, out of respect for you, Mr Manley. Mr Willis has men looking after everything up there so he's still making money out of it even though there's no one living there.'

Dad seemed proud to hear that and Thomas was really excited, I guess because he figured we could just go and move back in. *If only it were that simple,* I thought.

'Everyone else is fine. The Westerns had a third son and called him George. Oh, and Mr Cale's handed the general store over to his son, though they both work there.'

'William?' Jeremy and I asked together.

'Yes, he's come back from the city. And before you ask, no, no one's sure what's happened to Julianne or her family. William hasn't said a word about it – another time the grapevine has failed us. Harrington's becoming ripe with secrets at the moment!' Brigitte tried to laugh about it, but it made me concerned. Yes, I did resent Julianne an awful lot, but I was also terrified that she had or was about to share Emma's fate, for whatever reason. What if she died and I never got a chance to see her again?

'I want to go to the city,' I announced to Dad and Mum that night. It was a radical suggestion but that didn't even occur to me. I'd spent the whole afternoon setting my heart on it until it seemed I was already on my way. I couldn't stop thinking about Emma and Julianne. I couldn't eat. I couldn't convince myself that I was blameless for Emma's death or for Julianne's disappearance, or that there wasn't something about me inherently wrong. I couldn't forget the last time I'd seen Emma and how I had judged her while she fled from me as if I were Hanson or Willis.

'I want to find Julianne, and maybe Emma's grave. I'm worried that Julianne may be dying alone too.' As I heard myself say this, I realised I did still care about her. And I guess part of me just wanted to find out what was going on.

My parents stared as if I were crazy. 'What?' Dad said. 'Meghan, Julianne has a mother, father and brother to look after her – you don't need to do anything rash. It's not the same situation as Emma, the city is ages away and you've no money.'

'It's not that far and I could go with Brigitte's family. I'd only be gone two weeks. Two-and-a-half at the most.'

'No, Meghan,' Dad said, and Mum nodded in agreement. 'We're not splitting the family.'

'You won't even miss me! One less mouth to feed is all. And I'll be back before you know it.'

Nick, who was sitting nearby, was incredulous. 'Did Brigitte give you this idea?'

I shook my head emphatically. 'She doesn't know anything about it.'

'No,' Dad said with a tone of finality. Mum looked at me as if she wasn't sure I was still her daughter, and I felt something that was a mixture of guilt and irritation.

I couldn't bring myself to say goodbye to Dad when he left for work with the boys in the morning. I was embarrassed that my suggestion had been killed so quickly, and annoyed that they hadn't taken me more seriously. I wasn't the kid they imagined me to be anymore. I wanted to tell them that but didn't know how I could make them see it. I picked up some dry gum leaves off the grass and used them to start a fire to boil a billy over. Mum and Helen had gone to work at the hotel, even though Mum should have been resting – she still coughed terribly – and they had taken Amy into town to call on Emily.

I was well and truly on my own.

I looked up when I heard the ring of a bell later that afternoon. There were two men walking along the road and one was leading a bike. I kept my eyes on the road even after they'd walked past. It occurred to me then that I could just start walking to the city and hitchhike some of the way. No one was around to stop me. My heart pounded at the thought. Leaving the billy, I went up to the road to see if it would tempt me in any way.

But all our roads are new and strange,
And through our blood there runs
The vagabonding love of change...

That was from one of Banjo's poems that Tom had read to us. I couldn't remember the rest. Maybe I was becoming a wanderer and maybe Julianne was just an excuse for change. Maybe I was falling in love with the road, meeting new people all the time and even the sense of uncertainty. Maybe I didn't really care about Julianne as much as I thought I did. Maybe I was just tired of my half-existence, of being the middle-child in a family that didn't need me. Maybe I thought that by walking and walking I'd somehow get away from that and find a sense of purpose. The city was becoming a sort of Camelot to me, though what it could offer I didn't know. Its mystery was part of the attraction.

So, I started walking. I walked around a bend and then wanted to see what was around the next one. I realised that it could become quite addictive, always with another bend or another hill to get around. I don't know how far I walked but I hadn't brought supplies and I had no real intention of walking off without a word to anyone. I thought about Julianne and of Dad's firm no, and I walked faster. Then when I thought about Emma, I burst into a run. I ran until I couldn't breathe and then leaned against a tree until I could. I'd already been gone an hour or two. Finally, when I thought of Mum and Dad's terror in losing Thomas when he was six, I started walking back again.

I'd been gone longer than I realised. Everyone had come back to find me missing, and the last reported sighting of me had been at the road. They were starting a search for me. The first thing I saw was Dad looking like an angry bull. I wasn't sure I was brave enough to approach him but didn't get a chance to decide because Nick saw me and pointed me out to everyone.

Dad stormed over. 'Where were you?'

'I... I just went for a walk.' I wasn't used to being in trouble.

'We thought you'd gone off to the city or something!'

'Well, I haven't, have I!' I said angrily.

He was about to reply, when he realised that I was right and that he had been yelling at me. I think he was going to apologise but Mum interrupted.

'Meghan, promise me you won't just go off to the city!' She gripped my forearms like a vice. Suddenly I realised that they felt guilty because they thought they'd driven me off.

'I promise.' It wasn't a hard thing to say. I'd already made that decision when I'd turned and walked back. 'Whatever you may think, I am loyal to my family.'

'And whatever you may think, we only ever say no for a good reason,' Dad replied, but as usual that answer was never satisfying.

Matchmaker Meg, that's what they should have called me. At least, that's how I was beginning to feel when everyone started bringing their relationship problems to me. I mean, first there was Helen, and now Sam had cornered me alone to find out whether or not he should pursue her.

'I can't work her out,' he kept repeating.

'No one can, Sam. We gave up on that years ago. May as well try and fly to the moon.'

'I mean, if I just knew she was interested, I'd go for it.'

'She's interested, Sam.'

'Really? You really think so?'

'Yup.'

He laughed with disbelief, then relief. 'Oh, Meg, Megsy, that's fantastic. That's amazing! Thank you!'

Later that day I found Nick looking very sullen, sitting with the dog by the river and trying to fill it with pebbles. I sat next to him and patted Rusty. 'Wedding bells yet, Nick?' I was never a great advocate for beating around the bush.

'No, Meg, and I don't believe there will be.' He tried to skip a pebble across the surface of the river, but it sank. I realised Nick's sullenness was deeper than I thought.

'What do you mean?'

'What can I do? I love her so much, sometimes I think I'll burst. But, what do I say? "Brigitte, I have nothing to offer you, but marry me anyway and leave your education and wealth and position behind and come and live in a tent with me."' He ran his hands through his hair. 'Meg, it's not right. I love her too much to see her reduced to this. I mean, look around us. Everywhere there is pain and destitution. Some of society's greatest men have been reduced to nothing. Women who were hosting balls in beautiful gowns are now raising children in corrugated iron huts held together with mud and gum leaves. The coppers lock up anyone who looks at them sideways in Kently, and a steady job is about as hard to find as Mum's mean streak. But we're lucky, Meg. We at least have a van and two tents, not to mention clothes and jobs enough to keep us in food with a little left over. We won't have to travel for a while now, but we'll always be a little worse off than we were because now men pay lesser wages but want more work. The price of flour will soon match the price of a motorcar. But at least we have what we have, and each other.'

He fell silent, but not me.

'I'm sick and tired, Nick, of people saying we're lucky. At least this! At least that! I don't care if things could be worse or not. The point is they're not as they should be! We worked hard on that farm, Dad especially, and it was taken off us. Does that make us lucky? No, that's one man's grudge against another. We looked after Emma and she stole from us. Saying we're still lucky just excuses us from the need to fight for what's rightfully ours. Are we lucky because the tramp only took one sheep's life? If we keep accepting bad things that happen to us, we'll have nothing left to fight for.' I turned to face him. 'Look, if you love Brigitte but do nothing because we're lucky "the way we are", then that's stupid! You'll never get beyond "the way we are", and then what?' I wasn't really sure what I was saying. I was forming the idea in my head as I went, but Nick seemed to understand.

'I'm not giving up, Meg. I just want to offer Brigitte the world and I can't even offer her somewhere to lay down at night.'

'Well, then tell her that, so she knows where she stands. I'd have given anything just to have Julianne tell me she didn't want to be my friend anymore, rather than just leaving me to guess why she disappeared.'

He took my hand in his. 'It torments you, doesn't it?'

I nodded and closed my eyes. 'I just can't reconcile the Julianne I knew and the Julianne who lied to me. They can't be one and the same person, at least not in my mind.'

'Your mind is a very complicated, full place, isn't it?' he asked jokingly.

'And one that doesn't come with a compass and a map.'

After work, a few days later, Dad chopped enough wood for a small cooking fire. We had moved into the peak of summer and none of us needed the fire for heat. The days were long and always sunny apart from an odd evening storm that swept through like gossip in Harrington. He lit the fire and after the flames had died down, he shoved the camp oven in amongst the ashes. Rusty stood by him, staring at the fire with a tilted head and his tongue hanging out.

'How was work?' I asked Dad.

He glanced up at me. 'Good. They've promoted me to foreman, Meg, which means just a bit extra a week!'

'Dad, that's great!'

'It's not much, mind, but enough for us to consider renting a house in Kently.' He smiled at me proudly and scratched his nose. 'Who knows, Meg, might be the start of something new!'

'I hope so. Where's Mum?' She and Helen hadn't made it back yet.

The joy on his face suddenly left. 'She, uh, she got a letter yesterday. Some family business. Sorting it out in town. Should be back soon.' His short sentences were enough to perplex me but when Dad affectionately squeezed my shoulder before going to the van to get plates, I knew something was worrying him.

We were all eating dinner when Mum and Helen returned. They had Brigitte and Emily with them, who at least seemed a little more cheerful than Mum and my sister. Helen was staring at me with bright concern.

They all sat down and ate dinner with us. Emily and Amy were chatting away like a pair of parrots, Tom, Jeremy and Dad discussing books, and Nick and Brigitte talking in low voices. Helen was smiling at Sam across the camp and Mum was staring into her plate as if its scratched surface held all the answers to life. Afterwards, Amy and Emily went off to play with Rusty, laughing as they went. Tom and Jeremy decided to see if they could find a platypus in the river and I don't remember where Nick and Brigitte went; I'm sure they went for a walk or something. Helen, after glancing guiltily at our parents and then at me, decided she wanted to talk to Samuel. Faced with Mum and Dad on my own, I had this terrible feeling that I was in trouble.

Dad moved to sit by Mum on the long log and put his arm around her. They both watched me as if waiting for me to say something. When I didn't, they shared a knowing glance and Dad finally spoke. 'Meghan, did you still want to go to the city?'

My mouth must have dropped because I suddenly felt my lungs fill with warm summer air. 'What? Why?'

Mum pulled out a letter from her skirt pocket. 'Your Uncle Leroy and my sister-in-law must travel to Adelaide for two weeks on business. He doesn't say much about it, but Leroy has asked if either you or Helen would be available for that time to look after your cousins, Edward and Mary, at their townhouse.' Mum breathed out heavily as if fate was working against her. 'Helen does not wish to go, partly because of Samuel, partly because of her job, and partly because she knows it would mean more to you than to her.' She unfolded the letter, smoothing out the creases. 'So, it seems that God has passed the opportunity to you.'

'Well, I don't know about that, but yes, this is very fortuitous.'

'You'd be paid a minimal amount for your trouble but they'd also house and feed you,' Dad said. 'Brigitte has already agreed to allow you to travel with them when they leave in two weeks' time and to organise a way for you to return, which is to occur as soon as your uncle returns, okay?'

I nodded eagerly, the idea beginning to sink in. 'You're really letting me go to the city?'

'Only because we can now ensure your safety,' Dad said gruffly. 'You will have a place to stay and your Aunt Jane's elderly mother will be there to keep an eye on you.'

'And you on her,' Mum added. 'She's not well and needs care.'

'Harriet?' I asked. I'd met her once before. She'd spent the whole time ordering me about like I was a servant, so much so that I ended up running every time I heard her footsteps.

'Yes,' Dad said.

I interlaced my hands tightly and rested them on my lap. 'You know, Helen is better at playing nurse than I am,' I admitted.

Mum smiled warmly at me. 'You were great with Emma and with me. If it wasn't for you getting me to hospital when you did, I could have really taken a turn for the worst.'

I felt my cheeks redden.

'Meghan, we're not going to lie and say that this is what we want,' Mum went on. 'We don't want you to go but we give you our blessing if you do.'

'And you don't have to go. Let us make that clear.' Dad's eyes rested on me as if he was hoping I'd breathe a sigh of relief and forget the whole thing. Mum gave a small, sad smile, because she knew that that just wasn't going to happen.

———————

Brigitte's dad, Mr Robinson, drew up by the campsite fourteen days later on the first of February. Brigitte hurried out to help me with my things. Most of the camp had drawn around to say goodbye to me. 'Take care,' Larry and Jack said, each shaking my hand.

Molly kissed my cheek. 'Hope everything goes well,' I said, 'if the little one decides to come early.'

'With your mum nearby, I'm sure it will be fine.'

I put my small bag of things in the car. My family followed me, and after Nick had said goodbye to Brigitte, he got in the car to give us some privacy. Amy hugged me first. 'Can you bring me back something, Megsy? Please?'

'I'll see.' I patted her head gently.

Thomas handed me a piece of paper. 'I wrote this for you.'

I stored it safely in my pocket and hugged my 'little' brother as much as he would let me.

I saw Helen looking at me with concern, but before she could say anything I found myself buried in Nick's big arms. 'Brigitte will look after you, should you need anything,' he said proudly, releasing me just before I suffocated.

I turned to Helen then, and she had red eyes. 'Oh, Meghan, you worry me,' she said, taking my hand in hers.

'Now, remember, you can't go around looking like a country girl in the city. Remember what I said about standing tall.'

I rolled my eyes. 'Don't get married without me,' I whispered as she hugged me, and I felt her freeze with shock. She was about to chide me but Dad, who wasn't so good at goodbyes, wanted to hurry it up a bit.

'Take care of yourself, Meg. Get home safely as soon as you can. Make sure you're back for your birthday.'

'I will.'

He eyed me for a moment longer. 'It's not too late,' he whispered.

'Yes, it is,' I whispered back, thinking of Emma. He shook his head and hugged me.

As soon as he let go, Mum embraced me like her life depended on it. She didn't say anything at first – I don't think she could – but I could feel maternal concern falling around me.

'I'm not leaving you, Mum. Not forever. I'll be back before you know it!'

'Oh, Meg,' she muttered and held me again. I knew that I'd have to be the one to pull away because she never would. It occurred to me that none of us had ever been away from each other for more than a week, so this was a new thing for my parents and it was more important to them than to me. I know you will be okay.'

'Bye, Mum,' I said with a smile. I was about to hop in the car when Jeremy suddenly caught my arm and took my hand to help me into the car. Then, he quickly but tenderly kissed my cheek and closed the door.

———————

I opened Thomas' letter – that brother of mine who's just a little too clever – and I read it as soon as we were well and truly on our way, as soon as I was too far to turn back.

The open plains are hers
For out there she searches
For what she cannot accept here.
She is a loved sister
But she is also Meghan
And that she cannot accept here.
She is an Aussie battler
And the morning's still sunrise
And I know one day she'll return
And accept Meghan here.

11

THE CITY WAS BUZZING. IT WAS ALIVE. IT WAS filled with angst and joy and energy to the point where I'll even admit it scared me. There were trams and cars and people everywhere. I had been to the city once before, when I was seven, to visit Mum's other brother, Uncle Robert, but I hadn't remembered it like this.

I had dinner that night with the Robinsons at their aunt's place. The house was not large, but it was beautifully and richly furnished. It reminded me a bit of living on the farm with people all around, but really the place was very different. Instead of open paddocks and rivers and sheep out the front door, there was the road and many other houses and people who didn't know each other like they did in Harrington. Brigitte's mother and brother met us there and seemed genuinely happy to see me. I was tired from the travel, which had taken most of the day, and so I was almost joyful when Brigitte suggested we have an early night. I was to share her room before they took me to Uncle Leroy's place in the morning and hoped we wouldn't have time to talk about anything much.

As I lay down on the skinny but comfortable bed, feeling my body adjust to the position, I closed my eyes and tried not to think about my family. Already I felt the tug of wanting to be with them, of wondering if they were okay, but I told myself to be strong – I would be back soon enough. I thought about other things: whether or not I would find Julianne; what would happen if I did; if seeing Emma's grave would make any difference.

'Meghan?' Brigitte's soft voice called from the other side of the room.

'Hmm?'

'Will you be alright, really?'

'Yes.' As far as I was concerned, there was no question about it.

'Well, I'll come and see you when I can. Oh, and I found out something for you.'

'Yes?'

'Julianne Young. Mum said there was talk that she'd been working at a milk bar.'

'Is it far from where Uncle Leroy lives?' I asked.

'A bit. You could catch a tram into the city centre though. Take your young cousins with you, if you need to.'

After Brigitte gave me the details, I lay in silence for a while, wanting to sleep but remembering Julianne again. How we used to swap lunches sometimes. How she helped me with mathematics and I helped her with French. How we spent one whole afternoon trying to ride sheep when we were little, only to be yelled at by Dad. How she slept over once, helped me with the eggs in the morning, and threw one at me. It ran all the way down my back like a broken sun. I had thrown one back at her but before we got too carried away, Mum caught us in utter shock. Still, we giggled about it all day at school – mostly about the look on Mum's face.

I thought about how Julianne's brother, Peter, had taken us fishing one afternoon. When I caught one twice the size of his, he said that he 'couldn't be bothered with girls anyway' and didn't take us again. I remembered accidentally falling into the river and getting covered in mud and how Julianne jumped in too, just so I didn't have to bear my parent's aggravation on my own. I remembered going to a concert for her sixteenth birthday, seeing Jeremy and the other boys there and saying how handsome they were. Then we forgot all about them until William came and asked her over for dinner that day.

It felt like years ago but was really only four months. Four months we had been on the road camping. Lying in that room with Brigitte was my first night under a proper roof in four whole months.

'Brigitte?' I said softly.

'Hmm?'

'Thank you.'

'Meghan, is that you?' Uncle Leroy called, having heard me enter the foyer of his stunning townhouse.

I didn't get a chance to answer as he came bounding down the stairs with a smile that made me think of Mum.

'Meghan Manley, look at you! I had no idea my niece had grown into such a beautiful woman!'

I laughed at the thought as he hugged me and instructed his housekeeper to take my bag upstairs. He led me into the lounge room, talking all the while.

'We're so pleased that you've been able to come and do this for us. Edward and Mary are very excited to meet you – they were too young to remember you from when we visited that time. You look remarkably well considering all these months camping. How is Evelyn holding up?' I told him about her trip to the hospital and he shook his head. 'She never mentioned that. Typical. My sister always had this fear of worrying other people, when really she is the only one who worries too much. The letter she sent back to me about you coming was filled with more terms and conditions than the constitution!' He laughed again, in a way that reminded me of Mum. He had the same dark brown hair, but it was cut short and I could not tell if it was curly or not. Either way, I decided I liked him.

His wife was a different matter. As soon as Aunt Jane entered the room she filled it with a bitterness I could almost taste. She was gaunt and unfriendly and, like Victoria, she tilted her nose up at the sight of me, as if I were a common peasant and she the reigning lady. I don't think even Helen could have found something pretty about her. She only came up to my shoulder but that did not stop her silencing me just with her presence.

'Miss Meghan.' She spoke as if my name left a bad taste on her tongue. 'I am glad you have arrived at last. Mr Wright and I must take our leave as soon as possible.'

'Certainly,' I said, uncertainly.

'Mama is upstairs and unwell, but she will appreciate your company, I am sure.' It sounded as if she wasn't sure at all. 'Edward! Mary!' she called with a piercing voice that made me cringe. I heard them almost falling down the stairs, but when they came into the lounge room they both stood tall and proper next to each other as if they were on trial for something. Edward was ten and Mary only eight. I could see a lot of Uncle Leroy in them, probably because that's what I was looking for. They both chorused, 'Hello,' to me upon their mother's command, then left again to return to their studies.

'We plan to be back in exactly fifteen days,' Uncle Leroy said as he hoisted the last suitcase onto the back of their car the following day.

'We *will* be back in fifteen days,' Aunt Jane corrected with a frown.

Edward and Mary kissed their mother's cheek before she got into the car. I was glad I didn't have to. Uncle Leroy handed me a letter. 'This arrived today. No guessing who it's from.' He said goodbye and I watched them drive away.

I sent Edward and Mary off to play, thinking they would appreciate the chance, although they looked surprised and even a little scared to think that I was so liberal. I went into the sitting room and spent the next hour relishing the letters from Mum and Helen that had been enclosed together. There was even a note from Amy.

I took so long because, in actual fact, I was delaying doing what had to be done. I was supposed to make a pot of tea and take it to Grandma Harriet, a cantankerous old woman if ever I saw one. I'd only seen her once on this trip so far, when Aunt Jane had told her she was leaving her in my care. She'd just grunted and looked over me like Dad would look over his sheep. I slowly filled the pot and took deliberate steps up to the second floor. Every move I made seemed to send a thousand creaks through the wood grains and into the floor. But I kept going until I reached her room, that dusty, musty-smelling place that made me miss the open air.

Grandma Harriet was asleep, so I left the tray beside her bed and retreated much more quickly than I had come. I returned to the sitting room to read over the spines of Aunt Jane's book collection, thinking how long it had been since I had read a good book. I was about to pull one out when Edward and Mary appeared in the doorway. They stood staring at me very quietly to the point where I felt nervous.

'Yes?' I asked eventually.

'Meghan,' Edward began but stopped again. He looked to Mary for encouragement. 'Meghan, could you please read us this book?' He pulled one out from behind his back.

I reached out my hand for him to bring it to me. '*Pilgrim's Progress.* Of course I'll read it to you.'

They beamed at each other and sat on the floor in front of me, looking up with keen blue eyes.

When it was time for dinner, I put a bookmark in and told them I would finish it another time.

'Really?' Mary stood up and leaned against me.

'Yes. I promise.'

'Mother never reads us stories,' she whispered, like she was committing a sin. She leaned closer to my face as if trying to see if I was real.

'What about your father?'

'Oh, he does,' Edward said proudly, but then added a little vaguely, 'sometimes.'

'Well, I'll read to you as often as you like. As for tomorrow, I want to go into town to do some shopping. Would you like to come?'

'Shopping?' Edward appeared doubtful. 'We're supposed to be at school tomorrow.'

'Oh, of course.' I was embarrassed that I had already forgotten about the concept of school. 'Well, I shall go myself and bring you both home something.'

———————

Before I could leave the next morning after my cousins had gone to school, I had to check on Grandma Harriet again. She was awake this time and wrote me out a list of things to buy and do while I was in town.

'Don't forget to buy some new flowers for the dining room,' she finished at last, leaning back in her bed and squinting at me as if she didn't trust me for a second.

I was nervous when I first hopped onto a tram, not just because I'd never done it before and wasn't sure I was on the right one, but more because I didn't know if I was really prepared to see Julianne. I mean, what would I say? If she had a great explanation for everything, would I forgive her? How would I know if she was telling the truth or not?

When the tram arrived at my destination, I stepped off, suddenly unsure of the strength of my legs but determined to see it through. I walked along the busy streets, staring up at the tall buildings and feeling that they would topple down on me at any moment. There were young children under the age of ten begging on the streets. Men queued up outside hotels waiting to get their share of food waste. One fainted as I walked past, and he was carried to the side. There were women wearing fancy hats and men in business suits wandering here and there, ignoring the misery around them while reminding me that I was still a farmer's daughter.

I went into one milk bar and a few other small shops asking for Julianne Young but without luck. There were so many cars and people about that I developed a ridiculous fear of being pushed onto the road and run over. I walked faster, looking about me like a frightened kangaroo.

'Does Julianne Young work around here?' I asked at a small restaurant, since I was running out of ideas.

The Italian man frowned at me. 'Julianne? Julianne work across road in shop with white door. You go over there.'

I turned slowly to see the door he was referring to and the wide shop window where I saw people crowding inside, buying treats for the day.

I cautiously crossed the road and went into the shop. I stood on my toes behind the crowd to see if I could catch the glimpse of red hair that would tell me I had found her, but I didn't. Eventually I made it to the counter where a blonde girl waited to serve me. 'Is Julianne here?' I asked. 'Julianne Young?'

She stared at me blankly. For a moment I felt I must have made a terrible mistake, but then her eyes lifted and she looked past me. I turned to follow her gaze and saw my old friend, thin and tired, but my Julianne, looking at me as if she were faced with God himself.

12

I DIDN'T KNOW WHAT TO DO. HERE I WAS IN A strange city surrounded by strange people, and Julianne had become one of them. She continued to stare at me as if she were transfixed. At first, I thought there was the hint of a smile and she leaned forward, as if she was about to rush to me with joy. That passed, I think because she realised I was harbouring anger against her, so she looked to the floor and did nothing.

Taking a step toward her, I saw her glance over her shoulder, like she was looking for a way of escape. My steps quickened in case she found one without me speaking to her.

'Julianne,' I began as she backed into a corner. 'Julianne, what happened to you?'

She breathed in quickly and I realised she was trying not to cry. I also realised that while I had time to prepare myself for this, for her it was a surprise confrontation.

'I can't talk to you now,' she said. 'I'm working. Where are you staying? I'll come to you after work.'

'Just like you said you'd come to Coolibah?' I said more bitterly than I had intended.

Julianne recoiled, then straightened and led me outside. 'Meghan, I fell in love with William,' she explained quickly, conscious of how little time she had. 'I wasn't honest with you about that or… Oh, it doesn't matter.'

I frowned, trying to be patient, trying to make sense of everything. 'I was told that neither you nor your family ever intended to come to Coolibah. That means you lied to me.'

She pressed her lips together. 'Yes, I did. I lied, Meghan.'

'Did you get any of my letters?' I asked, still confused.

She nodded and glanced away guiltily.

'So why didn't you respond? Why didn't you just tell me that you wanted to come with me, but you just couldn't? I would've understood!'

Her eyes began to tear up. 'Because I chose William, okay? I chose William over you, because, for whatever reason, I decided he was more important than whatever your friendship meant to me. Is that what you want to hear?'

I was shocked by her bluntness and hurt in a way I'd never been before. 'Friends no matter what,' I said softly. 'That's what you said. No matter what. But the moment it got hard you walked away – for a boy you knew no better than the milkman.'

Julianne gritted her teeth and stared at me as if nothing I said had touched her heart. I suddenly realised how hard she had become, and cold, like Aunt Jane and Victoria. This was not the best friend I once had known so well. 'You can hate me, Meghan,' she said. 'But we can't go back. It would be better if we just pretended we never knew each other, starting now.'

My eyes prickled at her harshness. I had spent three months fretting about her, caring about her in spite of myself, being angry with her because deep down I still loved her, and now she was ready to dismiss me in a second. I felt so ashamed of myself that I had ever called her a friend; so embarrassed that I had wasted all that time thinking about her; so insignificant because the friendship I valued so much apparently meant nothing to her; so angry for having ever let her get close to me.

'Fine. I hope William will be there for you then, or your job, or this city; all those things you betrayed me for. I hope they will look after you when you're lying on your death bed or when you find yourself in a gutter or in a poor house – I hope they comfort you then, because I certainly won't waste any more of my time.'

Tears ran down her face now and I was proud of myself for keeping mine under control. 'I have already survived these past few weeks without you or my family or William. I don't need you, Meg, so just go away.'

As I walked down the main street again, I was altogether unprepared to bump into Victoria as well. I didn't realise it was her until we'd walked past each other. We both stopped and turned, neither of us believing what we had just seen.

'Little Meghan Manley?' Her scarecrow hair punctured the air as she tilted her head. 'What are you doing here?' Victoria cackled as she looked from me to the big city around us. 'A country kid in the heart of the city – you stick out like a sore thumb!'

'I... I was visiting a friend. Julianne.'

'A friend?' She laughed again even more patronisingly, if that were possible. 'That's funny because Julianne told me that she'd never been good friends with you and that she was happy to leave you behind! Besides, she's my friend now, if you didn't know. I'm teaching her how to be a proper lady so she'll get a proper husband. Nothing like that ignorant William.'

Again, Victoria succeeded at somehow paralysing my tongue so I couldn't think of a response.

I was shaking by the time I got back to Uncle Leroy's place. I saw to Grandma Harriet, who chided me for being late and forgetting the flowers, and then I went into the little room I had for myself and realised I'd forgotten presents for Edward and Mary too. I was angry at myself, at Julianne, at everything. All the things I wish I could have said to her and Victoria were now flying through my head.

I couldn't make sense of it. Julianne had left me for William but now she was alone. Had Victoria manipulated them? *What if she did?* I asked myself. *I don't care anymore. I can't care. This hurts too much already.* I stared out the window listening to Julianne's harsh words repeat again in my mind and my eyes clouded with tears. I hugged my knees and suddenly wished very much that Mum and Dad were nearby.

––––––––––––––––

'She said she had survived all this time without anyone?' Brigitte asked me one evening a few nights later after I'd spent half an hour telling her how angry I was with Julianne. She had come to visit me and I was actually glad of her company.

'Yes.'

Brigitte frowned and tapped her cup thoughtfully as we drank tea together in the lounge room. 'What do you think she meant? Why is she all alone? Did you ask?'

'I was too busy just going away,' I said, leaning back into my chair.

'Meghan, I think something might have happened to her.'

'What difference does it make? Even if I wanted to help her, which I don't, she wouldn't accept it anyway. I've had enough friendship thrown back in my face to last me a while. Victoria said...'

'Meghan, you know better than to believe anything Victoria Willis might have said. Look, I know you are hurt, but...' She frowned.

'But what?'

'Never mind. How is your family going?'

'Fine, as far as I know, though sometimes I think they won't be honest with me because they won't want to worry me while I'm away.'

'Well, I received a letter from Nicholas today and he didn't mention anything bad, only that they are missing you.'

'Me?' I scoffed. 'What's to miss?' Brigitte was about to say something predictable but I cut her off. 'Do you love my brother?'

'Very much.'

'Would you marry him?'

'If he asked.'

'He won't, you know, until he has something to offer you.'

'I know,' she said matter-of-factly. 'I love him all the more for it.'

A week into my stay, Grandma Harriet became more civil. She was feeling well enough to venture downstairs with the help of the housemaid, and I poured her some tea in the lounge room where Edward and Mary were quietly playing.

'Put it here, Miss Meghan.' She gestured elegantly towards the small table. As I did, I felt the sweep of her gaze over me. 'You're not traditionally beautiful, are you? But then, I think it is mostly those ghastly clothes. You have a lovely figure, only you hide it. If only you could have been educated as a lady...' She took a small sip of tea and breathed out heavily. Grandma Harriet was partly right – one good thing about living on the road was that I'd lost those extra pounds, but that did mean my clothes hung off me now. Still, it didn't bother me.

'You should go to Hanson's Wares and buy yourself some new things while you're in town,' she said.

'That's owned by Frederick Hanson, isn't it?'

She rolled her eyes at me. 'Of course. The newspapers say he has been in town of late. Something to do with the death of a family member.'

'Oh. Where's the graveyard from here?' The mention of death made me think of Emma.

I wrote down the directions Grandma Harriet gave me and went there the next morning. I was able to leave Edward and Mary with her since she was becoming a little more active again, despite her sickness and age.

Wandering the cemetery alone soon made me uncomfortable. It was a bright, still day and I was the only person there. I looked at the newly turned sods, knowing that her grave wouldn't have settled yet, but I couldn't find her. There was a grave of an old man who had died in a train accident, one of a mother who had died of old age, and another of a woman who had drowned in a river, but no Emma. I was about to give up, when I saw a tall man with a black cloak pacing up one of the paths not far from me. He apparently found the grave he was looking for and leaned over it. He had no flowers but took his hat off. There was something familiar about him.

He must have sensed my presence, because he straightened, turned and looked at me.

'Frederick Hanson?' I said, taking a step back.

'Meghan?' He shoved his hands into his pockets, looking very much as if he wanted me to go away. This, of course, drew me closer. 'What are you doing here? Where is your family?'

By then I was standing next to him and I looked down at the new grave he had been leaning over. The small white cross read 'Emma Wales'.

'Emma?' I gasped. 'Did you know Emma?'

Hanson snarled as if preparing to spit. 'What's it to you?'

'You did know her, didn't you? Why would a poor, destitute girl like Emma interest you? Did you meet her in town? Did you drive her to suicide? Did you heckle her, the way you...'

'Enough already!' he growled. 'No, I didn't know her. But I was her father.'

'Her father?' My mind reeled. 'But she was older than Nick...'

He glared at me and I got the feeling Frederick Hanson wanted to physically silence me, but he said nothing.

'Who was her mother?'

'It's none of your business, Miss Manley,' he said, suddenly realising he had already told me too much.

'No, but I bet I can guess.' I was already forgetting myself. 'You took advantage of a young girl, either when you were with Mum or just after...'

'Took advantage?' His voice soared. 'She lured me in! And then took off and didn't even tell me she had a child until Emma was two. Women must take pleasure in jilting and tormenting men, I tell you. Your mother was one of them.'

'My mother has always done what is right and just!' I felt my face flush with anger. 'Would you have supported this other woman, had you known she was pregnant?' He gritted his teeth and I went on before he had a chance to gather his thoughts. 'No, you'd rather spend the rest of your life blaming her for your lack of decorum and resenting my mother for seeing through you and finding happiness when you failed to offer it to her. And I'll tell you something else about my mother! She cared for your daughter when she was destitute and sick and ended up in hospital herself. She forgave her when she stole from us and cried when she heard of her death. And where were you? Evicting other good families? Living in the realm of the rich while your daughter starved and sank so low she couldn't bear to live anymore? You found out about Emma when she was two! You could have got to know her all those years ago. You could have helped her. She once told us her father had been killed in the Great War, so I'll bet she never even knew you were her father! And then you have the audacity to stand here and blame her mother and mine?' I felt tears forming in my eyes and my nails digging into my palms as I clenched my hands. Before Frederick Hanson could answer my string of accusations, I walked away.

Dear Meghan,

We were so glad to receive your last letter, although I think it made us miss you more. Everyone is fine, but I am writing now to tell you that the sawmill has closed down. Nicholas, Jeremy, Sam and I have lost our jobs and the only work we have heard of is apple-picking at Gunya, which, as you know, is even further away from you. We have to leave immediately because we are running out of food and need money desperately. The four of us men are in the process of getting the government's susso just so we have some sort of regular income, but it seems so complicated and it will be a while before we receive any actual benefit from it. What Helen and your *mother are earning at the hotel is barely enough for flour now.*

Meghan, I fully expect things to get worse. I'm being honest with you because I believe that of all my daughters, you can bear it best. There is nothing more we would like than to have you with us again as soon as possible – our family is incomplete without you – but I just want you to know that if Uncle Leroy invites you to stay on, that you have our blessing to consider it. From what I have heard about Gunya, it is a police-harassed slum, but we need the money. Should you decide to join us, then know that we leave this afternoon as soon as I post this letter in Kently.

We all love and miss you, Jeremy included.

God be with you.

Dad.

'Well, God,' I said out loud as I folded the letter again, 'if you are with me, I am at least grateful that you didn't give me Frederick Hanson as my father.'

When I'd returned from my encounter with that man, Edward and Mary were scared because I was so angry. For both their benefit and mine I'd read to them again, finding it calming although not quite the same as sitting by a river in the country. I had spent the rest of my time in the city looking after the children, Harriet and the house to the point where I hardly had time to think. When I did, moments of anger and hurt would sweep through me and I worried that if I didn't get back to my family soon I'd become an emotional wreck. So I held onto Dad's letter when it arrived and carried it with me, thankful for the sense of familiarity it brought.

———————

'Are you packed, Meghan?' Uncle Leroy asked, peeping into my room.

'Yes.'

Leroy and his family had returned the day before, on time, just as Aunt Jane had said they would. Since receiving Dad's letter, I was keen to go, slum or no slum.

'Well, the car's here to drive you to Kalridgery at the edge of town, where you said you had another ride, yes?'

'Yes,' I said, wondering if a half-truth was actually a lie.

He looked at me sceptically, but I held his gaze to convince him I could take care of myself, if nothing else. He hugged me suddenly and then paid me what we had agreed upon for the fifteen days.

'Give my love to Evelyn, and Nathaniel, and your brothers and sisters. I hope very much we will see them soon.'

'Goodbye, Meghan!' Edward said, hugging me too.

Mary was teary-eyed. 'But can't you read us more stories?'

'When I see you again next time, I promise.' I leaned down and invited her into my arms.

Grandma Harriet didn't say goodbye and Aunt Jane said a quick, rather ungrateful one.

'Thank you for taking care of everything so well,' Uncle Leroy said as I got into the car.

As we drove off, I thought about what I was leaving behind: Julianne, Emma, Edward and Mary, whom I had come to love; and Brigitte, who had been good to me. But then I thought about what I was returning to: Jeremy, whom I was surprisingly eager to see, and my family.

I stopped to post a letter to Dad with a quid and a short note: "I'm coming home."

13

'HERE WE ARE, MISS MEGHAN. KALRIDGERY. Gateway to everything else. You good to go?' The driver pulled over to the curb.

'Yup.' I grabbed my bag and got out of the car. I walked into the nearest building and waited until he drove away. I watched a man with a cart walk by shouting, 'Bottle-o!', and then a kid ran out and exchanged two bottles for a copper. The street cleared and became eerily quiet. Swallowing my fears, I stepped back onto the road.

It stretched out in front of me like a cow's tongue. After a few other town names, the signpost at the edge of town said 'Kently – 102 miles'. Gunya wasn't even mentioned. Suddenly I was feeling not half as adventurous as I'd felt back at Uncle Leroy's, where I had assured myself I could make the long trek back to my family on foot and save the money.

Surely, I could hitchhike.

Then it started to rain.

It was heavy and persistent. I'd gone only about two miles when I sought refuge under a bridge, blocking out thoughts of loneliness and concern and thinking good thoughts. How Nick had once brought me home a handful of wildflowers, 'just because'. How Dad told me a Bible story by the fire one night after everyone else had gone to bed. It was something about this woman who stood by her mother-in-law no matter what. 'Now that's mateship,' Dad had said.

When the rain eased to a gentle sprinkle, I made myself get up and keep going. A car went past but didn't stop for me. I could feel the water beginning to soak through my jacket and I was beginning to trudge in the mud. By the time I'd gone five miles, I had to stop again under a tree.

What are you doing? I asked myself, slumping into the ground. *You're not strong enough for this. You can't do this alone. It's raining and you're hungry already. What will you do when it gets dark?*

I sighed and leaned back into the tree. I had a real urge to pray but I just couldn't. I was still upset with God about the farm, Julianne, Emma, Frederick Hanson – everything. But I guess, deeper than that, I was afraid he would let me down too. And if God let me down, there was no hope for me. It was one thing for Frederick Hanson and Mr Willis to turn against our family. It was one thing for Julianne to let me down. It was one thing for Emma to steal from us. But if God didn't answer me, my whole empty frame would collapse. So I didn't ask for anything. Better to be empty and surviving than full and dying on the side of the road. I had to get to my family – that was what I had to concentrate on more than anything. I couldn't let my thoughts and feelings get in the way. I couldn't!

But I trembled slightly and felt my strength beginning to crack already. I fiddled with the cross on the necklace Jeremy had given me and suddenly missed him a lot. I was scared of myself, of dropping the china all over again so to speak. So I stood and walked on in the rain.

———————

I was glad the days were still long. I wasn't cold, only soaked and miserable. I started to hum as a means of keeping myself going. I wasn't following any particular tune but after a while I realised I was humming *Be Thou My Vision* out of habit. I stopped myself and started humming the anthem *God Save the King* instead but stopped again and sighed. *I can't escape you, can I?* So I sang *Botany Bay* out loud, relating to the convicts and their desire to fly back to the ones they loved.

I'll be the first to admit that I was scared that night. I made myself a bit of a fire under some gum trees and concentrated on cooking some damper rather than listening to the eerie sounds in the bush. I flinched at every owl hoot and rustling leaf, sure I wouldn't live to see the morning. I couldn't get to sleep so I sat up poking the fire, trying to make myself really tired until I had to sleep. When that failed, I gave up and hummed *It Is Well,* and somehow 'peace like a river' eventually allowed me to close my eyes.

My clothes were damp and my muscles stiff in the morning, and I was hungry. I ate a bit of breakfast, but I was rationing my supplies. I packed up my things in the bag and tried to picture my family to inspire myself to get walking, but it took a bit longer for me to find the strength to actually put one foot in front of the other. I dragged my feet over the gravel road and kicked the rocks, the bag on my back feeling as heavy as a bale of wet wool. The sky was still grey although the rain had stopped.

I'd only walked two or three miles when I came across a group of men working on the road and earning their susso. They seemed surprised to see a young girl who probably looked poverty-stricken and malnourished alone on the track.

'Lost your family, girl?' one of the older ones asked me as I approached them. He leaned on his shovel and frowned at me.

'Just on my way to join them.'

'Where are they at?'

'Gunya.'

'Yeah? You've got ages to go yet! Best get yourself a lift.'

'Yeah, I will,' I promised myself as I kept going.

The green farmland spotted with sheep made me homesick. I stopped for lunch next to a small creek and rubbed my arms with some gum leaves in hope of warning off the mozzies that had been plaguing me.

I felt so lost and scared. I wanted nothing more than to feel the warmth of Mum's embrace, the comfort of Dad's kind words. I wanted to read more of Thomas' poetry and hear again how much Nick loved Brigitte. I wanted to know if Helen was courting Samuel yet and if Amy still played with the other children. Instead, I walked on.

After a while, I heard a car coming from somewhere behind me and it stopped suddenly. Feeling a little nervous, I kept going but then someone got out. 'Meghan!'

I turned on my heel with surprise and saw her running towards me with eyes almost as red as her hair. The car set off again.

'Julianne?' I squinted to see if it was really her and didn't know what to do when I realised it was. She stopped just a few paces away from me. 'What are you doing here?' I asked.

'After you left I changed my mind, and so I decided to come after you. I've been asking after you and following your trail ever since, hitchhiking rides and backtracking occasionally until I found you!' She paused and took a deep breath. She looked like she was emotionally exhausted. 'I wanted to say sorry.'

I flinched slightly. 'Julianne, why are you following me? Go back to the city, to your job and the life you seemed to want so badly.'

'You don't understand!'

'No, I don't!' I said angrily. 'More than that, I don't know who you even are! You told me that we should just pretend we'd never met and now you're here, miles from anywhere, coming after me! What am I supposed to make out of that? You're the most confusing person I've ever met!'

'Meghan, I didn't think you'd understand. That's why I didn't tell you. I thought you'd hate me and persecute me like everyone else has. Even though you probably still will, I should have at least given you a chance. Now I've lost my job, I have nowhere else to go and I'm praying, Meghan, so hard, that you'll forgive me and give me a second chance.'

'What are you talking about?'

'Meghan, I'm pregnant.'

I felt my mouth drop but she went on before I had a chance to say anything.

'To William. After you left he… he convinced me to see his way on many things and I lost perspective on who I thought I was and what I believed in. I wish I could lie and say I meant to come to you at Coolibah, but it's true that it was a conscious decision to go with him to the city. Victoria encouraged me because she wanted company on her trip with Mr Willis. Both she and William convinced me you wouldn't care that much, and stupidly I believed them, even though I knew deep down that I was betraying our entire life of friendship.' She was crying now. 'It was just one night, one stupid night. And I realised, when William returned to Harrington next morning after a blue that Victoria started, that my life wouldn't be the same ever. I'd compromised everything. I didn't know then that I was pregnant. When I realised, I told my parents and they left me in the city to stay until the child was born. "Get it seen to or adopt it out," they said, otherwise they'd never speak to me again. When I eventually told Victoria, she left me instantly. But I can't abandon the child because it's not its fault. I don't know what kind of mother I will be – I'm seventeen, for God's sake. I'm not supposed to be a mother at all! But I have to do this one thing right.

'I've made more mistakes in a few months than most people make in a lifetime, but I want you to know that I did love you and still do. I've done and said things I'll regret forever and I don't deserve your forgiveness. But I shall ask for it all the same. Please let me come with you.'

'"I don't need you, Meg," that's what you said!' I reminded her, my mind suddenly very tired and cloudy. I could hardly understand what she was saying. 'Do you have any idea about the implications of what you say and what you do? Because I'm so confused right now, I can hardly think straight. Even if you mean what you say, where do we go from here?'

'The only way we can go. Forward.'

———————————

I hardly spoke to her for the rest of the day. There was too much to think about. I allowed her to walk with me but kept such a fast pace she was always lagging behind. I didn't want to look at her. I just wanted to get away from it all.

Pregnant? I exclaimed to myself every five seconds. I couldn't comprehend how the young lady I'd left at Harrington had gotten herself into so much trouble so quickly. Getting back to the sanity of my family became imperative and I hardly wanted to stop at all that night, even though every muscle in my body ached and I was dizzy with hunger.

'So, will you keep the baby?' I asked when we did stop, breaking the silence as we ate next to a small fire.

Julianne nodded, surprised to hear my voice. 'It shouldn't be punished for my mistakes.'

I swallowed. 'I respect that. But how will you do it? And where are you going now?'

'Oh… I was hoping you would let me… let me come with you and stay with your family, if you'll have me.'

'We're camping, Julianne.'

'Beats sleeping in the streets.'

'We can't afford…'

'I'll earn my own keep, thank you very much. Been doing it for this long.'

'What about William?'

'What about him?'

'Well, he does know, doesn't he?'

'I sent him a letter, but he didn't respond.'

'What about…'

'Meghan, please stop interrogating me.'

I bit my tongue and watched the fire, feeling old and weary.

'Meghan,' Julianne whispered a few minutes later. 'You will be able to look me in the eye again one day, won't you?'

I was silent for a long time, concentrating on the burning ashes of the wood. 'Julianne, you're asking a lot of me, you know. I have to get to know you from scratch again. More than that, I have to decide if I want to. What you've become is so far from who I thought you were… How am I supposed to trust you? I believe that you are sorry, but kisses don't heal broken bones, no matter what we want to believe.'

I heard her sniff. 'I've really have hurt you, haven't I?' she choked.

I nodded, taking satisfaction in her at least knowing it.

Still not meeting her eyes, I lay down by the fire, pulled my jacket closer around my neck and hoped that the spits of rain wouldn't turn into anything more serious.

Julianne hardly spoke to me the next day and lagged so far behind I was beginning to wonder if she was trying to decide between giving up on me and leaving, or sticking with me to avoid being alone in the bush.

You're being too hard on her, Meghan, a part of me was saying. *But look what she's done!* the other part countered. *Hurts me and then expects me to forget it! Why didn't she just tell me the truth in the first place?*

It had started raining but I ignored it and kept going until I was soaked and so tired that I would have had tears on my cheeks had they not been washed away. The bitterness I was harbouring was making me crumple inwards like some science experiment gone wrong. I realised in that moment that no matter who I was, I was not naturally harsh and terse. This thing I was carrying around was turning me into someone I didn't like.

I was so busy thinking about this and chastising myself for not realising how difficult it would really be to get back to my family, that I was surprised to find myself in a small town that I can't even remember the name of. I suddenly realised that there were people talking and bustling around me. It was nothing like the city, but after the aloneness of the bush track, I felt like I was back in the city's main street.

It was a Sunday and there was a travelling preacher telling a story in the park, three men busking together and little children running barefooted towards a small shop. Julianne went to hear the preacher's story and I followed her, but we had arrived only in time for the end.

'Haven't seen you young girls here before,' the preacher remarked as the small crowd scattered. It took me a moment to realise he was talking to us. He was not an old man but had a wise air about him that commanded respect.

He also had a young daughter clutching to his pant leg. He picked her up and said goodbye to a few people walking by.

'We're just passing through,' Julianne said.

He offered his hand and Julianne shook it. 'I'm Charles Dawson, but most people call me Travelling Dawson, or just Dawson. This here is my daughter, Gabriella.' The little girl grinned at us both and then put her head over her dad's shoulder so she couldn't see us. 'Nice to meet you both. Where are you headed?'

'Gunya,' I said.

'Gunya? Still a fair way to go, then. If you like, I can give you a lift to the next town. That's thirty miles you won't have to walk.'

Julianne's eyes lit up. She would have been excited to not have to walk one mile, let alone thirty. 'Would Mrs Dawson mind?'

He shook his head with an odd smile. 'Nah, not much. She died two years ago.'

'Oh, I'm sorry.'

Dawson shrugged and said nothing more about it.

Soon we were on the road with them. Julianne fell asleep with Gabriella, the two of them collapsing against each other on the back seat. I couldn't believe how quickly and deeply Julianne had gone down. Maybe my fast-paced walking really had worn her out.

I was sitting in the front staring out the window, grateful that my feet were getting a rest. My shoes were wearing out quickly and I didn't think my parents would appreciate me needing another pair as soon as I got back.

'Your friend,' Dawson said, 'she in trouble?'

'Yup,' I said, not caring what he thought.

'And what about you? What are you doing?'

'Going back to my family.'

'Hmm.' He was silent again for a moment. 'Julianne… she, ah… You don't seem to be on good terms.'

I shrugged.

'She let you down?'

'You could say that.' I tapped my finger idly against the windowpane and sighed. 'She broke a promise to me in favour of this bloke, completely disappeared from my life for four months, said some tough things to me, and now she's hanging around me again as if nothing even happened. I know it don't sound like much…'

'If it was important to you then it's more than enough.'

'I'm just hurt, I guess. It was more because I would've done anything for her. But… I didn't mean the same to her.' That realisation made me feel a bit numb.

'Yeah. It's a hard one.' Dawson nodded thoughtfully. 'I knew a bloke once. He had a small circle of friends who he trusted with his life, literally. They did everything together. They travelled together, ate together, worked together – you can imagine how close they would've been. Some people didn't like them much, this group of men; my friend, in particular. They did and said some controversial things, I guess. But then one day, one of his mates sold him off, literally, to this other bloke who didn't like him. Told this rival where he was, even led him to him. Ended up costing my mate his life.'

'Are you serious? His friend led him to his death?'

'Yup. Can you imagine what it'd be like, seeing him approach you and knowing what he had done? Real kick in the guts. And then all his other friends left him too.'

'Really?' Julianne's failures suddenly seemed very insignificant. 'They can't have been very good friends then. Not really.'

'Oh, but they were. They really loved each other. They were just confused and scared, I think.'

Like Julianne, I thought.

'What happened to the man who betrayed your friend?'

'In the end he was driven mad by guilt. Not a very nice story actually.' He shook his head and laughed it off.

'Did the man ever get a chance to apologise?'

'Not really. But I think my friend knew he regretted it, and he forgave him anyway.'

'Forgave him? Just like that? I wish it was that easy!'

Dawson laughed warmly. 'It's one of the toughest things in the world. But you know, it's no excuse for someone's bad behaviour. Forgiving someone is for your own benefit. It just means you'll stop hating them, stop treating them with condemnation and bitterness. That way your own bitterness can dissipate and you can breathe easy again.'

'But if you forgive, aren't you just leaving yourself open to be hurt all over again? Bitterness is my protection from being let down now.'

Dawson glanced at me as he drove. 'You have a very clear perspective of yourself, which is great. You just need to rise to a higher place; a place where you don't let your friends dictate your happiness in the first place. See, Julianne hurt you because you gave her power to. My mate, when he was betrayed, he was hurt, yes, but he could forgive because his happiness wasn't in his friend's hands. You can love someone and still not be hurt if they let you down. Just place your happiness in the Lord.'

It was my turn to laugh, but it was a cynical, sour laugh. I had known it would come back to this. One doesn't go for a drive with a preacher without expecting to hear something about God. 'Ha, what does he know?'

'Quite a bit, actually. He loves all of us even when we let him down, which, I bet, is all the time. Besides, it was his son, my friend, who lost his life at the betrayal of his mate, Judas, so I imagine he understands more than you credit him for.'

14

'JULIANNE,' I SAID, PRODDING HER. 'WAKE UP, we're here.' She opened her eyes groggily and I smiled at her. 'Come on. I'm not even going to make you walk much. Just a mile up to the campground.'

'We haven't got a tent,' she yawned, slowly unfurling.

'Come on.'

Julianne pulled herself out and thanked the preacher for the lift. I did too.

Dawson winked at me. 'My pleasure, Miss Meghan. I hope you both get to your families soon.' He walked over to the hotel to book in for a night, and that was the last I saw of him.

That night I spent a lot of time thinking about what Dawson had said while Julianne was asleep. I began to realise that I had been pretty hard on her. She was trying to make things right. As for the bitterness inside of me, I desperately wanted to let it go, to breathe easy again – I just wasn't sure how. In the end I decided to at least try and treat Julianne better. Mum had said it was 'Wright and Manley' not to hate and I didn't want to be the kind of person who did. I was hurt but that didn't mean I was no longer accountable for my actions.

So, I decided to start forgiving her by writing a short letter to William, telling him that we were going to Gunya and that he should meet us there. I was pretty sure that Julianne hadn't really told him she was pregnant at all, but I was hoping that he still loved her and that it would be enough. Without telling her, I posted it the next morning.

'Here comes a car!' Julianne called out to me. We were walking down a grassy hill littered with bark from a few gum trees. We waved at it, but it went by.

It was another hour before we saw another one. This time, I had an idea. 'Julianne!' I said urgently. 'Push out your stomach and lean heavily on your stick. Although you're not showing much yet, they might get the idea.'

She did as I suggested with a giggle, subtly holding her jacket out as well to make it appear that she was more rounded than she really was. To my amazement and pride, the car slowed.

'What's a mother-to-be doing out on the road?' a woman with a round, moonlike face asked, leaning out of the passenger window.

'Oh, we're on our way to Gunya!' Julianne said cheerfully. 'Trying to catch up with my husband! He's got work there, you see,' she added at the woman's confused look.

'Oh, well, that's something, isn't it? Come on, then, we'll give you a lift as far as we can.'

———————————

It was raining when we stopped again. The sign at the crossroads said 'Kently – 17 miles'. I couldn't believe we were so close! We'd probably make it the next day! Better than that, Gunya was now even mentioned, although it was still another fifty-three miles.

The car drove off and Julianne and I were standing in the middle of the road with our two bags. She looked up at the sky and crinkled her nose when the rain fell on her face. 'It's been raining too much lately. Look at the creek.' She pointed at the one running parallel to the road. 'It's going so fast.'

'High too,' I remarked, but without any particular interest.

It wasn't until the next day when we were following the road beside what was now Kently River that I began to worry. The rain was heavy and the wind was shocking, tearing through the trees like a grim reaper. Julianne was scared and I was only being strong for her sake. Water patches on the road were growing and we walked through one that was nearly up to our knees. I was afraid that Julianne would catch cold but there seemed to be nothing we could do but press on.

We went off the road at one stage because there was a paddock, and I wanted to walk there rather than under the trees. They were dropping their branches like Samuel used to drop hints around Helen.

Sheltering in a small farming shed, Julianne and I huddled together. 'If you had one wish, what would it be?' she asked me.

'To see my parents right now. What about you?'

'I just want the storm to be over.' I knew she didn't just mean the one outside.

The one outside did eventually settle a bit and lest we were caught trespassing, we kept going, eating the remains of damper I had cooked the night before as we walked.

Seeing Kently again was like coming home to a familiar old friend. It was just the same apart from the tree debris on the roads and the lack of people about. Even so, I felt more cheerful than I had felt in a long time, and I hurried along to the old spot on the river, a part of me hoping that my parents had changed their minds about moving on, and a part of me willing to be content just to find anyone I knew.

The campers at the river were only a few and they had all moved away from the river, up on top of a small embankment. I could see why – it was high, also full of debris and raging. I could no longer see the rocks that I'd slipped on in my moment of anger at Helen. The river had widened its embrace.

'Meghan?' a woman with a child in her arms called. She waved at me eagerly.

'Molly!' I ran to her and she hugged me closely. 'Oh, Molly, it's so good to see you! You've had your baby!'

'Yes, isn't he beautiful?' She let me hold him and he looked up at me with lovely big eyes. 'His name's Harry, after his grandfather. Looks like Dave, doesn't he? Your mum delivered him just before they moved on to Gunya. Everything went seamlessly and I was so glad to have her.'

I gave Harry back to her, afraid I'd drop or hurt him. 'How were they? Mum and all of them?'

'All well, though very disappointed with what happened at the sawmill and all. It was a hard decision for them to go on without you. Your mum fretted about it quite a bit. I must say, Meghan, they were looking a lot better than you when they left. You look like you haven't slept properly in a month! Have you been on the road alone in this weather?' she asked just like a mother would – caringly, but with a frown.

'Not alone. This is Julianne. She's travelling with me.'

'Hello, Julianne. Still, Meghan, two girls alone... Come on. It's going to rain again. Our tent is small, but it's better than nothing!'

———————

It was one of the most uncomfortable nights I've ever been through. Apart from general squishiness, it poured and thundered all night. I had never known a storm so ferocious, as if it were taking its anger out on the land. Once or twice I heard the crack of a tree as it fell to the ground, unable to withstand torrential rain and ghoulish winds.

The night was noisy – the river seemed to be getting faster and I was sure it would soon overflow to where we were, or that a branch would fall on us. I could see the outline of shifting leaves on top of the tent, forming horrible shapes that made it even harder to rest, although by then we had given up on that. We just wanted to get through the night and inspect the damage in the morning. Dave had to get out numerous times to fix the tent, and Harry cried so much, I decided then and there I would never have children. Then I thought of Julianne, who no longer had that choice. She had a child coming whether she wanted it to or not.

Her being pregnant took me so long to get used to. I suppose it's because I didn't have the usual things that help you get used to the idea of your friend being a mother; things like seeing them fall in love, get engaged and then married. Julianne seemed to have skipped all three, although I think she did love William. But the last time I saw her we were still kids wandering the streets of Harrington together. Life was simple and uncomplicated.

We'd certainly left that behind. Or perhaps it had left us. Either way, the storm had started now and didn't look like it was going to stop anytime soon.

I had never been so glad to see the dawn, even though it was still a cold, wet day. But had I known what sort of day it would become, I would have stayed in the tent. It was partly due to my impatience. My whole being was driven on getting back to my family. I was exhausted, stiff and sore, but I wanted to keep going. Although it had stopped raining, the river was higher again, broken trees and branches were everywhere, and it was a perfect day to find decent shelter and stay there. I was only thirty-six miles away and wanted to get going. Julianne begged me to stay put until the weather calmed and after having a bit of a blue with her about it, I walked down to one of the trees near the river.

There was a bird on the other side of the bank making a mournful cry and I took a step forward to get a better view. It seemed safe. The water by the tree was only shallow and the worst bit was in the middle of the river. I leaned on the gum tree, holding onto one of the branches tightly just in case, but the river was too fearsome for me to stay by it for more than a moment. Hearing Molly calling me, I was about to walk back and have another go at convincing Julianne to keep going. Whatever I felt when it came to her, I wasn't prepared to leave her behind now.

But the branch I was holding onto snapped. The ground beneath me shifted. I realised in a flash that I was standing on the tall bank behind which I had often bathed, only it looked different since the water was so high. It was falling beneath me and taking me with it. I lost my footing and could feel the river sucking me in. I clawed at the dirt and roots of the tree. I grabbed handfuls of mud that slipped away from me. I saw people running towards me, yelling at me, but I couldn't hang on. The bird I had heard flew into the sky with a shriek. It was a raven.

The roots slid from my fingers and in a terrifying moment I was drawn underneath the brown water. I felt myself bump into debris and get scratched on my arm, but I was most worried about breathing. I couldn't work out which way was up and I was tumbling like a rock down a hill. My foot landed on something. I instinctively pushed against it, propelling myself upwards.

The breath of air was like a kiss from God. I drew it in deeply but panicked when I realised that the people I'd seen were now out of sight. A moment later I heard yelling and looked behind me where they were running along the side of the river. One of them threw a rope out to me but the river was going too fast and I missed it.

'Grab onto a branch!' another man yelled. I think it was Dave.

It started raining again. The river carried me around a bend, and that was the last I saw of Dave or anyone else. I was shivering. I used all my energy in treading water and trying to keep my head above it. I looked around for branches and snatched a few but they didn't seem to help. As I continued to be dragged down the river, I was slammed into a tree, not because I wasn't paying attention but because the will of the river could not be argued with. Before I could grip it, I was swept on.

I tried swimming towards land but quickly exhausted myself. I felt my skirt tear under water when it caught on something and a piece of it was left behind. I tumbled further and further. Then I saw a low branch that had grown over the river. It had a piece of rope on it that I think had once been used as a swing, but the river was so high there was only a few feet between the branch and the water now. The branch was directly in my path and there was no way I could miss it. I just had to try to slow myself down enough so I didn't get thrown against it. I did my attempt at backstroke but don't think it helped very much. I still slammed against it.

I don't know how long I stayed there, my arms reaching over the thick branch, the water washing around me, but it wasn't until I saw half a tree coming down the river towards me that I suddenly had the energy to pull myself up onto the branch to avoid becoming a sandwich filling. I was just in time. The floating tree came to rest where I'd been just a moment before. I closed my eyes and clung to the branch I was now lying on, water flicking over me as it rushed past. For the first time in a long time, I prayed.

15

I REMEMBER STARING AT THE INTRICATE PAT-terns of the bark on the log I was clinging to, certain they would be the last thing I would ever see. I followed the creases with my broken fingernails and tore at it until there was just hardwood left. I watched some small insects scurry around at my disturbance and squished them when they got too close to me. I was completely waterlogged, and my teeth were chattering so much it was as if they had become bored with being in my mouth and wanted to get out. My muscles were tensing and tiring at the same time and I knew I wouldn't be able to hang on much longer.

I'm not sure how much time passed while I sat there unable to think clearly – it could have been minutes, it could have been hours. I do remember getting swept off the branch again and tumbling around under the water like a broken doll. I remember telling myself to stay awake, to not give in, but I failed because the next thing I remember is waking to find myself thrust against the side of the river with a terrible headache but no explanation as to why or how I had survived.

I was faint and so sore I wept with the pain. I'd never been so scared, so lost, so desperate as I was at that moment, lying on the side of the river and feeling it rage behind me, not entirely sure if I was alive or even if I wanted to be.

I drifted in and out of consciousness as the day wasted away. When I was awake I was engaged in an intense battle with myself, part of me trying to force myself up, the other telling me I'd never do it. Blood trickled down my face from a head wound that must have been responsible for the throbbing. In the end I guess the primitive will to live kicks in, and so somehow I dragged myself away from the water and onto some muddy grass.

It was only then that I realised it was no longer raining. There was a slight, warm breeze. Dusk had settled but this time it did not bring peace. My body ached and I tried to ignore it. My eyes flickered, struggling to stay open. I couldn't fight it any more. I drifted into a nightmarish sleep.

When I woke in the morning, stiff, cold and hungry, I wanted it to be over. My body felt like a wildflower field stamped by cattle. *God,* I thought to myself, since I was too tired to speak out loud, *Emma died alone and I know I must too. You can take me now. I don't know if I'll meet you or not, but what's most important is that you take care of my family.* I coughed tiredly.

My family... Thinking of them suddenly stirred me back to life. *I have to see them again.* The fixation ran through my mind over and over until I grabbed hold of it and somehow managed to pull myself to my feet.

I fell straightaway and realised that I'd moved more quickly than my body was capable of. I crawled for a bit and tried again. That time I was more successful and I stumbled away from the river up a steep bank until I was on top of a bit of a hill. I sat down amongst the long grass and felt the warmth of the sun on me. As I began to focus on the scene before me, I realised that the land was blanketed in water for as far as I could see.

I had never seen so much water or any other sight quite like that one. I felt insignificant: weak against the power of nature. Or was it the hand of God?

I could see some farmhouses with water almost up to their rooves. There were a few more small hills with livestock gathered on them. The land was wet and moody, drowning under more water than it had ever asked for or needed. It was silent and brooding, still coming to terms with its new burden. I wondered for a moment if this had hit Harrington and if we would have lost our livestock. At least that was not something we had to face.

I looked up to what was now a blue, clean, stunning sky. I could hear nothing but wind in the grass around me. Then, because nothing will kill the spirit of the land, a song disturbed the quiet air and brought into it warmth and hope. A pied butcherbird that sat high in a tree somewhere back towards the river sang calmly and beautifully to the point where I was physically drawn to him.

Following his warbling song, I was called not to the river but along a small track cattle once used. It was muddy and I slipped more than once as it had recently been under water. I appreciated its wandering guidance as I walked along. The butcherbird continued to sing and although I never found him, he did lead me to a road.

I first saw a man on horseback, a farmer looking for missing livestock. He was about to pass me by but groaned to himself. Without a word he turned his horse back and handed me a small bag containing bread and cheese, which must have been his lunch.

'You got caught in the river?' He looked me up and down with some concern.

I nodded.

'Our house is over that way,' he said, pointing behind him. 'The missus will give ya a hand if ya want, but we were flooded.'

I thanked him and he rode on. I dropped to my knees at that very spot and ate all of the food without pausing.

nach groaned under the sudden influx and I held it with my hand to settle it.

The food helped to clear my mind and gave me some strength. The first thing I did then was to rip torn pieces of material from my skirt and use them to bind a few of my more serious cuts. The worst one was on my right leg, which was making walking a tiring and painful exercise. I cringed as I pulled the cloth closely around it. Using another piece of skirt, I wiped the blood away from my head and found the source of it in my hair.

Standing in the middle of the road and holding the cloth firmly on my head wound, I tried to determine where I was. I couldn't see the farmer's house and wondered how far away it really was, and how much help they could offer me if they were flooded. I'd been carried down the river in the opposite direction of Kently, I knew that much, but where Kently was now I had no idea. I wasn't familiar with the land around me and it looked especially strange because of the floodwaters. Being on a road, I had the option of going either left or right. I chose left because it seemed to stay near the Kently River while heading upstream and it was in the direction the famer had pointed. There was a chance I might come across his house. I just had to hope the road didn't veer in the wrong direction later.

I could still hear the butcherbird singing. He seemed to be following me. I started thinking of him as my guardian; somehow his song made me feel safe. But by that night I hadn't found any sign of people. I was starving again and as darkness fell, so too did the song fade.

Had I been back at the farm at that time of day, I would have been heading back to the house with a pail of fresh warm milk from the cow. The smoke from Mum's kitchen would have been pouring comfortably out of the chimney and Amy would have been feeding the new kitten while asking me for some of the milk to give it. I would have found Thomas intently studying a new piano piece while Helen would have been either reading a book or helping Mum with dinner. I would have stood by the range to warm up for a moment until Dad and Nick returned from the paddocks. Then I would have blushed when Dad kissed Mum and laughed when Nick told me a story about his day.

I certainly would not have been caught in a river amidst a flood, and even if I had, I would have at least had plenty of people to comfort and look after me. As it was, there was nothing left to remind me of my old life. I was cold and alone.

That is, until I came across the small lamb stuck in the mud to one side of the road. Its small bleat immediately caught my attention. I stumbled over to it and awkwardly lowered what was once my healthy body beside it. It struggled against me when I tried to help it but soon gave up, and after much wrestling, heaving and groaning, I pulled it free.

It was exhausted and I knew enough about sheep to know that it would probably not survive the night. A good farmer would have put it out of its misery, but I was all out of practicality. I had been fighting death for hours – I was not about to invite it into my life now. Besides, if I were a sheep in my injured condition, they probably would have put me down too. So I hugged the lamb, remembering the one Julianne and I had played with in another world and time. I smiled, and decided to nurse the lamb as best as I could. I had nothing to give but warmth and affection, but at least it gave me purpose.

'So, the farmer's daughter turns thief herself?' a cool voice said behind me.

I turned on my heel, feeling my spine shiver in fright. It was made worse when I couldn't see anyone in the darkness.

'Even after her strong words to me that spring afternoon.' I heard the crunch of gravel as someone walked towards me. I took a step backward, gripping the lamb tightly.

He walked into a slither of moonlight and I wanted to vomit when I realised it was the tramp. God, how could this be? I shuddered and he smiled, enjoying my fear.

'Heard there was a girl near drowned. Didn't realise it was you. The searchers must have missed ya – they're further down the river. But I've been following you for a while.'

'Then you would have seen that I was merely rescuing this lamb, not stealing it.' I was ashamed at the tremble in my voice.

'Really?' His mouth twitched. 'Rescuing a lamb beyond help? I doubt it.' He coughed and spat on the ground. The lamb bleated pathetically in my arms and I realised I was probably crushing its bones in my fierce grip. I set it down on the path and then did something I will always regret. I ran. I abandoned the little thing.

Dad always told us that we had to confront our problems, but I had no strength to face the tramp. I was spent but the lamb paid the price. I returned to the spot much later that night and found that the little lamb I'd rescued had endured a far worse death than it would have had I let it be; its blood drained away to the side of the road. All at once, my hunger, fatigue, injuries, fear and emotions fell heavily inside me and I dropped to my knees and then my side. Lying next to the lamb, I closed my eyes, broken and exhausted.

I didn't want to open them again when I woke in the morning, but when I did I was more confused than scared. A steady fire was crackling a few yards from me with a billy on the boil. I then realised that my head was resting on a pillow, and not only that but I had the infinite luxury of a blanket around me. I smelled and heard a horse nearby and wondered who had rescued me. I propped myself up and looked about, but there was no one around. I heard the butcherbird call again. I smiled when I saw that there was also a camp oven in the fire, probably cooking damper at that very moment.

I was already getting excited at the thought of food, but nothing brought me to life more than what I saw next. A man with a worn and tired hat came walking through the trees towards me with a dead rabbit in his hand. He saw me sitting up and looked at me from under the brim of his hat, his deep brown eyes smiling at me.

'Jeremy!' I pulled myself to my feet and stumbled towards him, but he met me halfway and I threw my arms around him.

'You're alright!' he said, holding me tightly. 'I was so worried that you wouldn't wake!' I drew back and realised there were tears in his eyes.

'You're the best thing that's happened to me in weeks!' I hugged him again, unashamed of my sheer joy at seeing him. For the first time I was aware of his strong build.

Jeremy laughed and I let him go. 'Meg, are you really alright? Julianne rushed to Gunya to tell us what had happened to you. God knows we were washed out ourselves, but I've never seen your family move so quickly. We have been searching for you for what feels like an eternity. We must have passed you at one point and missed you accidently...' He grasped both my hands in his. 'Your father has hardly spoken a word since he heard of it. He's exhausted himself looking for you, and your poor mother – I've never seen her so distressed. And I was... I was terrified that we'd lost you.'

I smiled widely. 'You haven't lost me,' I whispered, shaking my head to emphasise the truth.

He gently touched my cheek. 'You are the strongest girl I have ever known. Now, come on, Meg.' He poured me a cup of tea. 'Drink this and get your strength back. I've got some damper almost ready and I'll cook this rabbit for a second course. We have to get you back to your family as soon as possible so I need you fit to ride.'

I realised a few moments later that Jeremy was definitely not a natural cook, but as I was starving I ate my share of the damper quickly. It wasn't until I'd swallowed the last mouthful that the terrible after-taste set in. And he had taken such pride in preparing it for me. I pressed my lips together, telling myself that it wouldn't be a good idea to ask him how he'd survived by himself for so long on this so-called food, no matter how much I suddenly wanted to know. Maybe that's why he'd been so happy to see Mum, all that time ago.

Being careful not to grimace and throw-up, to wash it down I drank as much tea as I could without making him suspicious. He started cooking the rabbit and I could feel my stomach turning at the thought of what that would be like, but he sent me down to a small, calm creek to clean myself up before reuniting with my family. Although I'd had enough of water for a lifetime, I did as Jeremy suggested and felt better for it. It was good to get blood off my leg and face, to distinguish between dirt and bruises and make some sense of the rags of my clothes. Jeremy lent me his coat when I got back and handed me a bowl of rabbit stew. Even though it was slightly better than his attempt at damper, I could hardly eat for the excitement of seeing my family later that day. Things had certainly improved since the night before.

'How did you find me?' I asked as we ate, feeling a strange connectedness with him that set me completely at ease. I guess after nearly dying and then realising what was most important to me, I didn't want to waste any more time feeling awkward around people. Hating Julianne certainly seemed like a waste now.

Jeremy put down his plate, shuddering as he relived the night before. 'I thought you were dead, Meghan, truly.' He couldn't look at me as he spoke. 'Like I said, we'd already searched this area, but I was sure you wouldn't be any further down the river. Logically, you would have been washed up before then, or otherwise... otherwise drowned. So I left the others and came back. Something drew me up that path, maybe God, and then I found you in the middle of the road with blood beside you...'

'No lamb?'

'Lamb?' He looked at me curiously. 'No, no lamb. I thought it was your blood.'

'No, it was the lamb's. He must've come back and taken it.'

'Who?'

'Never mind.' I was still far too tired to waste precious breath on the tramp. 'What happened next?'

'Well, not a lot, really. I carried you here, made you as comfortable as I could and got a fire going. It was quite early this morning, you see.'

'Early this morning? Jeremy, have you been looking for me non-stop?' I was filled with deep admiration for him, more so than ever before.

He nodded wearily. 'Many had given you up as drowned. But like your family, I... I hoped with all that was in me that you would have survived. You're a fighter, Meg. You're too loyal to people to give up on them. I couldn't give up on you.' He looked up at me with a crooked smile and I returned it with all the warmth I could muster.

'What's the date today?' I asked him with a sudden thought.

'February 26.'

Looking back at the fire, I breathed in deeply. 'Today's my seventeenth birthday.' I surprised myself with the realisation. 'Last year Mum promised me a party with all my friends – a picnic down by the river with cake and all good things. Now, here I am, spat out by a river, no idea where I am and certain of only two things. One, that seeing my family again will be the best present ever. And two, that you are a good man, Jeremy, and a good friend.'

His eyes glistened. 'Happy birthday, Meghan.' He touched my cheek again, leaned closer and kissed me.

———————

I certainly had no complaints when Jeremy asked me to sit behind him on the horse. I wrapped my arms around his waist, discovering a new kind of giddiness that didn't actually make me sick. Still smiling to myself, we set off to find the rest of those whom I loved.

It was a long ride and although the movement hurt some of my cuts and made my stomach even more unsettled, I was too happy and relieved to really notice the pain. We cantered across paddocks and paused on a hill that gave a good view of the land around us. I could see Kently, not too far off, tucked in between the gum trees.

'I set off a flare here at dawn.' Jeremy turned to me with a face flushed from the ride. 'We were all given one by the police in Kently to let them know if you were found and to return there. They should be there now.' He squeezed the hand I held around his middle.

For the first time, I saw the butcherbird sitting high in a tree. It cocked its head and suddenly flew off into the distance.

My heart was pumping so hard when we arrived in Kently. Jeremy and I got off the horse and he tethered him outside a shop. My eyes darted around at every person, desperate to find my family. I waited for the yell of recognition, the familiar voice, the open arms. My search became more quickened and desperate, and I actually jumped when Jeremy put a hand on my shoulder. Without looking at me, he pointed to something farther up the main road. My eyes followed the direction of his finger and saw a sorry, tired-looking group of people huddled together. I felt the blood fall to my feet and my veins fill with adrenaline and joy when I realised who they were.

I stood staring at them like the village idiot, unable to speak. When Jeremy whistled to them, they all looked up. There was a hypnotising moment as they stared at me, beginning to realise but hardly daring to hope. I'll never forget the energy and shock that filled them when the realisation actually hit. Someone shouted my name, but I don't even know who. I was running to them and they were running to me.

I couldn't see Mum, but Amy was ahead of the rest of them, waving her arms around in the air with a big grin. 'Meghan!' she called.

When I reached her I literally picked her up off the ground as if she were six again.

'You're alright?' Amy cried, but I was too choked to reply. I felt her small arms squeeze me tightly but put her down again, and taking her hand, I dragged her with me to greet the others.

Reaching them was kind of like what I had imagined heaven to be like: everyone so filled with love and thankfulness that there was no room for meanness or unhappiness and certainly not anger. I hugged Nicholas, Helen and Thomas in a daze, and then felt the secure embrace of my father. He squeezed me so tightly I lost my breath. I thought he would hold me forever. He whispered my name but couldn't say anything else.

'Where's Mum?' I asked when Dad did release me, but before he could answer I saw her rushing out of the nearby post office.

'Meg!' she called with a mother's desperation, descending the stairs quickly.

I rushed straight into her arms.

Mum was too choked to speak any further. I buried my face into her shoulder, letting the tears come. Dad wrapped an arm around her and I could feel him stroking my hair.

'I didn't think I'd ever see you again!' I said. I shook with a rush of relief and many other things they probably don't have a name for.

'I prayed for you every day,' Mum said, finding her voice again, 'but I hardly dared to hope!' She was struggling to hold back tears. 'But God returned you.' She kissed my temple but didn't let me go. 'My Meghan is home.'

16

MUM AND DAD INVITED ME TO SPEND THE NIGHT in the van but I insisted I was fine. I was looking forward to sleeping between my sisters again – that was inviting enough for anyone. But before bedtime came I sat with Jeremy and all my family, once again together, around the fire. We were at a spot on the other side of Kently and nowhere near the river. Mum was kneading my hand and leaning into Dad's embrace as if exhaustion had hit her and she could hardly sit up straight. The others were all singing happy birthday to me, and once they finished, Mum and Dad gave me a present. It was a bracelet of Mum's – one that her mother had given her and one I'd often admired. I was touched that Mum had chosen me to pass it on to, so much so that I didn't know how to thank her. She and Dad just smiled at me when I tried. I put the bracelet away carefully, not even game to put it on.

'I told you I'd be back in time,' I reminded Dad.

'You're a week later than you should have been!' he accused, but laughed and reached around Mum to tousle my hair. 'From the moment you were born, you always did things in your own time and way.'

'Even if it always succeeded in giving us near heart-failure,' Helen said.

'I don't do it intentionally,' I said.

'You're certainly an exciting sister to have.' Nick sounded proud. 'I think I said that if you hadn't drowned, I'd kill you myself for causing us all so much worry! I mean, first to go to the city all by yourself, then to travel all that way back to Kently, mostly by foot and with a pregnant girl in your care, and to then get yourself swept away in a flood!'

'I think she's a heroine!' Amy said dramatically, clinging to my arm.

'I think she's crazy,' Thomas said, not wanting to be left out of the discussion. He winked at me behind his shaggy brown hair.

I looked over at Jeremy. *I think she's lovely,* he mouthed at me discreetly and I felt myself blush.

'Oh, quiet, all of you,' I said, 'and tell me what it's like at Gunya?'

'You'll find out soon enough,' Thomas said gloomily, poking a stick into the fire.

'Have you all got work?'

Nick and Dad glanced at each other, and I felt something quicken my heart.

'You didn't lose your jobs, did you, on account of having to come and look for me?'

'We were able to come, provided we had someone look after our work while we were away,' Dad explained. 'Samuel, Jack and Dave are working extra hours to look after Nick's, Jeremy's and mine. Molly's doing Helen's share...' He hesitated with a hint of a smile.

'Who stepped in for you, Mum?'

She gazed at me softly. 'Julianne.'

Dad's smile widened, but instead of saying anything further he encouraged us all to get to bed. 'We'll head back to Gunya first thing in the morning.' He tried to get Mum to move off him so he could stand, but she was too tired to be bothered. 'Come on, woman, off!' he said to her with mock severity. 'There is only one cure to our exhaustion – sleep!'

170

My body thanked me when I laid it down in my old tent. Amy had gotten in before me and as soon as I was settled, she moved over and clung to my arm again. She didn't say anything, but I could tell she was feeling a lot.

'I missed you, Megsy,' she said some minutes later. 'I was afraid I wouldn't see you again. Do you remember the time you found a dead spider in your bed?'

'Yes,' I said with a frown that she couldn't see in the darkness.

'It was me! I'm so sorry, Meg! Please don't hate me for it!'

Knowing she couldn't see my smile in the dark, I put an arm around her. 'I already knew it was you, Amy. And I'm sorry too.'

'What for?'

'I forgot to bring you something back, like you asked,' I confessed.

'You're all that matters,' she said, snuggling into me.

Helen joined us and lay down with a deep sigh. 'Oh, Meg, I think these last two days have been the worst of my life!'

The three of us laughed together out of tiredness.

'You must tell us what happened after you were swept to shore in the morning.'

I thought about the tramp, Jeremy's rescue and his kiss, and wondered how much I would tell. 'You must update me about Samuel first.'

Before Helen could answer, Amy put in, 'Can't you tell us about the city and Uncle Leroy, and how you met Julianne? Are you friends again?'

I sighed. 'I don't know, Amy. But I'm not as angry with her. She's expecting a baby now.'

'We all got a bit of a surprise about that,' Helen said. 'But since then, we've hardly had time to think of it. She hitch-hiked a ride to come and tell us about your accident and we left to find you.'

There was a moment of comfortable silence while we just enjoyed being together again. Then, the flap of the tent drew back and Mum came in to say goodnight. She tucked Amy in and kissed her cheek. She asked Helen about something to do with the next day and said goodnight to her too. Turning to me, she pulled up my blanket and secured it around me while I stared at her, letting it sink in that I was really with her again, that I really had survived, that everything really was okay now. Mum rested a hand on my shoulder and gazed at me too with a faint, tired smile. She really did look exhausted. 'I'm sorry this happened, Mum,' I said. 'I know it would have been terrible.'

She nodded, stroking back the hair from my forehead. 'Sleep well, darling,' she said, and she leaned down and embraced me one more time.

Gunya was a much bigger town than Kently. The storm hadn't affected it as badly and it was busy with people, even when we arrived late in the afternoon the next day. There were many men holding up signs asking for work, a busker singing a song I didn't know and a few others who knew my family and were relieved to hear I'd been found. It was strange to think that my family was acquainted with people I didn't know. The few weeks I'd been away suddenly felt much longer.

We were all riding in the van except for Jeremy, who was riding his horse, one he had bought for a shilling from the owner of the orchard where he worked. 'He was going to send him to the knackers because he's just bought a motor vehicle,' Jeremy had told me. 'Didn't seem a right way to end a hard-working horse's life, so I said I'd take him.'

I watched Jeremy now, tilting his hat to various people as we went through the main street.

A bit later we arrived at 'the slum'. There were women with children living in the most appalling excuses for houses, men trying to work through sloppy mud and police dousing a man's campfire and yelling at him to, 'Get moving!' No material or scrap of food was wasted among hundreds of people. I felt so sad that my family had been reduced to this. It didn't seem fitting for Helen and Mum, such fine countrywomen, to be working amidst this. Just being there dampened even Amy's spirits, and since she was normally so bright, that made me even sadder.

No sooner had we pulled up to a spot slightly removed from the masses than some familiar faces engulfed us. Molly appeared first and held onto me for ages, muttering something about the terror of seeing me being washed away. 'I thought that was the end of you, Meghan, I really did!' She clicked her tongue, then turned to offer Mum some bread she had made since she knew we would be hungry.

Already the boys had started setting up the tents while Dad organised the van. Jack and Larry were there and they helped out too. It wasn't long before the whole site knew that 'Nathaniel and Evelyn's daughter' had been brought back safe. After being introduced to many people all at once, I was happy to get to bed early, away from it all. Only then did I realise I hadn't seen Julianne.

In the morning I was told she was in town looking for work. Like me, Thomas and Amy were out of work so the two of them walked with me to find her. When we did, Julianne impulsively threw her arms around me and told me how incredible it was that I'd survived. 'God must want you alive,' she said, 'because nature certainly wanted you dead.'

'God?' I was about to follow with a sarcastic remark but nothing came to me. I suddenly remembered praying while clinging to that branch. Now here I was, alive. I wasn't sure if that was coincidence or not, but a part of me at least wanted to give him the chance he had apparently given me. As I found myself unable to finish what I was going to stay, I realised everyone was looking at me. 'Have you found work?' I asked instead.

She shook her head. Avoiding eye contact, both of us were uncomfortable and unsure of what to say to each other. I felt a pang of hurt, knowing that once we would have found it hard to stop talking, especially after all that had happened. I knew then that our friendship would probably be stilted forever.

I was sitting in our tent about a week later, thinking about Emma and my conversation with Frederick Hanson. I hadn't told anyone about it, though I longed to discuss it with someone. I still felt guilty every time I thought of Emma and angry when I thought about her father. *Her father?* The concept was still so foreign to me. My family was out working for pitiful wages to buy even more pathetic portions of food, but at least we stuck by each other. How could someone with money be so cold and heartless, and not even accept the blame?

And then there was Victoria. *Julianne said she'd never been good friends with you and that she was happy to leave you behind!* Her words spun around again and again in my mind and I was angry that she could still have such a powerful effect on me.

I shuddered when I heard the police yelling at their new scapegoat outside the tent. Without even realising it, I brought my knees up under my chin and hugged them. I could hear them fighting, physically hurting someone. It seemed so unfair. These people were desperate – they were just trying to survive. The police complained that they were thieves or poachers or squatters, and were forever trying to find someone to arrest or demand to move on, mainly because they were eager to thin out the slum that this patch of Gunya had become. Their taunts filled me with anger. I willed them to be quiet so I could return to my thoughts.

Eventually the fracas did quieten, and despite the wailing of a hungry child, the camp returned to some sense of calm. I bit my lip, remembering how well off we had been. And now...

'Meghan?' Jeremy asked softly just outside the tent flap.

I scrambled out to talk to him, something we had hardly had a chance to do since I had rejoined my family. 'Hello. How was your day?'

'Fine,' he said with half a smile, as if I was keeping him from getting to his point. 'Meghan, I want to talk to you... about what happened after I found you...'

Some people were washing and cooking in their nearby campsites. They glanced at us, waiting for him to go on, and we both prickled at the sense of being watched.

'Wanna come for a walk into town?' he asked with an embarrassed look.

We found an almost empty park with a bench to sit on.

'Meghan,' Jeremy began again as we sat down, 'I need to know... I need to know if you... if you regret...' He gritted his teeth as if he was hardly able to speak it.

I knew what he meant. 'Do you?' I asked, feeling my body freeze over with apprehension.

'No, no, I don't. But… your parents' respect has come to mean so much to me, almost as if they were my own parents.'

'And they respect you. So…?'

'Meghan, I'll be honest with you because I know I can rely on your confidence. I'm afraid of getting you involved with me while you are, while we both are, so young, but I'm also afraid of losing you.'

I stared at some ducks making their way down to a pond and the small child that was chasing them. 'I know it would never happen, but I'm scared of ending up like Julianne, pregnant and alone.' I sighed and tilted my head to the sky. 'Perhaps it would be best on all accounts if we waited at least another year before we got too involved.'

Jeremy took my hand. 'You're a wonderful girl, Meghan. Certainly worth waiting for. You're my best friend, you know.' He looked at me with those brown eyes and I met them with mine. I saw a deep sadness there from his past, amidst great strength.

He squeezed my hand and leaned over as if to kiss me. Instead, he kissed my cheek. Even so I felt my heart flutter and realised how wonderful it was to think that a boy found me not only interesting, but also worth waiting for. Even though it would be hard for both of us, he was prepared to do it and so was I. The thought of having Jeremy's love at the end of the year had an odd effect on me, unlike anything I'd ever felt before. Suddenly a rush of happiness filled me, a sense of being wanted and needed. Perhaps I was not as unattractive as I thought I was. Perhaps I was not as harsh, unfeminine and clinical as some seemed to think I was. Perhaps there was a woman inside Meghan somewhere after all, one begging for acceptance so that she could come out of hiding and present herself to the world as a force to be reckoned with, a woman of purpose. Perhaps that Meghan would not be rejected, but rather embraced... Perhaps it was all a dream that was destined to be broken, but it was a dream nevertheless, and one that gave me the courage to hope.

———————————

'Should I be worried about you and Jeremy?' Mum asked as we did the washing together. She scrubbed my skirt up and down in the water. It was a new one, bought to replace the one that had been destroyed by the river. 'Your father and I both love him, but...'

'I know, and no, there is nothing for you to worry about.' I wiped back some soapy hair from my forehead. 'We... we've decided to just be good friends, for now.'

Mum paused to glance at me. 'Sounds very sensible.'

'Some things are worth waiting for.'

Mum wrung out my skirt and looked at it closely. She removed a grass prickle. Without looking at me, she said, 'I think my girl is growing.'

'I'm sure I'll still fit into it,' I said.

She rolled her eyes at me. 'That's not what I meant.'

———————————

'Miss Meghan, it's fantastic to see you looking so well!' Samuel said when he called on us the next day. I had seen him once before, but he had been so focused on Helen, I knew he had hardly even realised my presence. Apparently, he and Helen were much the same as when I left them – he still pursuing her and she still trying to decide if she wanted to encourage him. Still, his cheerful persistence was wearing her down – she had said as much... Well, I had read between the lines.

'Thanks, Sam, I feel fantastic.'

He grinned and patted my shoulder as he passed me. Helen blushed when he spoke to her and I rolled my eyes. Helen noticed and widened her eyes in a 'Meghan-don't-you-dare-say-anything' look. I laughed, but then silenced myself when her look became a glare.

Nick came and handed me a letter. 'It's from Brigitte,' he said a little scornfully, since it appeared he had not received one himself. His stern, unhappy look brightened when I revealed that his letter had simply been enclosed in mine. Nick grabbed it and took off to find somewhere to read it alone.

I sat by the fire Tom was making and read how she and her family had returned to Harrington with the intention to stay there. I felt nostalgic as Brigitte wrote about people we had once mixed with on an everyday basis.

'Dad is considering extending his land,' she wrote, 'but has yet to find the right opportunity. There is only your father's land, still owned by the bank, and it is not for sale. Even if it were, Dad would hardly consider it. Frederick Hanson and Mr Willis seem to have their own plans for the property, plans that, I'm sorry to say, will probably benefit no one but Hanson and Willis.'

'No surprises there,' I said out loud.

One of the things I had first noticed since joining my family at Gunya was that they had become weary, and not just because I'd nearly drowned. There was destitution and deceitfulness all around us and it didn't help to think of Hanson and Willis enjoying our farm back in Harrington. Helen, especially, was at the end of her tether.

'Dad, it wasn't me!' she yelled with vexation that evening when he discovered that the horse had been let loose and was found eating grass in a property down the road.

'You were the one entrusted with him!' he countered.

'And I did not untie him! Ask Thomas! He was with me!'

'I don't remember anything about it,' Thomas said unhelpfully, rubbing his forehead as if it hurt.

Helen glared at him. 'No, you just had your nose in a stupid book all day!'

'It's not a stupid book!' Amy said, defending her big brother.

'What would you know?' Thomas said, now angry with Helen and taking it out on Amy.

Amy's face darkened. She started to say something but then walked off in a huff.

'Now look what you've done,' Helen accused him.

'Helen, please,' Mum said, 'just explain to your father what happened with the horse.'

'So, you don't believe me either?' Helen's shoulders sagged. 'What does it matter either way? The horse was found safe!'

'And it's only due to the generosity of the property owner that we aren't in trouble for it,' Dad said.

They were all so tired and burnt out that they couldn't even see what they were doing. As they continued to argue, I walked over to the tree Clyde had been tethered to, leaned down, brushed back the tall grass and found what I was looking for. I picked up the rope that had been chewed in two and turned back to the others.

'Excuse me?' I said.

They didn't hear me.

'Oi!' I yelled, getting their attention by waving the rope about.

They stopped and stared.

'Clyde's eaten through it himself,' I said. 'It was neither neglect nor wilful misconduct.'

'See!' Helen said with red eyes. Mum and Dad both fell silent as she stalked off in the opposite direction to Amy.

Mum seemed to be trying to rally the mental energy to follow her.

'Oh, I'll go,' Dad said with a sigh.

I handed the rope to Nick, who was holding onto Clyde's halter, and retreated to the tent, wondering how long this heaviness over our family would last. The depressing surroundings did not help. Here, they did not sing around the fire together. It was every man for himself. The only thing to live for was tomorrow and the hope that it might be better.

17

FOR A FEW DAYS, NICK AND I WERE THE ONLY ones getting along. Having Brigitte as a common interest helped.

'I've decided I'll just do my best with what I can control,' he said next Sunday after we'd listened to a preacher talking to the campers. 'I'll let God handle the bit I can't control.'

I crinkled my nose. 'Do you think God cares about those kind of things?'

'Well, he cares about us, so he must care about the things that worry us too, don't you think?'

'I don't know what to think. It's still something I'm trying to work out for myself.'

'Even after a near death experience?'

'Yes. See, it's much easier for me to believe that Jeremy rescued me rather than God.'

'But have you considered that it may have been God who used Jeremy as a tool? Why can't both be right?'

I gritted my teeth. 'Because that would make me wrong.'

I was relieved to find that Thomas and Amy were friends again too when Nicholas and I returned. But Helen was pushing Mum to the limits in a way that was completely out of character. Helen hardly ever argued with anyone, especially not with Mum. She deplored conflict and went out of her way to stop it, not start it.

'Just tell me what's wrong!' Mum insisted. But Helen shook her head and walked off again. I saw Mum turn her head up to the heavens and let out a groan. Somehow this helped, because this time she went after her.

The four of us remaining started our evening chores. I scrubbed the copper frying pan until Dad arrived, while Thomas got the fire going properly.

'Kids,' Dad said suddenly. He was standing over Tom, watching him build the fire. 'I need to talk to you. You know that Nick, Mum, Helen and I have jobs here, but I reckon that ever since we arrived we've had nothing but trouble. First it took ages to get work, and then Meg... well, we're all burning low and being in this dump isn't helping. With the little we've earned, the susso and what Meg brought back from the city, I think we'd have enough to live on if we were to travel to find work elsewhere. Nick, Jeremy and I could certainly work for the susso in Darralong. Would you all be happy to move there? I'm almost certain it would be better living conditions.'

Amy burrowed into my side, already worried just at the thought of having to move on, but she didn't complain. Nick nodded solemnly, and Thomas was excited by the idea, so much so that I think he would've started packing at that very moment. Dad looked at me. 'Meg?' he asked.

I nodded. 'Anything's got to be better than here.'

He smiled at us and looked somewhat thankful.

Later that evening, just as we were going to bed, I heard Dad beckon Mum for a walk. 'Why do they do that?' Amy asked as we watched their silhouettes through the tent.

Helen was pretending to be asleep so I answered as best as I could. 'I guess sometimes they need a break from being "Mum and Dad" so they can just be "Evelyn and Nathaniel", people with their own needs and desires and hopes.' I smiled to myself, proud of my sudden insight.

Amy didn't really understand the difference but was satisfied to leave it and go to sleep.

For some reason, I was restless and could not sleep. I waited for Dad and Mum to return, thinking that would help. When I heard their footsteps and moved to peek out of the tent flap, I saw them holding each other as they stood by the dying fire. I watched as Dad stroked back Mum's hair and kissed her, then I turned away, wondering if Jeremy and I would ever love each other like that even amidst such despair. I still couldn't forget that the last friend I had counted on hadn't deserved my trust. Every time I thought of her, my face flushed with embarrassment to think that I had ever trusted her at all.

And yet so much had passed, so much had happened, and the hate and anger were fading somehow. Wasn't it wrong to keep holding a grudge against her when she needed support now more than ever?

'Darralong?' Jeremy frowned after Dad explained our plan to him. I was making my bed in the tent when I heard their voices. 'Mr Manley...' Peeping through the flap again, I saw him shove his hands in his pockets with apparent frustration.

'Nathaniel,' Dad insisted.

'I can't come with you. I can't afford to. The job I've got here is good and I just...' He covered his face with his hands for a moment as if trying to draw the right words out of his mouth. 'I want to come, Mr Manley, I really do. But I don't think it would be right for me to just walk out on my employer after he's been so good to me.'

Dad folded his arms as he listened and dug his boot into the mud.

'I also... I need to stand on my own two feet, if you know what I mean.'

'Jeremy, you've been standing on your own two feet ever since your father died when you were nine, ten years ago now. You've grown into a fine young man and you've earned my respect and many others'. Do you think there's anything else left for you to prove?' Dad used the voice he reserved for serious situations – a deep, articulate tone that meant every word he said was calculated. 'Coming with us now would be a sign of friendship, not weakness.'

'Yeah... thanks, I guess. I certainly don't mean to be ungrateful to you and your family, but the fact remains I have steady work here and a debt to my employer who took me on when he had others to choose from, and who allowed me time off to search for Meghan.'

'And what of Meghan, if you were to stay?'

What? I wondered. *How is it parents can see everything?*

I heard Jeremy sigh, as if he was intensely confused. I wanted to rush out and say that although I would miss him lots, I'd respect whatever he chose to do, but I knew Dad would chide me for eavesdropping.

'If I want to get married eventually then I need to start saving,' Jeremy said. 'But... Well, when are you leaving?'

Dad paused for a moment. 'Two days from now.'

'Can I let you know tomorrow?'

Dad must have nodded because the conversation stopped there.

I later found Helen sitting at the base of a lonely tree with her arms folded and her gaze empty. Sitting beside her, I said nothing, pulling up grass by the roots and digging my nails into the dirt. A memory flashed through my mind of being swept away by the river and trying to cling onto the roots, but I blinked it away.

'I'm not made for this, Meghan,' Helen said suddenly and softly, as if it were a secret. 'Always wandering, not belonging anywhere, living in tents. I've hated it from the moment we set foot off our property in Harrington.' She shook her head and a tear rolled down her cheek. 'I've tried, Meghan, I have. But I'm not strong like you. I wish to God I were. I've learnt a lot about myself since being on the track. What I want in the future is to never have to be reduced to this again. I want to know if this will ever be over. I want to know if our family will survive. First Mum was sick, then Emma died and then...' She shuddered. 'And then you nearly got yourself killed. And Sam...' She wiped away tears with the bottom of her palm. Helen shook her head and laughed uncertainly.

'Yeah, and Sam...?' I prodded cautiously.

'He loves this life. I don't think he'd stop travelling even if he had the means to get a house. He's a drifter, and that's all he has to offer me... and I'm so disappointed because... because I'd hoped.'

Hope deferred maketh the heart sick, I remembered again. Helen's heart was certainly sick, and I knew why. She had dreamt of a life with Samuel. She liked him, maybe even loved him – I don't know. But he was asking her to be someone she was not.

'He's a good man,' she continued. 'Don't think I think of him as anything else. He's just not... not on the same page as me. And worst of all, I wanted him to be and didn't even realise it.' She bit her lip and looked at me. 'I envy you, Meg. You seem so clear on what you want.'

I smiled doubtfully. I didn't get much chance to think about what I wanted, or at least, I didn't feel like I did. I didn't even know what I did want, come to think of it, except for Helen to be herself again. I want you to be happy. That's not so complicated.'

She took a breath and tried to draw herself together. 'I will be. As soon as we get out of this awful place. Darralong is becoming more and more appealing by the hour.' She drew quiet again, and then sighed with confusion. She rubbed her forehead and cringed. 'I've been so horrible to Mum and Dad that I don't know what to do. And how am I supposed to say goodbye to Sam, Meg? How do I kill something that once brought life to both of us?'

'Can't you still be friends? It doesn't have to be the end of the world, does it?'

Helen thought about this while she replanted the roots I had dug up. 'Sometimes it's all or nothing,' she said eventually. 'Sometimes it's no use pretending. Sometimes it's best to just leave things behind. The problem is, I don't know which time this is.'

Mum was carrying a load of washing towards the van when Helen went over and offered to take it for her, which was, of course, a way of making amends. As Helen walked to the van, Mum studied her for a moment, trying to work her out, but she gave a slight shrug, apparently deciding it was all beyond her. She rubbed her forehead as if she suddenly felt too old but then she smiled anyway.

Later, Amy was sitting on Dad's lap telling him something about goats she had learned from one of the other young girls whose father used to breed them. Helen was showing me a better way to make breakfast while Mum, Nick and Thomas finished packing everything up, ready to go to Darralong. Samuel and Helen apparently already had their conversation and he was nowhere to be seen. I put an arm around Helen, feeling a need for her to know that I understood and cared. She looked up at me and smiled, knowing my intention, then flipped the eggs over in the frying pan.

Rusty barked happily when Jeremy came over.

'Jeremy, I really do wish you were coming with us,' Mum told him as she instinctively leaned over and fixed his collar.

'I will, Mrs Manley, I promise. Just not straight away.'

'I shall hold you to that promise, Jeremy Bell,' Mum said with a pointed finger and a smile.

We ate breakfast together but then everyone was keen to go. Jeremy had to get to work and we had to get on the road. He waited until the others got in the van before saying goodbye to me.

'Thank you for rescuing me,' I said.

His smile was enigmatic. 'I think you may have rescued me. I was very alone until I came across you in the bush that day. I haven't been as happy in my life as spending these last few months with you and your family.'

'And yet you're desperate to get away from us.'

He shook his head. 'No, Meghan, don't think that. I just… this is just something I have to do. I just have to find out how to be my own man and when I've done that I'll come straight after you.'

I didn't really understand but tried to give him the impression that I did. 'I'll miss you.'

He suddenly hugged me tightly. 'I shall think of you often.' Pressing his lips together, Jeremy glanced over his shoulder to see if anyone was around. Deciding there wasn't, he turned back and gave me a last, quick goodbye kiss.

———————————

I hadn't seen Julianne. She knew we were going but had kept to herself in town pretty much since we had arrived

187

there. At first, she'd visited me a few times at the campsite, and I would see her at the post office shop where she had found part-time work on my few trips to town. But after a while we both began to lose hope in ever reviving our old friendship. The very thought of her often brought a heaviness over me. It wasn't anger or even hurt, just confusion. I didn't know what to do about her.

As we drove through Gunya, I realised that there was another reason why Julianne had been slowly disappearing from my life again. I saw her far off in the street and was about to call to her to invite her to come with us. Despite our differences, I didn't like the thought of a pregnant girl being alone in a strange town as she had been in the city. But then I saw that she was with a young man. Julianne didn't see me, but the man turned for some reason and I saw that it was William. I was surprised and couldn't say anything. He met my eyes as we passed and showed the same shock. Julianne had gone into the post office and William was about to follow. But he took his hat off to me, and mouthed, *thank you.*

I realised that he must have got my letter. It seemed he had come to do the honest thing. I nodded solemnly, and William turned and was gone.

I've done my bit for her, I thought. *Now, let this be over.* Helen, who was sitting beside me, had watched this take place and put an arm around me. She understood. *I have almost everything I need with me. There's no longer a place for Julianne in my life.* In that moment I did my best to emotionally dislocate her from my sense of self, to assure myself that she now meant nothing to me. But even then, I felt my heart sink because I still could not dispense of the love I had once had for her that easily.

18

I HAD TO CLOSE MY EYES WHEN WE FORDED THE Darralong River. Since my accident I'd developed a gripping fear of large amounts of running water. What had once been my source of peace now made me feel sick and I couldn't even hear a river without flashes of my near drowning coming to mind. Sometimes I dreamt I was drowning and would wake choking for air. I assumed that, as with most things, time would prove the greatest healer, but as we crossed the river that afternoon my hands turned clammy and cold.

'You alright, Meg?' Thomas asked with furrowed eyebrows.

'Yup.'

'We've nearly made it to the other side.' He took my hand and I held it tightly.

We started travelling through open farmland and most of it seemed to be used for dairy and wool. Amy was counting any livestock she could see but she frequently lost count and had to start over again, a game that became very annoying to the rest of us. At the front, Mum and Dad were involved in a deep discussion about who knows what, but just as we passed an old farm house and waved at the people there, we heard a familiar voice.

'Evelyn?' a woman called out. Dad stopped the van and we all looked around trying to see who it was.

'Mrs Fletcher!' Mum said, figuring it out before anyone else. It was the elderly lady we'd met at Coolibah, who'd been on her way to stay with her daughter. Mum jumped off the van and walked quickly to the old lady, who was pruning a climbing rose in her front garden.

'Evelyn, dear!'

'I didn't realise your daughter's family were sheep farmers!' Mum said as they embraced. The rest of us got out of the van and tried to make use of our legs again.

'Oh, yes. This is her husband, Daniel Gregson.' She gestured to a thin, tall man who tapped his hat at Mum. 'His family's been selling wool for years!'

We were all introduced to him and Mrs Fletcher's youthful, friendly-looking daughter, Margaret. Reuniting with her was not unpleasant, but really it was Mum and Mrs Fletcher who were most glad to see each other, who kept chattering incessantly.

'I never forgot how kind you were when I lost my husband,' Mrs Fletcher said, taking her arm and walking her towards the house. 'I thank God that I was able to come here. I'm far too old to be walking the track now!'

We never actually made it into Darralong's township that day. After a long afternoon of being polite and putting up with boring conversation, we were invited to dinner and had to put up with more boring conversation. It wasn't until Mrs Fletcher said she had 'forged the most wondrous plan!' that we five kids started paying attention again.

'Now, Evelyn,' she began as if Mum was her other daughter. Her shoulders crouched over her dinner as she spoke, and she reached over and touched Mum's arm to make sure she was paying close attention. 'It's already autumn and soon it will be far too cold to be out on the road with a family the size of yours.'

'I'm sure we'll manage,' Mum said, with an unsure smile. 'Besides, it's only mid-March.'

'Nonsense. All of your family's clothes are getting a little tatty and what will they do for warmth in the tents? Now listen, I have a suggestion.'

Mum opened her mouth to protest but she was cut off.

'I've already talked to Daniel and Margaret about it and they love the idea! You were both sheep farmers so you'd be a lot of help on the farm. And Daniel and Margaret had to sell a lot of their sheep, so the shearing could be easily managed between all of you. Anyway, the point is, if you stayed you could live in the shearer's quarters! There are five good rooms up there, all with fireplaces. You and Nathaniel would share, of course, and perhaps you two can share.' She gestured to Nick and Thomas, who did not look excited at the idea. Mrs Fletcher noticed and quickly added, 'Or perhaps Nicholas could have the van as his own room!'

This idea was much more appealing to Nick. In fact, we were all excited about the prospect. To have a roof over our heads again! And proper beds! And rooms all to ourselves! All five of us turned eagerly to Mum and Dad, trying to persuade them with broad smiles and wide eyes.

Mum's mouth had fallen open as if it was all happening too quickly, and Dad seemed to be trying to suffocate a laugh, though I'm not entirely sure what he found so funny. 'Nathaniel?' Mum asked, handing the decision over to him.

'Oh, uh... Well, we would not want to impose...'

'It would be no imposition,' Daniel said, giving his opinion on the subject for the first time. 'But I don't offer it freely. In return for accommodation and a small wage, I would ask that you work on the farm. I could do with your advice in the paddocks and my wife could do with some help in the house, having four children of our own to look after. What do you think?' He leaned back in his chair and folded his arms behind his head. Again, all eyes turned to Dad.

He looked at each of us, as if trying to gauge our thoughts. Lastly, he met Mum's eyes, and they seemed to come to a silent agreement. Dad turned back to Daniel. 'Well, I reckon that sounds like a fine deal!'

We all broke into excited chatter. Dad leaned over the table and offered Daniel his hand. They shook on it and the deal was set.

There was only a bit of light left when Daniel showed us to the shearer's quarters. The building was out of sight of the house and perched on the shoulder of a hill. It was a long building with five doors as promised. There was also a smaller building next to it, which Daniel said was the kitchen and lounge room, or 'common room'. They were both built of stone and although sturdy, they looked a bit run-down. The bull-nose verandah gave it a cosy look, but overall we were too excited about living in proper rooms again to notice much else.

Thomas and Amy raced each other to the verandah's steps, running through the long grass. Thomas won, of course, then was mortified to find all of the doors locked. He and Amy turned and looked at the rest of us, sighing when they saw we weren't in a hurry. Daniel jingled the keys in his hand while he talked to Dad about plans for the next day, and Amy called for them to, 'Walk quicker!'

Red-faced, Mum hushed her.

'Who gets which room, Dad?' Thomas asked as we stepped onto the verandah.

'Well, your mother and I will be getting the manager's room, if there is one.'

'That's this room,' Daniel said, referring to the one in the middle and reaching for the lock with his keys. He opened the door and we all crowded around the doorway while Mum and Dad walked around inside. It was dusty and old-smelling but Mum would soon fix that. There was a proper double bed, a chair and a small bathroom. The rest of us would have to use showers in the common room. Mum nodded her approval and we looked at the other rooms. There were more beds than we needed, and really the five of us could have fitted in two rooms but we didn't even consider that. Nick wasn't even looking at the rooms. He'd brought up Clyde and the van and was already in the process of turning it from Mum and Dad's retreat into a male paradise.

Mum was most excited to have use of a proper kitchen again and to eat at a table. When Thomas lit a fire in the common room fireplace, it became quite snug. There were a few sofas and even some dusty old books that, once Daniel had left us to it, Nick joked about throwing into the fire. As if on cue, Thomas reacted fiercely.

We spent the next couple of hours cleaning and setting up our rooms. Mine was the one at the end farthest from the common room, Amy was next to me, Mum and Dad next to her, Helen next to them, and Tom last at the opposite end. Nick had pulled the van up beside my room and I could see it out the window. I liked how the wooden floors creaked under my feet like the ones at home used to.

But the thing that I liked best was the privacy. I was excited at the thought of being able to lock my door whenever I wanted to, of being able to get changed without having to crouch in the tent, of just having my own space! Of course, at first we spent ages going between each other's rooms, seeing what everyone was doing and just 'visiting', and there was a strange quietness back in my room when Dad told us all to go to bed. But when I fell asleep that night, I was smiling.

The next morning, we shared a real, proper breakfast cooked over an oven that didn't smell or taste like smoke. In fact, the smell in the common room was delicious. Mum and Dad had both risen with the sun and cleaned it all up to be the best it could be. They were proud of their efforts. It seemed more like something that belonged to our family just because it had our few things in it: one of Mum's patchwork quilts draped over a chair, shelves that Dad had made, flowers that Amy had picked.

As we ate together, I did think of Jeremy and miss him. I wondered what he was doing, if he was feeling lonely, if he'd caught up with William yet or if he had thought of me at all. Nick caught my eye and smiled at me. I guess he kind of knew what I was thinking, because he was probably thinking of the same thing with Brigitte, only more intensely. Helen poked her breakfast a little sadly, and I wondered if she was regretting leaving Samuel behind. But she laughed when Amy made a joke and was eager to get to work for the day, so I decided she was coping okay. She certainly liked having a bit of a home to work from again, probably more so than the rest of us.

'What's happening today?' Amy asked.

'Well, we men are going into Darralong,' Nick began.

'You are?' Mum asked Dad casually as she took a mouthful of scrambled eggs.

'Yeah, Daniel wanted to introduce me to some of his contacts and pick up some things at the produce store,' Dad said. 'Thought I'd take Nicholas and Tom with us.'

'But I want to go to town!' Amy wailed. She folded her arms and Tom gave her a 'Well, too bad!' look. She glared at him.

'We'll have a girls' day in town another time, Amy,' Mum promised. 'As for today, I think you, Meg, Helen and I should do a proper tour of the property.'

This in itself didn't sound entirely exciting, but Mum was hiding a smirk that had us all waiting. 'On horseback.'

'What?' Nick and Tom both asked.

'Dad, why do we have to go to town when they get to go riding all over the place?' Tom demanded. 'They've got thoroughbreds here!'

Amy was already rubbing it in. 'There wouldn't be enough horses, anyway! They only have four. Mrs Gregson told me!'

'And why should you have all the fun?' Mum asked Dad with her tongue-in-cheek.

'Alright, you win as usual.' Dad leaned across the table towards Thomas and Nick. 'Don't worry, sons, we'll get to ride when we work with the sheep, and that will be all the time.'

'So there,' Thomas added unnecessarily for Amy's benefit.

'Meghan, would you stop getting so far ahead?' Mum called somewhere behind me as I rode up a small hill on a beautiful chestnut horse. I halted the horse on the ridge and waited for Helen, Amy and Mum to join me.

'Sorry,' I said, but I really wasn't. I hadn't had so much fun in ages and it also reminded me a bit of Jeremy and his rescue. Amy's and Helen's faces were flushed and smiling too. Amy's beautiful brown eyes, alight with innocent wonder, touched me.

Mum rolled her eyes at me and pointed to the van that was coming back up the road. 'They're home,' she said, and she set her horse into a canter back towards the homestead with the three of us following. Riding downhill was sensational. I could feel the breeze rushing through my hair and a cleanness that only comes from being under the sun in large, open paddocks. I felt awake and present, whereas for… well, for a long time I had felt simply empty.

'Here they are,' Dad said as we slowed by them. 'The elusive horsewomen of Darralong, who only appear in the presence of truly strong, handsome men.'

Mum laughed. 'In that case, I think we might have taken a wrong turn.'

We all returned to the quarters. As Mum and Helen started preparing dinner, the rest of us gathered at the table. Dad leaned back in his chair, apparently deep in thought. When there was a lull in the conversation, that is, when we had pretty much exhausted the boys of all they knew and saw of Darralong, he leaned forward, picking at a bit of wood that was flaking away from the table. 'We saw some people from the past there.'

Both Nick and Thomas nodded solemnly.

Has Julianne come after me again? I wondered. *Or has Jeremy come already?* That thought brought a quick smile to my lips, but of course he would have come back to the quarters with them, and the boys wouldn't have looked so serious about it. *Unless he's in trouble…*

'Well, don't keep us in suspense,' Helen said, draining some vegetables.

'There's a strike brewing in town,' Dad began. 'There seems to be one rich man who lives there, who owns the majority of the land around here except for this property and one or two others. His name is Humphrey Pole. Apparently, Mr Willis has a close interest in this man and may even hold shares in his company. He is a great farmer in the region – in fact, I've heard of him before. Anyway, we saw this man, dressed in a very fine, tailored suit and with a fine white beard, driving in an open vehicle through the centre of town. Mr Willis and Frederick Hanson were with him. Daniel doesn't know much about it, but he did say that he believes Mr Pole is now a main supplier of produce that eventually ends up in Hanson's Wares.'

We all looked at each other with dismay. To think we had come so far from home only to come across the very people who had taken it from us!

'But… but why would Mr Willis and Frederick even be here?' Mum asked, scrunching her apron into a tight ball.

'That brings me back to the strike. There is a lot of unrest in Darralong. Most people are employed at the Pole estate but he's not paying fair wages. Well, at least not what the men think is fair. The people have formed a union and are planning a strike soon. John Willis and Frederick Hanson have come to offer advice and support. Or at least, that's the best I can make out of it.'

There was a moment of silence as we all tried to process this, and it was only the smell of burning potatoes that drew us from our thoughts again. Mum returned to her cooking and although she wasn't saying much, I could tell she was thinking heaps.

'It seems we've left the frying pan and jumped into the fire,' Dad said glumly.

'What do you mean?' Amy asked.

'Well, we came here because Gunya was such a depressing place to be, but now it seems that Darralong has its problems too.'

Amy opened her rosebud mouth in surprise. 'But we have a proper place to live! And there's no yelling or hungry babies, or men fighting or living in tents, or having people so close all the time!'

'And we all have work and interesting things to do,' I added.

'And it's kind of like we're home again,' Helen said.

'Yes, you're all right, of course. And we shall just have to avoid town as much as we can. Especially John Willis and his cousin.'

'Did they see you?' Mum asked.

'Don't think so. I reckon they think themselves far too important to bother with the commoners.'

'You're twice the man they'll ever be,' Mum said as she started serving dinner, burnt potatoes and all.

'Depends what you think is the measure of a man. Here we are, broke and penniless, and there they are, enjoying both respect and wealth.'

'We are rich in other things,' Mum insisted, looking at Dad with concern. His dejected posture was not reassuring. Our conversation turned to other subjects, but still I worried in the back of my mind if we could really avoid them and, if we didn't, what Frederick might say after my last heated conversation with him.

19

IT WAS MY IDEA. 'GOOD OLD MEGHAN.' SEE, MUM and Dad's wedding anniversary was coming up on April 4, and since Dad especially hadn't been himself, I suggested to the other four that we should go into town for the day and leave them back at the quarters to themselves as an anniversary present. They had both been working hard since we arrived in Darralong – Dad with the sheep, Mum with the household. I relished all the words like 'considerate', 'thoughtful' and 'clever' that came my way. I even relished Mum and Dad's surprise when we told them the evening before. We crowded in their room before going to bed.

'I've asked Daniel, and he says he won't allow you to work tomorrow anyway now, so don't even try,' I said. 'It's a day just for you two.'

They stared at me as if unsure whether to thank me or to be suspicious. 'What will you be doing in town?' Dad asked.

'Dunno. Thought we could do a picnic or something.'

'Not near a river,' Mum said quickly.

I rolled my eyes. 'Mum, that was a one-off, highly unpredictable event. I promise I won't drown.'

'We'll be looking after her,' Nicholas said.

'I don't need looking after!' I said. 'Look, all I am trying…'

Mum hushed me with a hand on my shoulder. 'Alright, Meghan. Your father and I shall enjoy the chance to spend time together, but we'll also enjoy the chance to spend time with all of you when you get back after your picnic.'

We said goodbye to them in the morning, our basket packed with the best we had and the horse and van ready to go. I still remember Nick flicking the reigns against Clyde's back and the van jerking forward as Amy and I sat with our legs hanging off the back and Rusty in between us. He barked excitedly while we waved to Mum and Dad. They waved back and then Dad hugged Mum from behind, resting his chin on her shoulder. She leaned back into him and smiled. I heard her laugh, and then we were down a hill and out of sight.

We passed the time joking amongst ourselves but as we came into Darralong, we saw people all around. They were listening to someone shouting from a wooden soapbox. To see what was going on, Nick pulled the van over to the side of the road and we got out. The speaker was saying terrible things about this Mr Pole, and the people filling the streets yelled out their support.

'It's people like Mr Pole that has brought this country to its knees!' the man was shouting, pointing to the land behind him, which I assume belonged to Mr Pole. 'If we don't act now, we'll never stand again!'

The crowd cheered in agreement.

'It's bigwigs like Frederick Hanson who keep what they can for themselves while leaving the little people to starve!'

The men waved their fists in the air while we looked on cautiously. I felt on edge. I wanted to go. Dad had always spoken against this kind of thing and I trusted his judgement. 'Isn't there another way to go?' I asked Nick.

'Yeah, well, I reckon if we double back to that side street we can make our way to the park down by the river.' He and Thomas started heading back towards the van and

I would have followed straight away but someone said my name.

I recognised the voice and felt a chill slither through me. I put my hand on Amy's back, urging her to walk to the van more quickly and catch up with the boys before the voice called me again. This time Helen, who was beside me, heard it too and looked back. 'Victoria?' she said, confirming my fear.

I tried to keep walking, to pretend I hadn't heard a thing, when Victoria herself put a hand on my shoulder and forced me to turn around.

'Are you deaf?' she asked me.

I concentrated all my energy on keeping my emotions in check. I couldn't let her get to me.

'This is just the sort of thing I would expect you to be involved in, Meghan,' she said, even though I still hadn't met her eyes. 'I bet your family had something to do with the planning of this strike!'

'We haven't been here long! Besides, I'm only seventeen, Victoria – I'm just trying to live my life!'

Out of the corner of my eye I saw a police van pull up into the rowdy mob. Ignoring Victoria, who was shouting something at me, and the others, who were now back over near the van, I watched as a man attacked one of the policemen. They fell onto the road and a cloud of dust rose over them. I was transfixed when I saw three policemen hit and kick the civilian. He was no match for them but still they didn't stop. I saw the flecks of blood. I felt the confusion of the crowd. They were backing away. The body of the civilian was now limp but still under attack.

I looked at the crowd again. Why isn't *someone* acting? I wasn't sure about a lot of things but I knew that whatever this man had done, what they were doing to him now was just as wrong and if they didn't stop he would die! I felt myself growing angrier, especially when no one did anything. Victoria shook my arm to get my attention again. I pushed her away and, forgetting all about a little thing called common sense, I dove into the crowd.

I pushed my way through the men, getting shoved here and there as if I were back in the river. I reached the front line where people had stepped back to observe the fight. The policemen kept attacking him. I ran out and knelt over the poor man, crying for them to stop.

'What are ya doing, girl?' one of them asked. 'Defending a known criminal? Get off him now or we'll arrest you!'

'Whatever he's done I'm sure it's not worth killing him for!'

'He's a tramp, a thief and a troublemaker! Now move!'

Pausing for a moment, I turned the man onto his back and looked him in the face. It was *the* tramp! The same tramp who had killed our sheep, threatened me twice and who certainly was a thief. Here I was defending him without even knowing it, even though a part of me knew he deserved what he was getting. It was a moment of confusion, the same kind that had been plaguing me for months. Was I right to defend him? Did it make what he had done okay? Wouldn't it be wrong to let him take such brutal punishment? But was I the right person to stop it?

His small, dark eyes stared up at me, his face streaked with blood, and I suddenly remembered that moment when he had grabbed my wrist. Now he was reaching for my hand and trying to tell me something.

'What's going on here?' a new voice demanded.

The shouting of the crowd suddenly dulled. I looked up sharply and saw Frederick Hanson and Mr Willis standing over me. The police backed off.

Frederick looked at me with a mixture of shock and anger. 'Meghan?' he asked, but it was only by the movement of his lips that I knew he had spoken.

'Do you know this girl?' the copper asked.

I held Frederick's gaze, not sure I wanted to hear his reply.

'Yes,' he said clearly and loudly. 'She is a troublemaker and a vagabond. Feel free to arrest her.'

'What?' I gave a nervous laugh, certain that I had heard incorrectly.

'Arrest her.' Frederick snarled at me and Mr Willis actually rubbed his hands together with childish pleasure.

Like a puppet, the sergeant walked towards me, handcuffs in hand. I saw Victoria first, laughing with her bony arms folded. Behind her, Helen was shouting something while Nick was trying to push past two other coppers. I heard him calling desperately to me. I saw Amy's disbelief as they clamped my hands in irons. They were cold, heavy and foreign. I saw Thomas trying to get to me, telling the cops over and over that this wasn't right. I felt white with shock and couldn't move until they jerked me towards the police van. Pushing my head down, they made me get in. I hunched over, turned and pressed myself against the back bars. I saw the tramp trying to pull himself up. No one was paying attention to him.

'We'll come for you!' I heard Helen shout, but then they were all swallowed up into the crowd.

There was a certain irony to think that the first building of the Darralong township I got to experience was its only cell. Trying to keep my mind off what was really happening, and just so I didn't lose it altogether, I ran my handcuffs up and down the bars in a loud and distracted way.

In the end, I drove the constable insane and he came and took them off me, so it was worth the effort.

I started pacing the small room, my anger overflowing once the shock passed. *How dare he!* I yelled in my head, thinking of Frederick Hanson. *A troublemaker? After everything he has done!* I grabbed hold of the bars and shook them, imagining that instead of cold metal, I held the throats of Frederick Hanson and John Willis in my hands, those confounded men determined to ruin me and my family. *First they kick my family out of home and now they have me thrown in gaol!* I shook the bars again.

I kept an ear out for a family member, most likely Dad, to come charging in to rescue me. I felt rather guilty. I had gone out of my way to give my parents a chance for some time out, and now they were going to have to come and bail me out of gaol. *You're in gaol?* I asked myself, the words sounding so strange and unbelievable. I curled up into a foetal position on the small bed.

One or two hours passed. *Maybe they won't come. Maybe they think I deserve to be here.* A tear rolled down my cheek. I closed my eyes and thought of Harrington pre-Hanson and the farm, and when life was good and not complicated and I wasn't a prison-dwelling criminal. *You've really gone downhill,* I thought, but with half a smile.

The cell was white with just one small window, much higher than my modest height allowed me to enjoy. Outside I could hear a raven's mournful cry, as if he were dying slowly and painfully in the tree. I pulled the thin pillow over my head, trying to drown him out, but in the end I gave up.

The constable's name was John McIntyre. He gave me a glass of water when I asked for one and assured me that things had gotten a little out of control. 'Well,' I said through the bars, 'being thrown in gaol is not a regular occurrence for me.' That was my attempt at a joke, but it fell fairly flat. 'How do I get out of here?'

'You need a family member to vouch for you, and to go surety for bail until your charge can be heard at court.'

'At court?' I felt even weaker than before. 'But I'm not a criminal!'

He rubbed the shiny button on his sleeve. 'Yeah, I know. What's criminal is that you're in here at all. But what can I do? I'm just a constable.'

I leaned forward, pressing my face between the bars. 'If you don't do something, you'll always be just a constable.'

McIntyre laughed, but then stopped. He seemed to be about to say something but decided not to and walked back to his desk. I heard the chair creak under his weight and I knew that even though I had struck a chord, he still wasn't going to do anything, only now he was going to feel guilty about it.

I lay back down on the bed and, for want of anything better to do, started reciting the alphabet. I recited it backwards for an extra challenge. As more time passed I started feeling sick with worry, so I closed my eyes and hummed *It is Well,* in hope that I would feel that peace again, but I didn't.

'Were you ever falsely accused?' I asked God out loud, remembering something about Jesus remaining silent before the enemy. 'I guess if you were, you showed them in the end.'

Constable McIntyre came over to see why I was talking to myself. 'You haven't been in here long enough to go mad,' he said, leaning on the bars.

'Or I was mad before I got here,' I said, with a forced smile. 'Do you have a Bible, by any chance?'

'Yeah, somewhere.' He looked at me uncertainly. 'But you're not about to be hanged, you know, or meet your Maker anytime soon.'

'Wait until my parents get here,' I said.

He laughed and fetched the Bible.

'Do you know where the story of Jesus getting betrayed by his mate is?'

'Ya mean Judas Iscariot?' he asked, and I nodded.

McIntyre licked his finger and flicked through the thin leafed pages. 'Committed suicide, you know. Remarkable what guilt can do to you.'

Emma. I tried to beat down the thought that the same thing had killed her too – guilt because of what I'd said. I forced the thought out of my mind, scared of what I might feel or discover about myself if I dwelt on it too long.

Constable McIntyre found the page and handed me the Bible back through the bars. Thanking him, I sat down and read the passage in the Gospel of Luke a couple of times, liking Judas less and less each time. 'Judas, betrayest thou the Son of man with a kiss?' I could hear the agony in Jesus' voice. After all they'd done together, when Judas knew who he was and what he meant to the world... He was intentionally selling his friend off for thirty pathetic pieces of silver! I felt so angry about it.

I would've hit him, I thought, while admiring Jesus' composure and acceptance of what had to happen at the same time. *How on earth could you forgive him?* I knew that deep down I hadn't really forgiven Julianne, even though I wasn't as upset with her anymore, and it had been ages ago now, and she wasn't on the same scale as Judas. How could I trust her again? Did I have to? If Judas had lived, would he have remained as one of the twelve disciples? Jesus may have forgiven him but would he have welcomed him back into the fold?

Maybe I was thinking too far ahead, expecting too much. Maybe forgiveness couldn't heal every wound but only take the sting out of them. Maybe I was hanging onto my resentment towards Julianne because I knew that if I really forgave her, the last tie that was holding us together would slip away forever. She was my childhood friend and even after everything, I really didn't want to lose that. But maybe it was too late. All that was left was for me to release her with grace.

It turned out Jesus was falsely accused as well. I read through his death and resurrection, for once not getting bored with the Bible, and then hoped he would rub it in the faces of all those who had persecuted him. But he didn't, which was initially disappointing. Then I remembered what Travelling Dawson, the parson, had said about forgiveness and not putting your happiness in the hands of others. Jesus had obviously been deeply hurt by Judas, but Jesus didn't take that to the next level, because ultimately Judas wasn't integral to his sense of self or his purpose.

I would have done anything for Julianne, and I guess I'd expected her to do the same for me. In losing her I had lost a part of myself. Worse, for whatever reason, I had never been that important to her. Even worse, I had yet to form a new sense of self. I was lost. It seemed there was something about me that made people want to betray and reject me. What was wrong with me? I battled a heavy sense of failure. By burying all my emotions and keeping people like Brigitte away, I was trying to forget about it. Now all I had instead was emptiness, which probably really did turn people away from me.

Lost and empty. That's all there is to Meghan Manley.

But Mum and Dad still loved me, even if I was a lost failure. Yeah, as parents, they had to, but surely there was something in me they believed in. And there was Jeremy, that boy I had come to care about a lot. He loved me even though my faults were as numerous as salt grains and not half as useful. *They say God created me, so aren't my faults really his problem?* Well, at least he knew them and apparently cared about me anyway.

But then, I suddenly understood. This wasn't just about forgiving Julianne. It was about forgiving myself: for letting Julianne hurt me so much, for being so stupid sometimes, for not always saying the right thing, for holding on when I should have let go, for letting Emma down so irreversibly, for lacking compassion, for not being the person I wanted to be. It wasn't Julianne I was so angry with and confused about. It was me!

You talk about being hard on Julianne and Emma – what about giving yourself a break? I wasn't sure if that was my thought or God's but I embraced it with a sense of relief.

Hugging the Bible, I lay back down on the bed and laughed quietly. I was becoming free. I could feel again, and my feelings weren't horrifying or overwhelming but rather true emotions like sadness over losing Julianne and Emma, happiness in having the love of Jeremy and my family, and relief that perhaps I was not such a terrible, empty person after all. I was becoming less confused by the minute.

And all those barriers I had created to stop people finding out there wasn't actually a point to me… I felt them cracking. I consciously gave up fighting against myself and against God.

And that's when the peace came.

20

I'D FALLEN INTO A SORT OF BLISSFUL NAP WHEN the next commotion started. People were yelling outside somewhere, a few men and at least one woman arguing as they approached the police station. Suddenly the muffled noise burst through the door with the kind of conflict you can feel singeing the air.

'Get out of my way,' a ferocious-sounding woman growled, and I heard the voices of Mr Willis and Frederick Hanson protesting. Constable McIntyre was apparently trying to restrain someone but I couldn't see anyone or anything, even with my face pushed up against the bars.

The constable protested when whoever it was succeeded in getting past him. Then, my previously mild mother converged on my cell with all of the gentleness of a raging bushfire.

'Hi, Mum,' I said carefully, smiling because I was happy to see her and still enjoying my revelation.

She looked at me with sudden irritation. 'You get yourself thrown in gaol and have charges laid against you, yet here you are grinning at me as if this is just another ordinary day? Then again, Meghan Manley, these mishaps do seem to be becoming ordinary in your life. Even when Frederick came to tell us some "bad news", I somehow knew it would involve you.'

'Mum…'

She leaned on the door and gripped the bars tightly with both hands. 'You do realise, don't you, that the whole family is now all over the place? Nicholas and Tom have had to pay for a ride to Harrington to see if Mr Robinson will represent you in court! Your father and Amy have gone back to Gunya to ask Julianne, Jeremy and whoever else to come and vouch for your good character…'

'Julianne?'

'And Helen has gone with Daniel to pursue the tramp you were defending, who has taken off towards the next town – this tramp, if you remember, being the same tramp you were prepared to kill over a sheep!'

'Mum…'

'So with my family split all over the countryside and me trying not to think about it, I have come to see my daughter to find out why this happened, and how it is that after organising the whole day so your father and I could have some time together when he needed it most, after telling us with such conviction that "I don't need looking after", that we are now both here with you behind bars?'

'Mum, I'm sorry,' I said, as sincerely as I could.

Constable McIntyre now came to confront Mum. He opened his mouth to speak but she got in first.

'This is my daughter and if you have any intention of taking me away before I have extracted an explanation from her, you shall become fully aware of the term "a woman scorned".'

I stepped away from the bars, scared of this new, aggressive side to Mum that had apparently been lying dormant for years. The constable flinched.

'Don't listen to them, listen to us!' Willis bellowed from the office behind us. Constable McIntyre had to go back to calm him and Hanson.

Mum turned to me again, rubbing her face in an effort to calm herself. 'I'm sorry, Meghan.' She beckoned me to come closer to her. I carefully approached the bars again and let her take my hand. 'I didn't mean to attack you. I'm just... well, scared, to be honest. Now, tell me what happened. I've only had Fred's version.'

Recounting the event to her only seemed to make her more upset. Mum had not realised that it was Frederick who'd had me put in gaol. It seemed he had gone straight to tell her that I'd been thrown in after committing numerous dreadful acts.

'You know most things don't upset me, not really. But I cannot stand it when people are so... so awful. I'm sorry, Meg. I think you may be suffering from a man whose pride I apparently dented more than I ever realised. Your father and I have been married twenty-two years today.' She paused with a faint, fond smile. 'You'd think Fred would have moved on by now.' Closing her eyes, she shook her head.

'I think he's just so angry at the world, he can't even remember why he hates us. But I still don't understand,' I mused. 'I mean he obviously had other things distracting him: Emma's mother and who knows how many other women.'

Mum frowned at me. 'What?'

I bit my lip, wondering if I'd said too much. But no one had made me promise to keep silent. I had done that of my own accord. As Frederick, Mr Willis and Constable McIntyre approached behind Mum, I cleared my throat. 'Frederick was Emma's father, Mum. He told me so himself, upon her very grave.'

The men stopped walking and if looks could have killed, I would have been trying to talk my way out of hell. Frederick stared at me with such disbelief that my confidence wavered. Maybe I had gone too far.

Mum held my gaze. She drew a deep breath, piecing everything together in her mind. Then she shook her head in bewilderment and closed her eyes for a moment. When she opened them again, she lowered her hand. 'Then he must be in a great deal of pain,' she said finally, turning towards him slightly. She met his eyes. 'I cannot imagine what it would be like to lose a child, let alone in such a way.'

My mouth fell open, not only because Mum was sincere in her compassion and had just taken 'turning the other cheek' to a whole new level, but because it had such an effect on Frederick Hanson. His eyes filled with tears at her words. Mr Willis tried to speak but he too could only flounder. At a moment when I would have really let them have it, Mum returned to the quiet, warm person I knew and loved.

'Would you please release my daughter?' she calmly asked Constable McIntyre. I will go surety for bail and we'll be sure to be there when Meghan's case comes before court.'

Constable McIntyre glanced toward Mr Willis and his cousin. When neither of them responded, he nodded dumbly and opened my cell.

On the way back to the shearer's quarters I told Mum what I had learnt about forgiveness. She listened patiently and told me she was proud of me. But following her footprints in the dirt along the track up to our rooms, I felt bad all over again when I saw a table modestly but beautifully set for two on the verandah. The plates of food remained untouched except by flies, and the chairs were pushed back from the table as its occupants had left in a hurry.

'Mum, I'm sorry for ruining your anniversary.'

She squeezed my shoulder but said nothing.

Mum made us both a modest tea that night but there was a terrible silence in the common room. She was at a loss without a lot of people to fuss over and I knew she was praying that everyone would be okay.

'I didn't mean to split up the family,' I told her.

She shrugged it off and we decided to call it an early night.

Except I couldn't sleep. I was beginning to worry too. It was only now that I was starting to realise the implications of what was going on. One small action from me and everyone was all over the place. I had to face charges in court. What if I lost the case? Would I go back to gaol? Would Mum and Dad have to pay some horrific fine that would make us even more destitute? What if something happened to any of the others while they were all gone? No wonder Mum could hardly think straight.

I walked outside and gently knocked on her door.

'Yeah?' I heard her call.

Opening the door, I found her sitting up in bed, her dark curls falling over one shoulder. She still had one kerosene lamp burning and I knew she hadn't been able to sleep either. She'd been reading an old piece of paper which she now carefully folded and slipped into her Bible.

'Mum, will it be alright?' I asked.

She sighed heavily. 'I don't know, Meg.' She patted the bed as an invitation for me to lie beside her. 'I just wish you... Oh, I wish for a lot of things.'

'What do you wish for most?' I lay on my side and looked at her.

'For us to survive this, somehow.'

'Well, we've done it for this long without too many problems.'

She turned her head with a you-have-to-be-joking look. 'You don't think you nearly drowning and then getting thrown in gaol is a problem?'

'Oh… that? Yeah, I could see how that could be a problem.'

'And you're only one of my children. I have Nick, who's so much in love with Brigitte it's hurting him; Helen, who finds this life so taxing and misses Samuel more than she's willing to admit; Thomas, who should be in a school for gifted boys but who has to put up with a life of drudgery; my sunny little Amy, who I think could keep smiling in the face of the devil, but who deserves so much more than this. Your father beats himself up every day because he still feels like he's failing us no matter how much I tell him we love and respect him.'

'Did you always love him?'

'Always,' she said without hesitation, 'and each year our love only deepens. He's my best friend. He's everything to me. We've hardly ever been apart.'

'I'm sorry,' I said again.

'You don't have to keep apologising.'

'Sorry,' I said, and we both laughed. 'Do I still worry you more than all the others put together?' I asked a moment later.

She thought about this. 'Well, admittedly the others haven't nearly died or been gaoled. Yes, you do a bit. Partly because I know that you feel lost. I was the middle child too, after all. I can see you stuffing feelings so far down that you forget they exist and I worry that this will keep you from experiencing things like love. And I know you keep things from me even when you are hurting. Perhaps especially then.'

I was too surprised at Mum's observations to respond.

'Take Victoria, for example. I mean, she always gets to you. I know she's not very nice, but neither is her father or Frederick or that tramp, and yet you don't hesitate to put them in their place.'

'Did I tell you I saw her again in the city?'

'No. You don't tell me much at all anymore. I mean, what happened with Julianne? How is it that she ended up pregnant? Where do you two stand now? And how is it that you found out that Emma was Frederick's daughter and yet you didn't even tell me?'

Mum was getting quite passionate now, so I relented and told her everything: what Julianne had said; what I had said; how Brigitte was becoming a friend to me; my conversation with Victoria. I realised it was true that I didn't know how to tell Victoria where to get off.

'Why?' Mum persisted. 'You're stronger, prettier and smarter. Why do you let her get to you?'

I wasn't used to being interrogated like this, especially when it came to something so personal, and emotions I didn't like rose in my chest. 'Because she's spent her whole life talking down to me! Every day at school she would come over and pick on me about something. I remember on my first day how she tipped my lunch into the dirt and then made fun at me in front of everyone. Another time, she convinced all the boys to write nasty stuff about me and then handed me the letter just before I had to get up and do a speech in front of everyone. I cried and all I remember is people pointing at me and laughing behind their hands. And instead of chiding them, Mr Timms yelled at me for getting upset.' I hugged myself and rubbed my arms. 'Victoria got her hold over me long before I even knew how to stand up for myself.'

Mum stared at me with her mouth open and propped herself up with an elbow. 'Meghan, I had no idea that she was bullying you like this!' I could see she was hurt that I hadn't confided in her when she could have done something about it. 'Why didn't you tell me?'

'I don't know,' I said honestly, but then I thought about it some more. 'I think it's because there was a part of me that thought I deserved it, that thought what she said about me was right, and that no one would believe anything else anyway.'

'But you know that's not true, don't you?'

'Now that I'm away from her, yeah, I guess I do. The whole thing with Julianne though... that made me doubt it. It made me feel all those things Victoria used to always make me feel, which is probably what made me so angry.'

'Hmm. Actually, I think you haven't known how to take Julianne because she doesn't fit into either of the "right" or "wrong" categories that your mind seems to divide everything into. But you know, she can't pay you back the debt she owes you. That's expecting too much. Nothing she can do will help. Only God can pay us back other people's debts and give us the grace we need to forgive them and let go of our desire to hurt them back. We can't do it alone because it goes against human nature. Anyway, Julianne is so confused at the moment, she really doesn't know what she's doing. I wouldn't pay that much attention to what she says and does until she gets her life under control again. Having a child is a huge adjustment, especially amidst everything else that's going on.'

'Do you ever see the bad side of people?' I asked her with a perplexed look.

'I try not to,' Mum said.

I rolled my eyes and snuggled into her a bit. She lay on her back and I put my arm around her waist.

I remembered when Mum was sick and how I had meant to ask if her life had turned out the way she wanted it to. I asked her now, and she wrapped an arm around my shoulders and drew me close.

'Better,' she said. 'I dreamed of a life with a loving husband and children enough to surround us. I got that and much more. I can't say living on the road was part of the dream but I am still content with my lot.'

She smiled at me, and a few minutes passed in silence.

'So... since we're having this long-overdue conversation, are you going to tell me about Jeremy now?'

'What's to tell?'

I saw her roll her eyes. 'I don't know, Meg, but I think you need to know that he loves you very much. I'm sure he has for a long time. Just be careful with his heart. And with yours.'

'I love him a bit too, you know,' I admitted. 'I'm just scared.'

'Scared of what?'

'Of... I don't know. Of loving someone so much, only to realise later that they never loved me at all, I guess.'

'He's not Julianne, Meg. And Julianne did love you once.'

Both of us fell into our thoughts again, and I finally started to feel a bit sleepy. 'Do you think I'll go to gaol, Mum?'

'No,' she said firmly. 'No child of mine is a criminal. I will not let you be treated as such and neither will your father.'

But somehow, I knew it would take more than that.

21

MUM WAS STARTING TO LOOK DRAWN WHEN, BY the end of the second day, no one had returned. We both went about our jobs on the farm, but our hearts weren't in it and I knew Mum was fretting more than was natural to her. She was living through one of her biggest fears and prayed each hour that her family would be okay.

God must have heard her, because later that evening we heard Daniel's dray coming up to the quarters. Both Mum and I ran out to the verandah as Helen jumped off the dray and hurried towards us, her eyes bright and pretty with adventure. 'Oh, Meghan, I'm so glad you got out of gaol okay. I was so worried. The tramp's taking up your cell now. We found him all right and he didn't even put up much of a fight when we told him he was coming back to Darralong. I think what you did has really been playing on his mind, Meg.' She smiled at me and put an arm around Mum's middle. 'I'm glad to be back.'

Mum held her close. 'I'm just glad you're okay.'

'Of course I am. Everything was fine. I even enjoyed it! Not the worrying about Meg, just the hunt.'

'Helen!' I said. 'You're getting wild!'

She laughed and we all went into the common room. 'They haven't dropped the charges by any chance?' she asked me.

'No. My case is tomorrow.'

'Tomorrow?' she echoed. 'So soon? Mr Willis must have pulled some strings! But... but Dad and the others aren't back yet!'

'We know,' Mum said heavily. 'Let's hope they all get back before 11am.'

––––––––––––––

Darralong was buzzing with gossip and distress when we arrived at 10:15, but not because of me. Splashed across all of the papers were pictures of Phar Lap. Two days earlier, our wonder horse had died. Mum bought a copy of the paper and, for a moment, thinking about the sad national loss overshadowed our own trial.

This does not bode well, I thought as I stared at the picture of Phar Lap winning his last race in a foreign country.

At 10:30 there was no sign of the rest of my family and I put the paper aside as Helen, Mum and Mrs Fletcher's family waited with me in the foyer of Darralong's small court. It had a dusty smell and the wooden panelling on the walls was fraying. I ran my finger over the rough edge of a panel and pricked my fingertip.

'Don't you worry, Meghan,' Mrs Fletcher said, patting my arm. 'Good always triumphs. Isn't that right, Evelyn?' She rested her hand on Mum's forearm.

'Hmm?' Mum said distractedly.

Feeling my confidence taking a downward plunge, I beckoned Mum aside and we moved to an empty corner. 'Mum,' I begun, with questions running around in my mind that I couldn't express. *What am I going to say in court? What if the fate of my family rests on my words?* I did say, 'I'm not sure I can do this.' A flashback of the river swept through my mind and I saw myself lying on the bank.

'Meghan!' Mum put a hand on my arm. 'I know I said you needed to feel things more but now is not the time. You are strong…'

'I'm tired of being strong,' I whispered, a tear rolling down my face. 'How can we win against men like that? We've already lost so much at their hands. I've resented this every bit as much as everyone else and still I tried to endure it but…'

'Be strong yet, Meghan. After all this is over, you can cry and fall apart and do whatever you like. You have earned every right to that. We've all had emotional meltdowns except you. But right now we have to get through this. God will bring us justice.'

I swallowed hard and tried to compose myself. 'Well, may he give me strength to survive and receive it.'

'Mum!'

We all turned and looked at the doorway of the court. Nick was standing there, leaning on the architrave while he caught his breath.

Mum hurried to him and hugged him hard, and then Thomas, who had come up behind him. 'Thank goodness you boys are back. How did you go?'

Nick turned and pointed out Mr Robinson, who was getting a briefcase out of his car. Brigitte and her mother were with him and Brigitte made a beeline for me. 'Meghan Manley,' she cried, hugging me, 'I leave you alone for two minutes and you go from being pulled out of a river to being thrown in gaol!'

Her father smiled and indicated for me to sit down. 'I must say, Miss Manley, I normally have more than half an hour to prepare a case with a client, but your brother has been good enough to tell me all the details along the way and I have an idea of how we should approach this. Now, we'd better get the story straight…'

By 10:47 there was still no sign of Dad and Amy, but having Mr Robinson there brought us confidence. He finished making notes and I sat there, asking God to calm the nerves that were fluttering at the thought of what was coming.

'It should be a fairly quiet event,' Mr Robinson said, 'providing the papers haven't heard about it.'

'Why would they be interested?' I asked innocently. 'Aren't they busy with Phar Lap?'

'Well, nothing personal, but it would be less to do with you and more to do with Frederick Hanson, who is more of a public figure than we give him credit for.' As Mr Robinson spoke, Mr Willis and Frederick entered. Unfortunately, though not entirely unexpectedly, Victoria was with them. Ignoring us, she and her father went straight into the courtroom while Frederick lingered for a moment. When he looked at me, there seemed to be something different about him. He gave Mum half a smile and then went into the next room.

By 10:58 Mum was white and numb with apprehension. Mrs Robinson was trying to reassure her but really, all she needed was Dad and there was no sign of him.

At 11am, on the dot, the court clerk called us in. I followed Mr Robinson into the empty, cold courtroom, relieved to find that it wasn't as big, imposing and unfriendly as I'd expected. The magistrate, Mr Lawrence, sat up in his chair and looked down at me over his glasses. I could have sworn he looked surprised. He raised his eyebrows and frowned, perhaps because he had been anticipating a hardened criminal. I quickly prayed that he would be a compassionate, astute magistrate who would see Willis and Hanson for what they were.

Standing by Mr Robinson, I listened to the clerk read out my charges.

'Miss Meghan Louisa Manley, you are charged with participating in an unlawful strike, defending a known criminal and interfering with police business.'

When he finished, I pleaded 'not guilty'. As the clerk stated that I had no prior record, I realised I was shaking. I was starting to feel like a real criminal. I felt judged before I had even been tried and I could feel Willis' and Victoria's dark, hateful eyes staring at me.

But just when I was about to lose my confidence altogether, I heard a sudden influx of excited voices in the foyers. We all turned our heads, expecting someone to burst in, and they did a moment later.

'Dad!' I cried out.

Without a word, he hugged me quickly and went to Mum. Behind him came Amy, who did the same. She was smiling brightly, and I felt a little annoyed that she could be so cheerful while her sister was facing court.

But then I realised why.

A small crowd of people filed into the court. First came Molly and Dave, with their little son. They smiled at me and took a seat. Next was Julianne, with William by her side. She was getting quite large now and although she didn't smile at me, I could tell she was emotional and even a little scared. William guided her to a seat and helped her sit down.

My mouth dropped when I saw who came in next. Uncle Leroy appeared and winked at me. Behind him were Aunt Jane, Edward, Mary and even Grandma Harriet. I wanted to tell them right there and then how touched I was that they had come all the way from the city, but I couldn't. Mum was as amazed to see them as I was. Young Mary waved at me furtively and continued to do so right throughout the case.

Next were Jack and Larry, then Ian and Jenny with their son Danny, all of whom had travelled with us on the road. Then Samuel walked in. He grinned widely at me as if he thought it was all a lot of fun, and for the first time I found I could smile myself. I watched as Sam searched for, and found, Helen, who stared at him as if he were a ghost.

I took pleasure in seeing doubt and concern spread across Mr Willis' face as he realised that I was being rallied around. I smiled my thanks at each of the people who had come, friends from every part of my life who meant many different things to me. But a shadow filled the doorway once more.

There stood Jeremy, tall, strong and more handsome than I remembered him to be. Nicely tanned, he was wearing relatively new clothes, and his hair, instead of being a little floppy and unruly, was clean cut. I felt my heart do something unusually out of control at the sight of him, and I was so happy he had come that I began to realise how I really did love him far more than I had ever thought myself capable of. Jeremy had meant something to me for some time, and I already thought of us as somehow belonging together. But this was something more, something that made me wonder if we really had to wait until that year was up.

'Miss Manley, are you expecting any more people to arrive in your favour?' the magistrate asked dryly.

I shook my head, unable to speak. Pretty much everyone I knew was already there.

———————

The procession of the court went fairly easily at first. I was asked questions both by the sergeant who was acting as police prosecutor, and Mr Robinson, who was so clever and quick that I admired him instantly. I was feeling steadily better and more confident about the case, especially when the crowd made disapproving noises as Mr Willis stepped up into the witness box. I could tell that got to him, giving me a smug sense of satisfaction. Unfortunately, he noticed that in turn, and I think it made him inclined to be nastier. He told the court a fabrication of lies: that I had instigated the whole riot, that I was a malicious criminal who had physically assaulted his daughter and that I was motivated by bitterness from losing the farm.

It hurt to hear him speak of such things, but I think it insulted my parents more. I watched as Dad's face clouded with anger.

'Now, as I understand it,' Mr Robinson began thoughtfully when Mr Willis had finished his ranting, 'the Manley farm could perhaps be considered as some of the best land in its district. Is that right?'

'Yes,' Willis spat, 'though I don't understand how that's relevant to anything.'

'It might explain why you were so proactive in evicting the Manley family…'

'Objection, your worship,' the sergeant cut in. 'Mr Willis is not the one on trial.'

'Granted. What is your point, Mr Robinson?' Mr Lawrence asked.

'My point is that perhaps some underlying motive exists for Mr Willis to insinuate that this young girl is malicious, and for him to twist a situation in which she had only been defending a helpless man from terrible assault, to make her appear as the instigator of the strike in the first place. This is clearly incredible and vindictive, suggesting that Mr Willis' accusation was made on a personal basis and not a legal one.'

This caused loud murmuring throughout the crowd. Brigitte caught my eye and smiled encouragingly while

Frederick Hanson suddenly got up and left the room. I looked back at Dad, who was gripping Mum's hand tightly. He nodded at me, to reassure me that I was doing okay.

Others were called up next. Many people had been at the riot scene. Some had written statements and a few had been called in as witnesses. Swearing before Almighty God, they gave a truthful account while Frederick was gone. Once they had been interrogated with painstaking detail, we broke for lunch.

When court convened again, Mr Robinson invited people to give character references for me. He started with Uncle Leroy, who told him of my 'upstanding and lasting contribution' to his household while he had been away. Then Mr Robinson invited Julianne up.

'For the record, could you please state your full name?'

'Mrs Julianne Rachel Cale.'

I looked at her and she covertly pointed to the ring that was now on her fourth finger.

She got married and didn't even tell me!

'And what is your relationship with the accused?'

She hesitated. 'We were friends. Best friends.'

'Were?'

Julianne cleared her throat, looking down. 'Yes. We had a falling out, but that was mostly my fault.' Her eyes were already tearing up. 'But even though I hurt Meghan, she let me travel with her and quietly brought me together with my husband. So I came here to defend her and to say that no matter how much she may want to do anything different, she will only ever do what's right. And she's very clear on what is right. Always has been. There's no grey area for Meghan Manley. If anything, that's her only fault.' She smiled and twisted some of her red hair around her finger, but her gaze was pained, as if it was my lack of 'grey area' that had caused many problems for her.

She went on, 'It's why she went to defend that man, probably without even thinking. She saw something wrong and went to fix it.'

'In your opinion, is Miss Manley a malicious and disruptive person?'

'No! She just does what the rest of us are too scared to do.'

'Perhaps that's what people find threatening,' Mr Robinson said under his breath. 'Thank you, Mrs Cale.'

After a few more very flattering references, Constable McIntyre called the tramp to speak and for the first time I realised he had a name, 'George Harold Smith'. He gave a truthful account of what had happened the day of the strike.

'Look, I'm the criminal,' he confessed, leaning heavily on the door of the witness box. 'I killed one of their sheep when they still had the farm, encouraged to do so by Mr Willis. I even let loose a few of their others without them knowing. Miss Meg tried to warn me off and I threatened her, as I did another time after I knew she'd been nearly drowned in the Kently River. I found her half-dead and I did nothing but scare her.'

I glanced at Mum, realising this was another of those things I had neglected to tell her, or anyone else for that matter. Both she and Dad appeared angry and upset.

'But she never made a big deal of it. I'll never forget when she came over to stop them hitting me. I couldn't believe that she did it.' He shook his head. 'I still can't.'

I thought back to that event. Even though I hadn't known who he was at first, I realised I probably would have done the same thing even if I had known.

Frederick Hanson was next to speak. Even the mention of his name caused everybody to whisper with wide, gossiping eyes. He had to be fetched, and when he came back into court he held in his hands two books that made Mr Willis abruptly sit up, red-faced with confusion. Frederick glanced at him and drew a deep breath as he walked up into the stand.

He stated his name, swore to tell the truth and answered the first basic questions without fuss or emotion. When he was asked about Mr Willis, Frederick fell silent for a moment. His gaze turned towards Mum. Finally, he looked at me, but I could not read him.

'Mr Willis is my cousin,' he began. 'He and I have been involved in many business ventures together, some successful, some dismal; some acceptable, some not so clean. Please allow me to give some background information that may explain why this case is currently before the court.'

The magistrate gave him permission. I had no idea what he was going to say.

'About nine months ago, John brought to me the prospect of owning and working rich farming land which he promised would soon be in his possession. He said that it could bring us both great wealth. This land belonged to the Manley family, and if I'm honest, it was that knowledge that prompted me to agree to his prospect of taking it for ourselves.

'The Manleys… are a good family,' he went on vaguely. Staring straight at Mr Willis, Frederick seemed to come to some sort of decision and went on. 'I hereby tender these documents to the court as evidence.' He handed the two books to the clerk. 'One ledger is a truthful account of what the Manleys really owed to the bank, which in reality was very little. The other is a list of outrageous fees and interest that their bank manager, John, put on their small loan, using these uncertain economic times as an excuse. After giving them an impossible amount to repay, he also suddenly recalled the loan to ensure they never could. For pure greed, he fabricated their accounts and misused their money without their knowledge until they were forced into insolvency. In simple terms, this means that in truth they should never have been evicted.'

Before the magistrate could say anything, Mr Willis stood and began yelling insults at Frederick. Dad, who was fuming, took a step towards Willis with a look of a predator about him. Constable McIntyre had to restrain Dad and Nick as well. For a confusing few minutes, the court was in total uproar. Helen had tears on her cheeks. I just couldn't believe that Fredrick was doing this.

Why now? I wanted to know. *Why at all? And does that mean these past months have all been because of one man's greed? How could one man possibly influence the happiness of so many others? How could he have the audacity to charge me with disturbing the peace? How dare he?* My eyes filled with hot, angry tears and I found myself snarling at Victoria, who was looking daggers at me with even more hate.

'Order! Order!' Lawrence called angrily.

'It is because of Mr Willis that the Manley family has been subjected to destitution!' Frederick raised his voice to be heard over the indignant noise of the crowd. 'Admittedly, shamefully, I helped him. But if it were just up to me now, I would drop the charges. If the whole country were like Meghan Manley and her family, there would be no crime. We have had our differences, that's for sure, but Meghan is no criminal. What I heard Mrs Cale say is true. She just does what the rest of us are too cowardly to do. That is not a crime. It's just a wake-up call.'

Court was adjourned that afternoon so both Mr Willis and Dad could calm down. Once again, Constable McIntyre had to separate them. I had never seen Dad so furious before. All the pent-up feelings of shame and failure were being channelled into his fists and he just wanted to hit something. In the end, only Mum could stop him. Standing between him and Mr Willis, she interceded, 'Nathaniel, stop! You know getting violent won't help any of us.'

He swallowed and finally managed to take her advice.

I went outside for some fresh air, secretly hoping that Jeremy would come after me, but it was Victoria who did.

'Why are you following me?'

She shoved me hard and I tripped backwards, ending up in the dirt. Scrambling quickly to my feet, I dusted myself down. I saw Julianne standing at the doorway of the court but when she saw what was happening, she simply turned away.

'How dare you insult my father in this way?' Victoria snarled. 'What did you do to get Frederick to side with you? Or should I say, what did your mum do while your father was away?'

'Don't you dare speak another word, you vile, disgusting excuse for a person.' My anger was rising into my mouth like a bubbling volcano. 'How dare you stoop to insulting my family when it is you and your father that have been the cause of our circumstance! You've been the

229

instigators, the leaders, the masterminds in our deliberate destruction! If it weren't for you we'd still be at Harrington! Julianne and I would still be friends! You and your father are criminals of the worst kind – you feed off other people and take pleasure in bringing them down. All this time I thought you might have been right about me, when it's *your* soul that's empty and tainted by the devil himself. How dare you attack my reputation to cover yours? How dare you try to blame me for bringing out the truth about who you truly are? Frederick Hanson spoke up of his own accord, a man I've always thought of as a lowly snake, but now I know that the Willises are even worse than him.'

The crowd inside the building had converged outside in time to hear the second half of my speech. At least I had plenty of witnesses when Victoria raised her hand and slapped me so hard I dropped to my knees. I longed to stand up and take her down, to show her just how strong I could be, but something deep inside told me not to react. All at once, I knew that I couldn't try to control someone else's actions. I couldn't make everyone see things my way. I would never be able to convince Victoria what was right and wrong. She had to make that decision for herself.

So, in the middle of that road in Darralong, I turned the other cheek and invited her to hit me again.

22

STUNNED, SHE TOOK A STEP BACKWARD AND stared at me.

I could feel blood trickling over my lip and into my mouth, its acidic taste making me cringe and sicken.

'Don't blame me for what you failed to be,' I said to her.

She raised her hand to strike me again and I heard Mum cry out. Then, instead of hitting me, Victoria let out a sharp growl and walked off.

Dad rushed to help me to my feet. 'Are you okay?' he asked, getting his hanky out. I took it and wiped the blood away.

'Yeah.' I gave a shaky smile, not entirely sure what I'd just done or if it was worth it. I caught Julianne's eye again and she looked down. I realised then with a saddening heart that the remaining whisper of our friendship had just faded away.

Once court resumed, I pulled together what was left of my strength. I was immediately called to the box. In short, straightforward sentences I told them what had happened with the tramp, just in case they hadn't got the idea yet, and then the sergeant asked me why I had done it. It seemed like a simple question but I had to think about it for a minute. I tried to come up with something intelligent to say but had nothing to offer but the truth, so I cleared my throat and spoke it.

'Almost every day since we've been on the road, I've met people who do amazing things, survivors who look out for each other and stick by each other. Some of them are here today doing that very thing. They're sticking by someone who may or may not deserve it but who, at least in their eyes, isn't being given a fair go. Whatever Mr Smith is, he wasn't being given a fair go that day and I saw it as my duty to do something about it, because if none of us ever do anything to make a stand, then people like Mr Willis will take over the world and we'll have nothing left to defend. We'd have no pride or integrity, and without that we'd be nothing.'

'Do you see yourself as a woman of pride and integrity?'

Again, I hesitated. 'I see myself as Nathaniel and Evelyn's daughter, as my siblings' sister, and we were raised to do what is right no matter what. So yes, I guess I am. But really, when it's all said and done, I'm just a young girl trying to grow up and find my place in the world. If that place is in between people like Mr Willis and every Aussie battler, then so be it. But my place is also over there with my family, and they have been wronged by that man.' I pointed at Mr Willis. 'All I want is for us to be given a fair go. It's not much but everyone deserves at least that.' Looking at my parents, I forced a smile. 'It's what we would call the Wright and Manley thing to do.'

———————————

There were a few quiet moments as the magistrate made some notes and looked over some others. I sat next to Dad, who put an arm around me, and Mum leaned across him to squeeze my hand affectionately.

'Normally, I would take more time than this to consider the evidence,' Lawrence called suddenly and loudly to get our attention.

When the chatter quietened, he continued. 'But the verdict of this case is so clear to me that I'm disappointed it was even brought before court. Miss Manley, you and your family have endured poor circumstances since last spring, as have many Australians across the country. Indeed, this phenomenon is worldwide. Yet you have endured this with more conviction and upstanding than those who call themselves the cream of society. I am disappointed that it takes a seventeen-year-old girl to remind us of what we believe in, of what is right and wrong. You are a credit to your parents, Miss Manley.' He picked up his papers, tapped them on the bench to form a neat pile, and then, after taking a deep breath, Mr Lawrence announced, 'I am dismissing the charges.'

As everyone cheered, I was momentarily suffocated between my family members. The magistrate brought our attention back to him once more. 'Sergeant, I hope that you will pursue any subsequent charges that have arisen in this case, including assault of the defendant and sheep theft, and that you see that Mr Willis' business is looked into scrupulously. Frederick Hanson, if I were you I would ensure that the Manley family are given what is owed to them as quickly and as painlessly as possible.'

'I regret to inform the court that their farm has recently been divided and sold,' Frederick said, looking down.

I wasn't too shocked, only saddened, but I glanced at Thomas, who slumped in his chair with disappointment. Breathing out slowly, Dad gripped his hands together. I hadn't realised until then that he hadn't completely given up hope either, and it was sad to see him feeling let down all over again.

Lawrence frowned too. 'Then I order that you help them to start again and pay them what is owed out of the profits from the sale, as well as compensation. You will report back to this court in one month to discuss your progress.' He put aside his notes and nodded at me solemnly. In fact, I'm almost certain he winked at me.

The press were waiting for us when we went outside again. I was asked a thousand questions and separated from my family, and it wasn't until Dad came over to collect me that they left me alone. Then they flocked to Frederick and Mr Willis. Victoria trailed after her father, crying. Mr Willis was so white I thought he was going to faint. He knew his career was over, and worse, that he'd brought it all upon himself.

'Are you happy now?' Victoria hissed as she passed me.

I opened my mouth to reply, but then just said, 'God bless you, Victoria,' and walked on.

My family stood in a circle and all talked at once, trying to make sense of what had happened.

'You got off!'

'Does this mean we're not broke anymore?'

'No, but it means we will get money to start again.'

'Who knows how long that will take.'

'But this is all over?'

'Phar Lap's dead?'

'What do we do now?'

'You did so well, Meg!'

'I'm very proud of you, Meghan.'

'Dead? I mean, really, really dead?'

'Can you believe that about Mr Willis?'

'And what about Frederick, coming clean with all that stuff!'

'Don't know what changed him!'

Uncle Leroy and his family joined us. He kissed Mum's cheek and said a proper hello while little Mary ran into my arms and Edward clung to my arm tenderly.

'Well done, Meghan,' Uncle Leroy said. 'He got what he deserved. Who would have thought that a child born on the side of the road would grow into such a fine woman?' he joked with a provocative grin.

Mum slapped his arm half-heartedly. 'I never doubted it for a moment.'

'I must say, Miss Manley,' Grandma Harriet remarked, looking me over, 'you look quite lovely.'

I smiled and stood a little taller. 'Thank you.'

I don't know how long it was while I stood there, being tossed between everyone, listening to congratulations and many other things, but I do remember watching Mr Willis and Victoria being taken into the police station up the road, and how they both glanced back at me, grimaced, and then disappeared from my life forever.

I saw Jeremy standing with Samuel to the side and was about to go to him, when I heard Frederick Hanson call, 'Evelyn, will you come here, please?'

Dad tried to hold Mum back, but she reassured him and went over. He handed her a file with some papers in it. Frederick continued talking for a moment while looking at the ground. Mum was nodding. She put her hand out to him, to shake as friends, but as he grasped it in his, he leaned forward and kissed her cheek.

Standing next to Dad, I felt him tense up and knew he would have gone over there to tell him off, but I held onto his arm. 'He's just saying goodbye, Dad. And he's sorry, I think.'

Frederick walked away, towards the police station, and Mum came back over to us with a sparkle in her eye. She kissed Dad warmly to put his mind at ease and handed him the file Fred had given her. 'He thanked me for looking after Emma, and he's given us this outline of what will be owed to us. We have enough to move on from this life, Nathaniel. Just think of it. Enough to start again and build a new home.'

'That is the best news I've heard in a long time!' Dad kissed her and wrapped his arm around her. 'But so long as I have you and our children, I really have more than enough to be content with anyway, you know.'

'Then why haven't you been?' Smiling, Mum poked his chest accusingly.

'Ah.' He pretended to think about this. 'That would be because I'm stupid sometimes.' They laughed together and I left them to it, wanting to get to Jeremy.

He was waiting for me near the edge of the small crowd.

'I didn't realise you'd become a celebrity since we saw each other last,' he began with a laugh as we hugged. Jeremy held me onto me tight for a bit longer. 'I missed you,' he whispered.

'And I you.'

'You did?'

'Yes. I think I love you, Jeremy Bell.'

'Yeah? I reckon I love you, too.' I think he would have kissed me then, but Dad was coming over with Mum in hand.

'Did Jeremy tell you how he rounded up all these people?' Dad asked.

Jeremy's face turned slightly red.

'No...'

'Well, he's the reason everyone's here.' Dad patted my shoulder as he and Mum walked on.

'Jeremy...' I began once they were out of earshot, not quite sure what to say.

He squeezed my shoulder. 'You're worth it,' he said.

23

THAT NIGHT DANIEL AND DAD MADE A BIG FIRE just clear of the shearing shed and invited everyone up. Jack and Larry provided us with music and everyone sang together, just like we used to at some of the other campsites.

I was even a little sad that this lifestyle was coming to an end. We were going to start looking at land to buy. No more adventure. No more travelling. No more new people. 'This was never forever,' Nick had already said to me. 'And this is the best possible way for it to finish. Everyone gets what they deserve.'

Although I understood that, I also knew I'd have to readjust again. I was thinking it over when Amy came and joined me. 'Megsy, you're not worried, are you?'

'Yeah, I am a bit,' I admitted. 'I mean, where are we gonna go? Where do we even start? How do you pick up the pieces and start all over again?'

'But there's nothing we can't handle,' she said so comically that I laughed and drew her close, brushing her fair hair out of her happy face.

After recovering from his initial disappointment, Thomas soon became the most optimistic of us all. 'I don't even mind that we can't get the farm back now,' he said, sitting beside Amy and me. 'It's exciting to think we will have a new place, and our own, proper house! I don't think I could go back to Harrington anyway, when I think about it. I feel like too much has changed.'

'It has,' I agreed.

'But a new farm... I can't wait to belong somewhere again.'

Listening to him, I realised that I already belonged, with my family and with Jeremy. I'd be happy whether we were living on our own farm or sheltering in the van on a rainy day, so long as they were with me.

'Aren't you happy, Meg?' Thomas asked with concern.

'Very happy, Tom,' I said truthfully. *But because I'm no longer at war with myself.* I looked up into the clear bright stars, closed my eyes, and smiled.

Helen dragged me aside for a private talk a bit later. 'Guess what,' she whispered, but didn't give me a chance to try. 'I've just been talking to Sam!' Her eyes were teary but she was smiling.

'And...?'

'And he said that he still loved me, and that if that meant settling down in one place, he'd do it for me. Meghan, he's coming with us! Wherever that might be!' She threw her arms around me. 'Can you believe it?'

'Yes, yes, I can! So, I take it you love him then?'

'Yes, I think I really do!'

I rolled my eyes. 'You're hopeless,' I said with a laugh.

'Oh! Like you can talk! Miss I-can-hardly-look-away-from-Jeremy!'

I opened my mouth to defend myself but nothing came out. Helen laughed. 'Where's Mum and Dad?' she asked. 'I want to tell them!'

When I realised they weren't at the fire, I looked over at the shearer's quarters and saw them going into their room and carefully shutting the door behind them. 'Um... I think you'll have to tell them later,' I grinned. Helen saw what I meant and covered her mouth to suppress a giggle.

Back at the fire, the group had begun singing *Waltzing Matilda*. Mary came and sat on my lap since Amy was playing a game with Edward. Even Aunt Jane was smiling and seemed to be enjoying herself. Mr and Mrs Robinson were singing along while Nick and Brigitte sat close to each other, whispering and smiling together. She looked beautiful with the glow of the fire on her cheeks and her copper hair moving in the cool, gentle breeze. If she hadn't been so intensely involved with Nicholas at that moment, I would have gone to hug her and tell her how happy I would be to have her become part of the family. But, as it was, that would have to wait.

Over the next few days, everyone went back to where they had been before their lives had been disrupted by my little escapade. Ian and Jenny and their son left to go to Kently early on. Before they went, Jenny told us she was expecting another child. Molly and Dave headed back to Gunya but we later found out they had changed their minds and settled in another town. Jack and Larry went back on the track but didn't have any plans. 'We'll just see what's around the bend,' Jack said, swinging his swag over his shoulder.

The Robinsons left next. 'I'm sure we'll see each other soon enough,' Mr Robinson said with a proud glance towards Brigitte and Nick, who were saying an intimate goodbye. 'Glad to think you'll have a place of your own again.' He shook my hand. 'Well done, Meghan. It was an honour defending you.'

Uncle Leroy and his family said goodbye later that day. He hugged Mum for a long time, shook Dad's hand, and promised to come and visit us in a month or so when we had a new place. I said goodbye to Mary and Edward, promising to read to them when they came to visit.

At first, I was scared that Jeremy would go back to Gunya and continue his determination to stand on his own two feet. When he asked me to go for a walk with him four days after the court case, I thought that was what he was going to tell me.

'No,' he said when I asked him. We were walking along a track down the side of a grassy hill. 'I just want to be with you.' Turning away from the views of the rolling land, he looked at me. 'When your dad came to find me in Gunya and told me what had happened to you, I was sorry I'd ever let you go. I mean, I still think it's best we wait out at least the year before we get too serious, but... Well, we may as well get to know each other real well in the meantime. I'll start saving for our life together, if that's what you want.' I indicated that I did, and he went on. 'I had a good chat with your dad. He said that part of being a man is doing what I did in Gunya, standing on my own two feet, but that it's also sticking by your family. And your family's as good as mine so I'm going to try both; I mean, sticking by you and your family while being my own man as well. Is that okay by you?'

Feeling a little daring, I stood on my tiptoes and kissed him.

'Is that a yes?' he asked, bemused.

'Much more than that.'

———————————

I still cringed inwardly when I thought of Julianne, and it was no different when she came to say goodbye. I couldn't deny there was still some sting in the wound. She and William were going back to Gunya.

'I just want to thank you for writing to William. I don't think I would have done it myself,' she said, standing out on the verandah outside the shearer's quarters the next morning. 'You knew that I hadn't told him I was pregnant, didn't you? I was scared that he wouldn't come even if I did tell him. I would have felt even more helpless.'

I nodded my understanding but said nothing.

'I'm sorry, Meg. With Victoria, I should've... Well, I should've done a lot of things... but I'm not like you. I'm not strong.'

I studied her, feeling the weight of differences between us.

She had become a stranger to me. She didn't have the same values as me. Maybe she had never had them. Maybe I had been too hard on her, maybe I didn't know how to repair what had been broken and maybe every time I thought of her I still felt the shadow of hurt, but at least I'd tried.

'I'm sorry too, Julianne. I know I can be strict in my thinking. I can't pretend to understand why you did some things, but I know you didn't plan for it all to happen. But... it's all different now.'

'I know. Maybe it's best if we just keep walking our own paths for now.' She looked at me hopefully. 'But not forever?'

I hesitated, but said, 'No, not forever. One day I'm sure we can try again, once my family sorts though this mess. I think we will all need a fresh start. In the meantime, I shall always remember you, Julianne, and the fun we had. I will think of our childhood friendship and treasure the memory.'

She smiled weakly. 'I'm glad you got some money back to start again.'

'Thanks. And I'm glad you and Will are together. Hope everything goes well with the baby,' I said, indicating her stomach. 'Maybe you… and the little one can come and visit when our family settles somewhere.'

'Yeah, that would be nice,' she said. She turned to go. 'Take care, Meghan.'

I watched as she carefully descended the steps, her bright red hair and pretty blue eyes tinged with a heaviness that made my heart ache for her.

A part of me was still her friend and wanted to hug her and say it was all okay, despite everything. My body was tense with the things I wanted to say to her. Even so, for now, I had to let her go.

'Julianne?' Mum called, coming out of her room.

Julianne paused mid-step while Mum went down to meet her. She handed her a small package, which Julianne opened. It was a pair of little white booties. 'For the baby,' Mum said.

Julianne's shoulders sagged with emotion. 'Thank you,' she whispered.

Mum patted her upper arm and then came and stood next to me. We waved and watched her walk down to William, who was waiting to take her back to Gunya.

As Mum put an arm around me, I leaned into her. 'You know, I really just want things to work out for her.'

'They will, Meg. She'll be just fine.'

Mrs Fletcher cried when we told her we were leaving to find a place of our own. It had been eight days since my case had been closed. We had finalised things in Darralong and were ready to go. We'd also heard that Mr Willis was now facing the district court, and rumours were suggesting that his business dealings had been so bad that he may yet end up in the city court. Frederick Hanson's name had also been sullied, his one good deed not enough to redeem him from a lifetime of spitefulness. The difference was that he was now accepting his fate, while Mr Willis was still fighting.

Jeremy and Samuel were mounted on their two horses as we stood outside Daniel and Margaret's home saying goodbye. Mrs Fletcher clung to Mum while Daniel shook Dad's hand, sorry to lose him. 'Thank you for all of your help on the farm. Wherever you go, they should be proud to have you.'

Eventually we piled into the van one by one, Clyde tugging at the bit and eager to go. Rusty jumped up with an excited bark while Dad and Mum climbed up onto the front. With one last wave back, Dad flicked the reigns over Clyde's back and the van lurched forward.

———————

Living off some of the money we had been paid, we made our way along the track, Mum and Dad visiting farms for sale and trying to make a decision that would benefit all of us. We went through some familiar towns, including Kently, where I walked back to where I'd fallen into the river. The water was no longer fighting for space with the land, no longer raging for a way to express itself, no longer full of debris or tainted with waste. It was clean, calm and peaceful. Up above, the butcherbird sang in the gum tree. Being near a river didn't even worry me anymore. Somehow, it reminded me of God. *I guess that was just your way of getting my attention. A dramatic baptism.*

The only way to wash away your barriers. I smiled up at the sky, looking for the voice, even though I knew I had heard it only in my heart.

Instead of heading back towards Harrington, we turned north, where there were wide-open paddocks sprinkled with blossoming eucalypts and little wild yellow flowers. At a quaint town called Bridgewaters, Mum and Dad began routinely enquiring about land for sale after we set up camp at the local site. We'd arrived just in time for lunch, and after stoking up a fire, cooking something to eat and enjoying it, we all walked into the township.

'This could be nice.' Nick nodded approvingly as we walked along the main street, leaving our parents to talk to the local land agent. 'Only an hour or so by car to Harrington, I think.'

'You mean to Brigitte,' I teased.

'Maybe...'

Up each side of the road were huge elm trees whose leaves were blowing around in the breeze. Amy jumped on the fallen leaves on the path, liking the crunching sound they made.

'I grew up not far from here,' Samuel said suddenly.

'I didn't know you once belonged somewhere,' Helen told him.

'That's because I'm a man of mystery!' he laughed. 'Nah, I lived with my grandmother here for a while, you know, Mum's mum. Dad had a temper, see, and he'd take it out on Mum, and then, well, he belted her too hard one day. So Nan took me in and I spent my days getting in trouble at school. Last thing she said to me before she died was, "Keep smiling and make sure you get yourself a good woman, treat her right and give her a nice home." And I thought, *Yeah, right, like that could ever happen to me.* I didn't know what a family was, so I drifted. But then I met a good woman after all, and now I've just got to work out what a "nice home" is.' He laughed again and Helen linked her arm through his.

245

'I hope your parents like this place,' Sam went on, hardly drawing a breath. 'Seems fitting that I should end up back here.'

When we met Mum and Dad back at the campsite, they were smiling. 'Reckon we found a good place,' Dad said, throwing a log onto the fire. 'Nice plot of land, house in reasonable condition, nice river and enough left over to buy a fair amount of sheep. Yeah, I reckon we could make a good go of it.'

'We think you'll like it too, Nick,' Mum said mysteriously, without adding why.

When we all went to look at it the next day, it did seem special, like home, but different somehow. Farther down the road from the homestead was a small, independent cottage which was technically on the property.

'See that, Nick?' Dad asked as we tumbled out of the van and leaned on the sturdy fence in front of the little house. 'Your mum and I have been talking, and we reckon you could use that cottage. We could lease you a couple hundred acres. Could start running your own property. You'd have to pay some rent, of course, but I reckon it'd be a nice start.' He glanced at Nick, who couldn't believe what he was hearing. 'Well, what d'ya reckon?'

By the time we got back to our camp at Bridgewaters, we all had our hearts set on it. Nick was beaming and I'm pretty sure he was already rehearsing what he was going to say to Brigitte when he asked her to marry him, now that he felt he had something to offer her.

'Do you like it?' I asked Jeremy as we went down to the nearby creek with two buckets.

'The farm?'

'Bridgewaters in general.'

'Yeah, I do, actually. I'd be happy to stay here.'

'Me too. I think I'm even getting a bit excited about it.' I watched as Mum, Dad and Nicholas left to go and negotiate with the land agent in town. The house on the farm had been a nice, cosy place before it got a little run down. No one had been living there for a while and the land was a bit wild as well. It would make a beautiful, welcoming home in time but would need a lot of work, so Dad was only prepared to offer a certain amount for it.

'You know what I like best about the new place?' I asked Jeremy as I scooped some water into my bucket.

'What?'

'Well, we'll be working on something that we get to keep. Not like shearing other people's sheep or picking their fruit and then moving on. We get to keep the rewards of our labour. And even better, there's no Willis, Hanson or Victoria around to ruin it.'

'If only they'd never come to Harrington,' he said, setting his bucket on the grassy bank and sitting beside it.

I washed my hands in the creek. 'To be honest, I've hardly thought about them. I already know they'll get what's coming to them. Besides, I just want to get on with our life. No more looking back. I've forgiven them already, quicker than Julianne.'

'Yeah, but she meant much more to you than they did.'

'She still does.'

We sat on the bank in silence until Jeremy picked up his bucket to go back to the tents. I stood and did the same.

'Oh, Meghan?' he called, and I turned to face him.

'Yeah?'

'I've been meaning to give you something.'

'What?'

He lifted his bucket slightly and I saw what was coming. I took a step backward but it was too late – he got me good. My whole front was soaked and dripping.

'Jeremy!' I yelled, trying to glare at him but failing. I could hear him laughing at me but missed the look of delight on his face as my wet hair was now covering my eyes. Without a word, I pushed the plastered hair out of my face, stepped towards him and shoved him with all my strength. His laughing stopped as he slipped into the creek and landed on his back. He tried to get up but kept slipping everywhere. The creek was shallow, so Jeremy sat and looked up at me with mock disdain.

'Meghan! I thought you were a lady!'

'What about you?'

'I've never thought of myself as a lady!'

It was my turn to laugh and when Samuel came over to see what we were doing, he laughed as well. He offered a hand to help Jeremy up. With a sly grin, Jeremy pulled him in too.

24

DAD SETTLED ON A PRICE FOR THE NEW FARM and it was soon ours. We had to wait a few days before we could move in, and in that time Nick got himself to Harrington and asked Brigitte to marry him. When he returned he was more elated than I had ever seen him. He sprinted across the campsite like someone about to miss a tram in the city, and we didn't need to hear his shout, 'We're engaged!' to guess his news.

As we cheered for him, I realised that instead of being scared of losing Nicholas, I was excited for him and eager to have Brigitte finally become family. She had written each of us a brief note that she sent with him. 'It did not come as a surprise,' she'd written in mine, 'but I am still amazed at the immense joy this has brought to my family, and I really hope it brings the same to yours.'

Just after Nick returned, we were given keys to our new farmhouse, so we packed up our tents and loaded the van one last time. We drove out of town, Samuel and Jeremy riding along beside us, and all of us eager to start afresh. Mum and Dad were laughing together at the front of the van for most of the trip, and we were doing the same amongst ourselves in the back.

We pulled up outside the front door and rushed towards it. Mum and Dad raced us and we let them win. Just as Dad opened the door, he swept Mum off her feet and carried her over the threshold.

'Nathaniel! Put me down!' she laughed.

He did so but kept his arm around her. As we followed them inside, their laughing came to an abrupt stop.

Naturally, we had expected the house to be empty, and it was except for one thing. Right beside the door was Mum's old dressing table and a note that she picked up.

'Courtesy of Hanson and Robinson,' she read out. 'Look, Nathaniel, they must have found it and had it delivered!' Inside one of the drawers were a few newspaper clippings. 'These are still here!'

We spent a few minutes going through them. Mum handed me one that was about my surprise arrival at Jeremy's mum's place. Another was about Mrs Bell's death. There was a nice photograph of her, and when I passed it to Jeremy he spent ages staring at her. The last bit of paper was the announcement of Mum and Dad's marriage.

'Wright and Manley...' Dad read, leaning over Mum's shoulder to see it. 'Sounded smart at the time but it's been well and truly tested since.'

'Oh, we've done alright,' Mum said.

Dad smiled. 'Would you marry me, Miss Wright?' he asked, looking at her reflection in the dresser's mirror.

'Oh... I suppose so,' she said, smiling back at him.

Mum opened the other drawer then, and inside was an article not previously there. She held it up. In big black letters was written, 'Young Lady Challenges Frederick Hanson to be Manley'. There was a photograph of Frederick and John Willis slinking into the police station at Darralong and another one of me with Dad.

'You're famous, Meg!' Amy said excitedly.

'Harrington's Meghan Manley (aged 17),' the article said, 'has called magnate Frederick Hanson to return to a sense of morality in a court case that may serve as the undoing of Hanson's wealth as well as that of his cousin, John Willis. This comes after Hanson's confession that Miss Manley's family was wrongfully evicted from their family property of twenty-two years last October...'

250

At first, I was embarrassed, but then felt myself glow inside. Who would have thought that a girl from a town most people haven't even heard of, in a family that I thought didn't really need me, was now on the front page of a newspaper challenging a public figure and being admired for it?

Dad patted my shoulder solemnly. 'Meg, what would we do without you?' He put an arm around me and drew me close. 'It's thanks to you that we've been given this chance to start over. You've given us a reason to be proud again. Willis and Hanson have been shown for what they really are. And right now, what I'm most proud of is you.'

After putting all the clippings away again, we spent the afternoon cleaning, sweeping, opening windows and letting the fresh air in. There was a bit of a bite in the breeze, reminding us that we were heading into winter. Amy and Tom made a fire in the hearth, arguing over the best way to do it.

When we finished, the empty place was spotless. We dragged in our pillows and blankets and set up beds on the floor. Mum and Dad made theirs in the master bedroom, using the thin mattress they had had in the van. We were all thinking how nice it would be to actually get proper beds again, but I appreciated the roof and the warmth of the fire in the room. We cooked dinner in the flames and ate together on the floor. When it came time for us to go to bed, the five of us plus Jeremy and Samuel pulled our beds together so all our heads were in a circle. We spent ages laughing and whispering when Dad called out for us to shut up. We chatted and laughed some more until he yelled again. Finally, we fell silent, and with Amy and Thomas on either side of me, I thanked God for blessing us more than we could ever have hoped for.

––––––––––––––

Overall, 1932 was one of the hardest years. Almost half of Australia was unemployed and more and more people fell to travelling, as we had done, just to survive. Mum and Dad struggled with finances for a long time after getting our new place, but we were still one of the lucky families. We didn't have to beg, fight or worry about where we'd be sleeping every night. Dad told us we were blessed, and I believed him. We really were rich in other things: in each other, in God.

All around were terrible reports of suicides of men and women who could not cope with the depression. Reading the newspaper one morning, I discovered that Mr Willis had lost his court case and, unable to bear the shame, he had become one such man and taken his own life.

On that same day, Mum received a letter from Molly, who told her that Julianne had given birth to a daughter. She had called her Meaghan, adding an 'a' for 'amity', Molly wrote. I think she wanted me to know that. When Mum told me, I smiled and realised I had completely forgiven her. Yes, I still cringed to think how our friendship was lost, and a bit of hurt still ached every time I thought of her, but I did not hate her. Somehow, I had let it go and started becoming who I wanted to be.

––––––––––––––

The morning after we moved onto the new farm, I left everyone in the house and went for a walk to check out the property, to see what the river was like and if there was a place I could call my special spot. As I wandered out into the front yard and onto the driveway, Tom called, 'Meg?'

'Hmm?'

'I've decided I'm not really cut out for writing after all. Would you like this?' He handed me the pencil and writing pad that Dad had bought him all those months ago and before I could answer, he ran back inside.

Carrying them with me, I wandered down the lush hills, picking some of the yellow flowers. There was no big, beautiful willow tree by the river but there was a nice patch of green, burr-free grass that served as a little welcoming bank. I sat there and watched the water flicker over the rocks, listening to the beautiful butcherbird sing. I thought about all of those whom I loved. Brigitte, who would soon be a sister. Nicholas, who had become his own man. And Helen, who was still the classiest of us all even though Samuel's easy-going nature was teaching her practicality.

Sam still talked a lot. He had woken me up that morning while serenading the property's beauty: 'Geez, this place is nice!' he had said, standing by a window. 'Do you like it? Yeah, it is pretty beautiful. I can see myself settling around here, having eight or nine children. Ten? That's fine by me. Yup, this place, it's got something special about it! But you know what's even more special? The people you get to share it with. That's right. Can't have one without the other, you know...'

I smiled to myself and then thought about Thomas, who was hoping for a chance to study again if there was any money left after buying furniture, sheep and everything else. In the meantime, at sixteen, he was happy just beating all the other boys in cricket.

And then there was our Amy, who was not so little anymore. She wouldn't turn fourteen for another few months but was still becoming quite the lady. I'd watched her that morning, laughing with Sam, and hoped that nothing would ever sully her innocence.

As for me, I felt like I was only just coming to life. I still thought about Julianne, still felt bad about Emma, still felt useless sometimes. I was still learning to forgive myself daily. I was also learning to stop expecting so much of myself. As I sat by the river that day, I cried. It was unexpected, sudden, and not like me, but I guess they were tears that had to be shed. All the bitterness, unforgiveness, resentment... it all rose to the surface. Lying down on the grass, I let myself feel the impact of those months on the track, and by the time I'd run out of tears, I felt as if a burden had been lifted off me.

I flicked some water from the river onto my face, and when the ripples subsided, I looked at my reflection in its silvery surface. What I saw was not as disappointing as it once had been. I was less ordinary, less plain; more unique, more beautiful. I saw a young woman who was loved, who had a future and who knew something about integrity and doing right. I saw Meghan Manley, a girl at peace with herself and with God, and with the ever-flowing river.

Watching insects flicker through the sunrays and dance on the river, I felt the warmth of the new morning beginning to settle in. I made myself comfortable back on the grassy patch, and feeling the blush of the Australian sun, I opened the writing pad to a fresh page. I fiddled with the worn and chewed pencil and wondered what I was supposed to do. I didn't know anything about writing or where to start, or if I should even try.

Tapping the pencil against the paper, I thought back to Harrington and how my family had sat by a river much like this one. I thought about the people we had met, the people I had loved, the people I had lost. I thought about how some things really ought to be recorded.

So, I lowered the pencil and began to write about me and my family, and how, to the best of our ability, we had pursued the Wright and Manley thing to do.

Acknowledgements

With thanks to all who so generously helped and
supported me with this novel:

My family,
especially my parents, my sister, Shirley Gray,
and my grandfather, Clifford Adams;

And my friends,
especially Cherise Wakely, Stephanie Burton,
Robyn Bust and Lisanda Harris.

'The Wright and Manley thing to do' was a phrase coined
by my great, great-grandfather John Manley, upon
marrying his wife, Emma Wright – a phrase that resonated
with me enough to borrow it to use within this story, even
though it is set after they lived and not based on them.

About the Author

Born in 1987 in the Hunter Valley (NSW), Trudy has always been passionate about the power of words and working with young people. She began what would become her first novel, Desolate Beauty, at 17, and completed the draft a year later. She achieved her degree in English literature in 2007. Desolate Beauty was published in 2009 and won third prize in the Australian Christian Book of the Year Award. Her second novel, Judging Meghan, followed  in 2010, and Broken Melody was released in 2013. The Sunshine List won second prize in the Australian Young Christian Writers Award (2015).

Having finished her youth work postgraduate degree in 2010 and worked with disadvantaged young people for more than seven years, Trudy is now a caseworker who endeavours to provide children of all ages with safety and security.

She currently lives in the Lake Macquarie region of New South Wales, Australia.

Read more about the author on her website:
trudyadams.squarespace.com

Or scan the QR-barcode below with your smartphone:

Also by the Author

The Sunshine List
ISBN 978-1-911086-65-9

"I must say, Caitlyn, I have heard from some of your other teachers that you have"t been as attentive as you used to be, and that you're missing more and more assignments. It's not lack of skills, so why are you letting it get away from you?"

Spending more time in the deputy principal's office was not what 14-year-old Caitlyn had in mind when she began Year 9 in her semi-arid Australian town. As far as she was concerned, life was perfect until her wayward cousin joined the household, her parents started fighting, her best friend turned into Public Enemy No. 1, and her mum started making her write to-do lists.

Surely growing up wasn't meant to be this complicated. Now not only does Caitlyn have to navigate the unforgiving wilderness of school, but find a way to preserve the ties that are only just holding her family together.

www.onwardsandupwards.org/the-sunshine-list